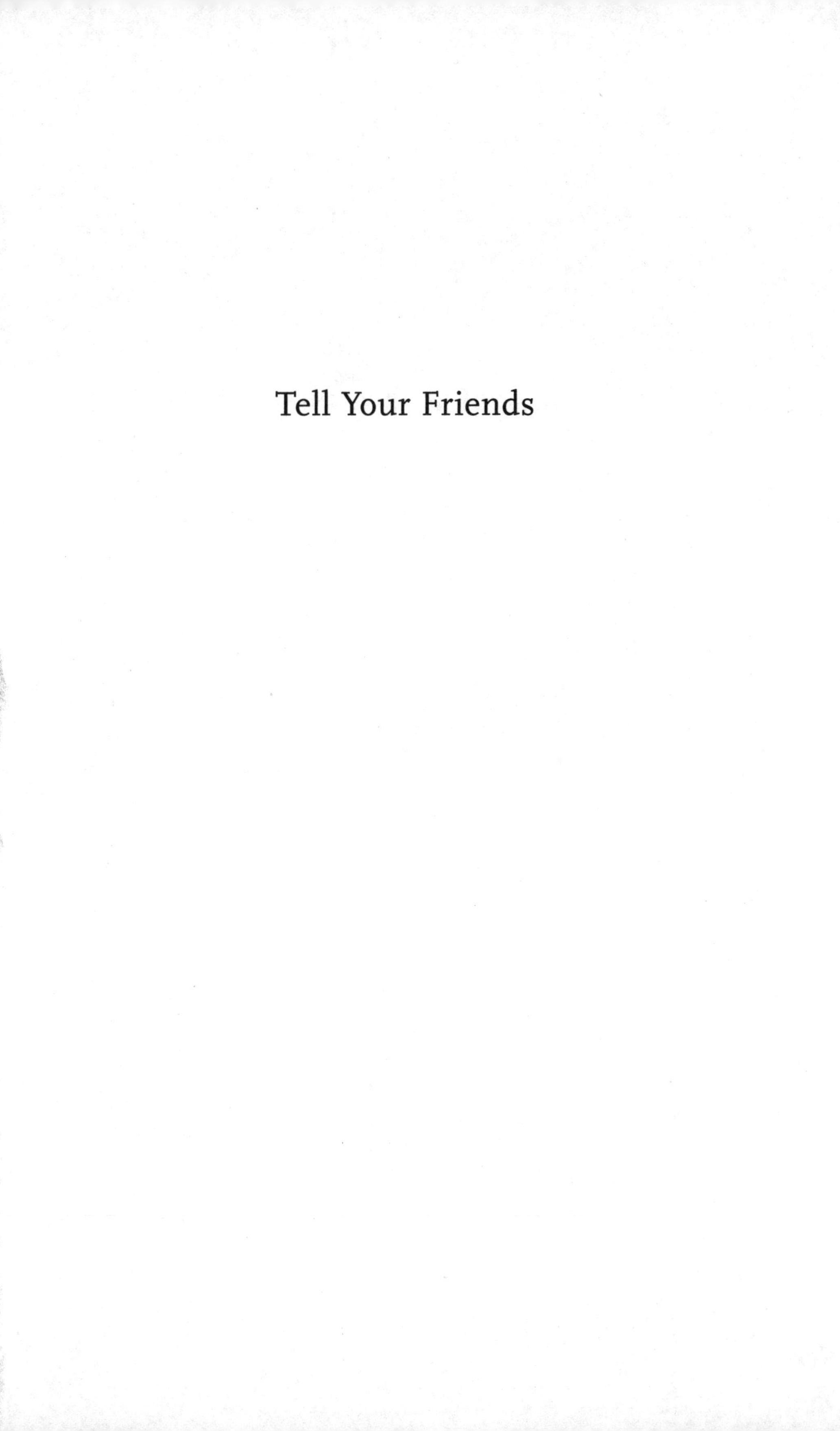

Tell Your Friends

ALSO BY LAUREN WILSON

The Goldens

Tell Your Friends

A Novel

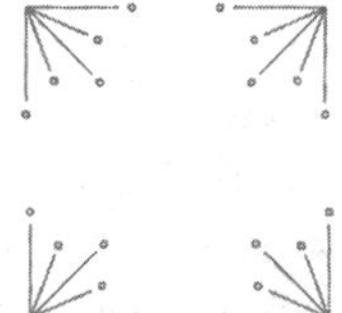

LAUREN WILSON

PINE &
CEDAR
NEW YORK

This is a work of fiction. All the names, characters, organizations, places, and events portrayed in this work are either products of the author's imagination or used fictitiously.

www.flatironbooks.com

Designed by Susan Walsh

The Library of Congress Cataloging-in-Publication Data is available upon request.

ISBN 978-1-250-36248-3 (hardcover)
ISBN 978-1-250-36251-3 (ebook)

First Edition: 2026

10 9 8 7 6 5 4 3 2 1

For Jack

Thank you for always being there

Tell Your Friends

PROLOGUE

IN THE KNOW

The UK's #1 lifestyle & entertainment magazine
16 April 2009

SOCIAL MEDIA STAR LEXIE SHAW DIES FROM "MYSTERY ILLNESS"

Alexis "Lexie" Shaw shot to stardom on her family's vlog, *At Home with the Shaws*, where she featured in dozens of videos alongside her younger sister Crystal, aged six. To date, the channel—which is run by the siblings' mother, Marjorie—has nearly 300k subscribers.

And now Lexie has died, aged just seven years old.

In videos spanning more than two years, Marjorie described Lexie's illness as "complex," "complicated" and "with a range of symptoms" which had left doctors "baffled."

Lexie's tragic death was confirmed by her parents on their social media channels this morning. The post, replicated on each account, reads: "We are heartbroken to announce that our beautiful Lexie passed away this morning at home, surrounded by her loving family. Our angel was incredibly brave, but she couldn't fight any longer. We are utterly devastated."

Fellow vloggers in the parenting niche have paid tribute to Lexie, with popular figure FiveKidsAndCounting—whose television docuseries premieres next month—posting: "Today we're sending our heartfelt sympathies to the wonderful Shaw family, who lost their beautiful daughter, Lexie, this morning. Lexie was a beam of light, and her personality shone in every single video. All our love."

Chapter One

CRYSTAL

I was three hundred miles from home, and the sky was glowing pink and gold.

The setting sun reflected off the glass buildings and transformed the skyline into a miracle of color, skyscrapers like a row of upside-down icicles. It was as if the city had dressed up in its finery, all for me.

It was years since I'd been in an actual city, with cars and buses and people and buildings more than two stories high. I hadn't been in a city since—

I didn't want to think about it.

University was supposed to be a fresh start. It had taken weeks to persuade my parents to let me study in London—so long, in fact, that I'd missed the course start date. I would be joining a month late, and I had an inkling that this would put me at a strong disadvantage. I could catch up on missed assignments easily enough, but I was more concerned about my social life. Would it ever recover?

I'd taken a taxi from the train station, simultaneously too tired and wired from my day of traveling to even consider navigating the complicated Underground system. Instead, I leaned back in the passenger seat and listened as the driver regaled me with stories from his many years as a cabbie, gazing out of the window at the glittering skyscrapers and blinking brake lights of rush hour.

It felt like an eternity before we reached the apartment block where I'd be living for the next ten months or so, and my eyelids were starting to droop. They shot open again when the driver popped his hazards on and got out to help me unload my bags. I did the same, and hovered somewhat awkwardly beside him.

The driver heaved my two ostentatiously brand-new suitcases and bulky, overstuffed backpack onto the pavement, and indicated with a gesture that I should take one of the suitcases. He threw my backpack over his shoulder with a grunt and took the other case, rolling it toward the main entrance.

I followed behind and, as I did, allowed myself to take in some more of the city around me. I'd never been to London before—not even for a university open day. Litter drifted past my ankles in the breeze, and the windows in the buildings around us appeared to have been weeping: damp streaks marked the stone, and moss grew around their edges.

I found myself wondering, for probably the hundredth time that day, whether I'd made a terrible mistake by moving so far from home. And it wasn't just the distance; the city was the complete opposite of the island where I'd grown up, which had been mostly empty of both buildings and people.

I didn't miss my parents—not yet, anyway—but I did miss Opal and Oliver, my twin younger siblings. I knew they'd be thrilled to be in the city with me, their mouths gaping open as they looked up at buildings taller than any we'd ever seen.

As I imagined this, one of my suitcase wheels got caught in a crack in the pavement. I stumbled, nearly losing my balance entirely, but was saved by the taxi driver—who helpfully righted the suitcase and then set my other one beside it. We were at the door.

"All sorted?" he asked. He patted the suitcase, once, as if it was an unruly wild animal and not just a top-heavy rectangle on flimsy plastic wheels.

"I think so," I said. "Thank you so much."

I reached into my pocket and handed him several notes, wadded together. I knew that tipping was important in the city, but I wasn't entirely sure how much was appropriate. With a look of mild surprise, he counted the notes and peeled a couple off the top, then handed the rest back with a gruff nod.

Before I could ask if he might be able to help me carry my bags inside, he was already heading back to his taxi. I watched, somewhat longingly, as it merged slowly back into the city traffic.

Inside, through a set of automatic doors that opened with a smooth *swish*, the reception area was warm and welcoming. It was dimly lit with glowing lamps; jungly potted plants filled the edges of the room, and light wooden paneling on the walls all gave the impression that I was in a fancy spa.

A pink neon sign above the unattended reception desk read STATUE HOUSE. I was in the right place. I lugged my bags across to the lift, stepped inside, and looked at the floors. The pool was located in LB, the lower basement. The gym was on B. Floor ten was the roof terrace. Already, I could picture myself sitting up there in the summer with a cocktail in hand, surrounded by a horde of new, glamorous friends.

I'd received my keys a week or so earlier in the post, and I slipped them out of my backpack to double-check which floor I'd be living on. Once I'd confirmed it was floor three, I hit the button and the doors slid closed.

In the mirror, I caught a glimpse of myself—my cheeks were flushed, my eyes sparkling with excitement. I was going to *love* living here.

My parents had agreed to let me attend university on two conditions. The first, which weighed heavily on my chest, was that I was still "part of the family" and would act accordingly. The second was that I lived somewhere that suited me, i.e. somewhere clean, comfortable, and expensive. We'd mutually decided on Statue House because it had recently been renovated, looked brand-new and luxurious inside, had cleaners and a laundry room, *and* had security staff on call twenty-four hours a day. The pool, gym, and roof terrace were all just bonuses.

The lift let me out on the third floor. It was bright and there was a healthy-looking cheese plant in the corner, which made me smile. Apparently, the residents of Statue House liked their plants.

There were two doors on this floor, one to my left and one to my right. Each door was painted blue with a shiny silver number: 3.1 and 3.2. My keys told me that 3.1, the door to the left, was mine.

I put my key in, twisted it, and then stared as I opened the door. The place was enormous.

The door led straight into an open-plan living space with a tall, arched window surrounded by exposed brick. On one side was the kitchen, packed with dazzlingly shiny appliances and glossy counters, and in the corner right beside the window was a large bed. The floor underfoot was potentially actual wood, or otherwise very high-quality laminate.

My mum had been very firm about me living in my own apartment. She wanted to prevent any potential "distractions" like fighting with flatmates, and although outwardly I'd agreed with a smile, inside I'd had to force down the flare of injustice, the childlike voice in my head that shrieked, *But it's so unfair!* I was good at silencing that voice. I'd had a lot of practice.

I was mostly worried because flatmates would have been built-in friends, people who could show me around the campus and whom I could spend time with on an evening before I made actual friends. Living on my own cut me off quite effectively from other people whenever I wasn't at university.

But there was something to be said, I supposed, for having your own space.

I left my suitcases beside the door and went to explore. In the main living space there was a flatscreen TV, a desk and chair, and even a fully stocked mini bar—like this was a hotel. Opposite the kitchenette was a door that I discovered led to an ensuite bathroom with a monsoon shower.

Less glamorous, but equally important, was the stack of cardboard boxes piled haphazardly in the middle of the room. It would've been impossible to get everything on the plane and then the train, so we'd sent some things ahead—pots and pans, toiletries, other essentials I'd need for the first few days. My parents had also paid extra to have my fridge stocked, something that I was desperately grateful for. I was *so* hungry.

However, there was something I had to do first. I eyed the queen-sized bed and took a running jump at it. It was already made up with the generic Statue House sheets, and I slowly sank into them, awed. My duvet cover and pillowcases were in the boxes we'd sent ahead, but the ones the building used were silky soft. I didn't see myself changing them straight away.

I padded back across to the kitchenette to investigate the fridge and, as I did, there was a knock on the door. I froze, half-convinced I was hearing things, but then it came again—three taps, light but insistent.

I crept across to the peephole and peered through it. A girl around my age was standing on the other side of the door, her arms folded. "Hi," she said as soon as I opened the door a crack. "You're my new neighbor, right? I'm Hayley."

"I am," I said. "I'm Crystal. Hi."

"I was wondering when you'd get here," Hayley continued. "They told me someone would be living next door, that I wouldn't be totally on my own up here, but then you didn't show up."

"I'm just starting a little bit late," I said. "Family stuff."

I hoped she wouldn't ask for details, and she didn't. "Oh, right," she said. "Well, I'm sure you'll catch up. We're, what, a month into the term? And the first two weeks are pretty pointless anyway, with everyone just going out and getting drunk or whatever." She hesitated, peering at me. "Have we met before?"

Before I could respond, she brightened with recognition. "Oh!" she cried. "You're on that channel, right? The family one? With the girl who died? That's it—*At Home with the Shaws*!"

It wasn't the bluntest way that somebody had addressed Lexie's death to my face, but it stung all the same. "Yes," I said. "The family one. With the girl who died."

Hayley at least seemed embarrassed when I repeated her words back to her, the color rising in her cheeks. "I'm so sorry," she said. "That came out *totally* wrong."

I let her apology hover in the air between us for a moment before I relented. "It's fine."

It wasn't. But I'd grown used to my sister's death being a touchstone, a point of reference that strangers brought up in conversation with me as casually as if they were asking me my favorite color or telling me what they'd had for breakfast that morning.

"I used to watch your videos when I was younger," Hayley said, clearly trying to steer the conversation back to steadier shores. "I was so jealous you got to live on that island!" She laughed. "I don't know why you'd want to come here, when you're from somewhere like that."

How to explain it? The island was a paradise, yes—but it was also a prison. A warped, broken finger of land some miles from the mainland, the pale beaches studded with shells, the sea turquoise in the watery sunlight and the hills purple with heather. Our house: enormous, white, with a floor-to-ceiling glass window that overlooked the sea. How could I possibly explain what the island meant to me, how much I loved and loathed it? The island had made me who I was, but I knew instinctively that if I stayed, I would never become anybody else.

"Anyway," Hayley said. "I know you've literally just got here, so I'll leave you to it. I just wanted to introduce myself, since, you know, we're neighbors." She pulled a face, making fun of herself. "I'm sure we'll see each other around."

"Absolutely," I said.

She wiggled her fingers in a little wave, and retreated back inside her own apartment. I closed my door, then slumped against it with a relieved sigh.

I'd wondered if anybody would recognize me, put together my name and my face. A few thousand of the vlog's followers had grown up with me and were beginning to disengage, no longer interested in my family's goings-on. But a far larger number—into the hundreds of thousands, even—still clicked on the latest video every week, religiously hit the like button on every photo one of us posted.

Maybe I had expected to be recognized, but I hadn't expected it to happen quite so soon. And I hadn't expected it to invoke such strong memories of Lexie, either. They were like a gut punch: the stale yellow air of the years she'd been sick, the ferry trips to the mainland for appointments at the children's hospital, the jungle mural there with the scary tiger that had made me cry. The endless paper pots of chalky pills she swallowed down with orange juice, her face pale and set like a martyr's.

Lexie's illness, and her subsequent death, had been the catalyst for everything that had come later. Lexie was the reason that I was here. And I had to do her proud.

I sat on my bed and looked at the room around me. Outside, it had started to rain.

Chapter Two

ALYSSA

It was a mild morning, the air fragrant with burned coffee and fermenting rubbish and somebody's pumpkin-spice vape, the cloud of vapor hanging eerily above the pavement like a left-behind ghost. I joined the queue at the bus stop, which was already three deep. I didn't recognize any of the faces. Behind us, an empty shopfront yawned, dark and cavernous.

I'd really made an effort this morning. My ballet flats were the most demure pink velvet, my white blouse was crisp, and my hair was pulled back neatly from my face with a velvet Alice band. I'd thrown a carefully selected secondhand leather satchel over my shoulder, filled with pens and battered notebooks and loose change and ticket stubs—all the workings of a journalist.

When the bus arrived it was packed, and after I flashed my pass at the driver, I hovered in the aisle. I held one of the handles above my head, my face uncomfortably close to some middle-aged businessman's armpit, and absentmindedly rocked on the balls of my feet as the bus sped up and slowed down in the morning traffic. I gazed out of the window at the glimpses of buildings and people flashing by, and let myself daydream. I liked to pretend that I was somebody important, somebody who mattered—a secret agent, a film star, the object of an attractive stranger's desire. But, as with all my fantasies, reality continued to be disappointing. The bus was filled with other commuters, everybody glued to their phone or their newspaper or their book, all of us trying to ignore the presence of one another in the cramped, swaying space. Once again, I had to face my mundane reality: nobody had taken a special interest in me. In fact, nobody was even looking at me.

As I stepped off the bus, the door closing behind me with a belch-like hiss, I allowed myself to stand on the pavement for a moment to catch my breath.

The newsroom was housed in a tall, glossy building across the road, and when I arrived early enough I liked to watch from the bus stop for a minute or two as people came and went. They always looked as if they were doing something really important—yelling into their phones, rushing into the building with takeaway paper cups from the coffee shop next door, all their actions conducted with a keen sense of urgency.

I crossed the road and went inside, then nodded at the guy on Reception as I swiped my coveted access pass. The building had six lifts and there were rarely queues, so I was able to step straight into one and let it whisk me up several floors. The double doors to our office were on the left, all gleaming metal and frosted glass, with the newspaper's logo stark in the window: *Local Times*.

Inside, on a busy day, the newsroom was all hustle and bustle. It energized me, hyped me up, made me commit to the part I'd signed up to play. I was a *journalist*.

On a quiet day like today, though, I was reminded that I was only a spare part. I wasn't a *Local Times* journalist—I was a first-year university student, gaining experience in the industry by helping out with reporting one or two days a week, unpaid. I was the lowest in the newsroom's hierarchy, and yet I was constantly reminded how lucky I was to be there.

One day, I was sure, my hard work would pay off.

It had to.

I'd always had books growing up. When my parents were busy working or socializing or otherwise being entirely uninterested in me, I'd immersed myself in fantasy worlds. Sometimes, I'd read for so long I'd forget who I was, where I was. I'd emerge from heady adventures and bursts of danger to find myself in my dimly lit bedroom, alone. And I'd wish I could sink inside the book itself, slip through the tiny, spiked letters on the page and be absorbed into the story.

As I grew older, I kept reading—anything I could get my hands on. I stole my parents' magazines, their newspapers, and I became obsessed. There was something about them: the sheen on the magazine pages, the double-page spreads, the enormous, bold headlines. And the *writing*. It introduced me to a whole new world, one of celebrity gossip and natural disasters and exciting new technologies and family tragedies. It introduced me to lives I hadn't known—or imagined—could exist.

I knew then that I wanted to be a journalist.

More than anything, though, I needed change. I was desperate for something to elevate me out of my disappointing life and into a shiny new one.

Morning, Alyssa," Bradley said as I slipped into the meeting room after everybody else. It was hard not to hear the shade of disappointment in his voice, the way it said, *Seriously, you're still here?* He smiled as he spoke, though, and I was grateful for the way he kept his dislike for me just under the surface. That way, I could almost convince myself I was imagining it.

"Morning, Bradley," I replied, perching on one of the plastic chairs pulled up to the conference table.

When I'd first started at *Local Times* at the beginning of the summer, I'd had an idea that Bradley might become a mentor figure to me. I'd pictured us poring over my copy together, him praising my eloquent turns of phrase and gently suggesting improvements. Fat chance; he'd seemed to like me at first, but the longer I stayed on, the more displeased he seemed with me, picking holes in everything I did. I wasn't sure why. Part of me wondered if it was just projection, if he was pushing his unhappiness and insecurities onto me.

Although he was in his mid-thirties and was already deputy news editor, Bradley oozed dissatisfaction: with his job, with the staff, with his life. I'd heard murmurs that his dream was always to work in television news. Instead, Bradley was stuck watching his former colleagues and friends making it big, smiling with their bright white teeth from behind their desks at six o'clock covering the exact same news that we were, only—in Bradley's opinion—better. And he hated it. God, he hated it.

"So," he said, and his nasal voice made me want to grind my teeth together. "We've got a few options today. There's a presser at one of the council offices, something to do with"—he checked his scribbled notes—"a new green initiative they've got going on. There's a protest about some bollards going up on Prospect Avenue to fully pedestrianize it—that'll be decent. There'll be signs, chanting, that sort of thing. Some good visuals for socials." He sighed. Bradley hated socials. "And, of course, there's a hearing for that post office head thing."

That post office head thing. It was an interesting way to describe a recent case in which a man had allegedly decapitated his brother, and then taken the head to his local branch of the Royal Mail to try to post it. By all accounts, it had been quite a shock for the poor woman behind the counter.

A couple of months earlier, I might have winced, quickly volunteered to go to the presser or the protest. But instead, I found myself piping up, "I'd be happy to go to the hearing."

I'd come to prefer covering the crime stories, the tragedies, over anything else. They felt important—*human*—unlike the vaguely promotional content they asked me to churn out. I didn't think I could survive another council presser, smiling mildly as I wrote down insipid quotes in my sloppy attempt at shorthand. I'd die on the spot. Of boredom.

Bradley eyed me. "I think we need a more experienced reporter there for this one."

What he meant: an *actual* reporter, with *actual* qualifications and experience.

"Oh, come on, Bradley," said Davina. A senior reporter, she had straight, dyed-black hair, a signature red lipstick, and a nose piercing, which was normally not allowed in the business-casual office. I got the impression that Bradley had asked her to remove it, she'd said no, and that had been the end of it. "How's she going to get court experience if you never let her go to anything good?"

"We need someone at the protest. And the council presser," Bradley said, but I could see him weakening. A presser would last an hour, tops—if he assigned me to the hearing, he could potentially get rid of me all day.

"I'll go to the bloody council thing," Davina continued. "Let Alyssa go to court. It's only a hearing, anyway, not a big deal—they'll just confirm a plea and a trial date, if he's fit enough for that. Which I doubt, considering the circumstances."

She had a point.

Bradley didn't look at either of us when he spoke. "Fine. Alyssa, you're going to the hearing. Davina, I want you at that council presser. Thomas, you'll be at the protest. Davina, can you join him after you're done?"

"Of course," Davina said. She glanced at me, and winked.

I smiled back. I wanted Davina to like me—properly, as a friend. I wanted us to compare notes, to roll our eyes at each other when Bradley was being difficult, to go for drinks after work to wind down from a hectic day. A bond like that was still yet to materialize, but her sticking up for me was a start.

Bradley rattled through the rest of the agenda: the other content that was planned for the day, tomorrow's potential headlines, what was in the calendar for the next few days. Eventually, he dismissed us all with a wave of his hand, lingering to dial into a conference call with the news editor.

As I took a seat back at my desk—the hearing wasn't due to start for another hour or so, and that was if it was on time—I caught Bradley looking at me through the glass wall of the conference room.

His expression was irritated and slightly bemused at the same time, like he couldn't work out who exactly had decided to hire me in the first place. Spoiler: it was him.

"Don't mind Bradley," Davina said as she passed, stopping to rummage in the black leather tote she had hung over the back of her chair. Her fingernails were also painted black, sleek and glossy. "He's always got a bee in his bonnet about something."

The vision of Bradley in a bonnet was enough to make me smile. "Thanks for taking the presser."

Davina laughed. "I fancy an easy day," she said. "Decapitations are *not* my idea of a good time. Besides, you need the experience. You've only been to court, what . . . twice?"

"Once," I said. "Today will be the second."

I didn't add that the other case was attempted robbery, and had been decidedly less gory.

"See, a good local news reporter needs to know the courts," she said. "We're lucky we have Magistrates and Crown here. More serious crimes. More interesting, generally. Anyway, are you coming for a coffee?"

Here it was. An opening.

"Sure," I said. I reached into my bag for my card, and Davina tutted.

"My treat," she said.

"I'll get them next time," I said.

"When they start paying you, then maybe."

When they start paying me, not *if*. That was a compliment.

We buzzed out of the office together and waited for the lift, side by side. Out of the corner of my eye, I could see Bradley watching us from the conference room, his arms folded in disapproval.

Chapter Three

CRYSTAL

I came to with a gasp, my heart pounding.

I couldn't remember what I'd been dreaming about, exactly, but there'd been a blur of medical equipment and needles, and Lexie's cold hand in mine. I'd had these dreams a lot after she died, but I hadn't had one for a long time.

I rolled over and tapped my phone, squinting at the bright light of the screen. It was only five o'clock, the sky just beginning to lighten into a cool navy outside the window.

Lexie's death had devastated my parents. It had torn the ground from beneath their feet and sent them rocketing into an unknown land: the land of losing a child. But I, too, had been left drifting. Was I still a sister when my sister wasn't here anymore, when she'd gone somewhere I couldn't follow her?

And afterward, once she was gone, when my parents were finally able to spend more time with me and give me the attention I'd always wanted, I was consumed with guilt—because the only reason they were able to do so was because Lexie was dead.

I knew I was never going to get over Lexie's death. I just had to live with it, wrap my pain and grief in smooth layers of time, like the grit of sand inside an oyster shell. The oyster covers the irritant in swathes of material until it's smooth and glossy, eventually creating a pearl. I didn't expect my grief to result in anything beautiful, like a lesson taught or an experience shared. It just was.

I lay with my eyes closed for a while, but the tinge of panic from my dream had filtered into my bloodstream, and I was wide awake.

One good thing about having my own place, I supposed, was that I wouldn't disturb anybody by getting up so early.

I padded across to the kitchen and opened a sealed jar of instant coffee, then filled the kettle. As it boiled, I gazed out of the enormous window at the buildings around Statue House, their lights slowly flickering on.

On the island, my bedroom had a view of both the land and the sea, and even then the only lights were from fishing trawlers passing by on their way to the deeper waters farther off the coast. And, if it was a clear night, I could see the stars—an arrangement of constellations, and the pale stripe of the Milky Way stretching across the sky. I probably wouldn't be able to see the stars here, only clouds tinted orange from the light pollution.

I poured the hot water into my mug and stirred, thinking about my plans for the day. I didn't have any lectures or seminars—my first was the following day—but I did have one thing on my agenda. The Journalism Society was meeting up, and I was keen to join.

Their page on the Students' Union website promised exciting opportunities, including work experience at newspapers and tours of the big television news studios on the other side of the river. But, as well as that, I wanted to bond with my course-mates outside the lecture hall—and, since I'd arrived a month late, this was a golden opportunity.

Deciding that I wanted to study journalism at university hadn't been difficult. It meant I could use the skills I'd developed from a lifetime of vlogging to actually make a difference. I didn't think the childhood videos of me opening Christmas presents or, when I was older, reviewing beauty products, had had much of an impact on the world, no matter how much my parents assured me that they had. The only thing those videos had an impact on was my parents' bank account.

The meeting wasn't until four, so I puttered around the apartment most of the day and ate half a packet of custard creams at lunchtime in lieu of a meal. Then, at two thirty, I dressed in what I hoped was a cute but approachable outfit: a rose-pink T-shirt I'd been sent from a brand that made everything organically, a hand-knitted chunky cardigan (from a different but just as environmentally conscious brand), jeans, and a pair of white trainers. Then I pushed back my hair from my face with a faux pearl headband.

Beside me, my phone lit up and I saw that I had another text from Mum. That made today's total four. So far. I hadn't read them, but I knew what they'd say. I couldn't delay it any longer.

I applied some lipstick in the mirror, propped up my phone, and opened up my usual app so that the camera was facing me. Then I forced my lips into a smile, and hit record.

"Hi, guys!" I said. "Sorry I've been so quiet the last day or so. But guess where I am? That's right. I'm checking in from my new place—at *university*!"

Even as I spoke, my tone falsely bright and cheerful, my mum's hissed encouragements echoed in my mind. *Smile, Crystal. Be more confident. Remember, you're talking to* friends.

The Students' Union stood out on the Cradlewell University campus. Nestled between a quadrangle of grass and some older stone buildings, it was a startlingly modern arrangement of glass and metal. As I stepped through its doors, I could see students lounging on colorful beanbags with laptops in front of them, reading books and comparing notes, sipping coffee from paper cups. I took the stairs up to the second floor as instructed over email, following the signs for the dance studio.

There were fifteen or so people inside, spread out in little groups across the smooth laminate flooring, when I cautiously pushed open the door. A window the length of the room bathed the studio in afternoon light.

A tall boy approached me with a clipboard. "Name?"

"Crystal Shaw."

He scanned his sheet without any sign of recognition, and then crossed my name off the list. "Awesome," he said, flashing a smile that showed slightly crooked teeth. "Welcome! You didn't come to the last session, did you?"

I shook my head. "I'm starting a bit late," I said.

"No worries." He had a floppy fringe, chestnut brown, that he kept pushing out of his face. "It was mostly housekeeping, but I can fill you in. Basically, we meet up here every two weeks. Sometimes there'll be a guest speaker or a training session, and we ask you to sign up for those in advance. Otherwise, like today, we'll just mingle. You know, get to know each other a bit."

"Sounds good," I said, and smiled to show I mostly meant it.

"Can I grab you anything to drink? There's coffee, tea, water . . . or we probably have wine, somewhere. You look like you need it."

Ouch. Did I really look that drained?

"Coffee would be lovely," I said. "I'm fine getting it myself, though. Thanks so much."

"Sure," he said, and gestured toward a folding table by the wall. "It's all over there."

As I approached the table, I saw that it held two metal urns presumably filled with hot water, a jar of instant coffee, and a basket holding a mixed selection of teabags, plastic spoons, and tiny paper packets of sugar. I picked up a mug.

"Did Jasper just offer to get your drink for you?"

On my left, a girl with shoulder-length dark hair was pouring herself a coffee. She tore open a sugar packet and stirred it in, and then added another. I wasn't entirely sure she was speaking to me until she glanced my way, smiling.

"He did," I said.

The girl picked up her cup. "You've made an impression, then," she said wryly. "I've heard he only offers to get drinks for the girls he fancies."

I tried to ignore the heat rising in my cheeks. "Is that still the case if one of the drinks he offered me was wine, because I 'look like I need it'?"

She tilted her head to one side, a gesture that emphasized her pointy chin and sharp jawline. "I guess we'll have to wait and see," she said. "I'm Alyssa."

"Crystal."

"So, do you want to . . ." Alyssa nodded, indicating the others who were starting to gather in a loose circle.

"Sure," I said. I tried to sound casual, but secretly I was thrilled.

Together, we approached the group, Alyssa one step ahead.

Over the next two hours, I got to know the members of the Journalism Society.

Like most of the group, Alyssa was also studying journalism. She also volunteered two days a week, and lived in an off-campus flatshare. It seemed, to me, incredibly grown up. Alyssa was an eighteen-year-old with independence. Meanwhile, I was still living off the money my parents funneled to me and staring at the adulthood instruction manual, utterly bemused.

As the group debated what the following term's journalism trip should be, my phone started to vibrate in the pocket of my jeans. It was an intermittent buzzing, which I knew meant I was receiving multiple texts or notifications, and suddenly I couldn't concentrate on anything else. Was it my mum again? No, I reasoned. It wouldn't be. She would've checked my location by now, and seen that I was on campus. She'd leave her performative sadness at my lack of response till later, when she could guilt-trip me in private.

"Crystal?" Jasper said, and I had the impression he'd said my name more than once.

"Sorry," I said. "What was that?"

"I was wondering what kind of journalism you're into," he said. I must have looked lost, as he added, "Television, radio, newspapers, magazines? Online?"

"I'm not sure," I admitted. "Online stuff, I think? Or magazines, maybe."

He nodded sagely. "Not everyone has their mind made up by the time they come to uni," he said. "That's why the syllabus here is *so* good, I think—you get to try a bit of everything."

"Jasper's done a lot of volunteering," another girl, this one with a mass of blond curls, said. "He's done a bit of everything already, so if you need some advice he's the one to go to."

Jasper looked proud, but I wasn't interested in flattering him with questions. I wanted to find out more about my new potential friend.

"That's cool," I said. "And Alyssa—you said before you're volunteering somewhere, too, right?"

It was Alyssa's turn to preen. "I am, yeah." She said it off-handedly, but her eyes were sparkling. "I'm volunteering at *Local Times*."

"I didn't know that!" the blond girl exclaimed. "How'd you get in there?"

"I applied for a job there at the start of the summer. I didn't get anywhere because I didn't have any qualifications—obviously." Alyssa snorted. "But the guy who interviewed me, Bradley, said I could help out there while I'm at uni. You know, to try to get some experience. I was actually down at the Crown Court today, reporting on a murder case."

There was a cacophony as the group expressed their shock and admiration.

"A murder case?" said an athletic-looking boy with dark hair. "Would we have heard of it?"

"Oh, maybe," Alyssa said lightly, "if you've heard of the guy who took a decapitated head to the post office?"

There was another group-wide exclamation. Clearly, everybody had heard of this case, and I was surprised I hadn't.

"That's been in the *national* papers," the blond girl said with awe. Jealousy curled in my chest, sour and sticky. While the case itself seemed horrific, going to Crown Court to report on it must have been a fascinating experience. I'd never had the chance to do something like that—over the summer, I'd been too busy watching Oliver and Opal, or recording and editing videos. I'd spent hours taking part in mandatory family activities, repeating the same actions, the same words, over and over until we had the best possible—but still "natural"—take.

Technically, maybe it *was* experience. I'd quite literally grown up on camera, and over the years I'd no doubt developed some skills that my peers perhaps wouldn't have. But *At Home with the Shaws* didn't belong to me. It wasn't mine in the way that *Local Times* was Alyssa's. I'd never have that same look on my face, that glow of elation, when I talked about my parents and their vlog. I'd participated because I'd been made to, not because it was my dream.

A voice broke into my thoughts. Jasper, again, who'd wandered across to the refreshments table. "We're nearly out of hot water," he said. "Anyone fancy the pub instead?"

Around me, there were nods of assent.

"I'm up for it," said Alyssa.

Jasper looked at me. "Crystal? Fancy it?"

I hesitated. Mum would be furious if she found out I'd been to a pub. She was a clean-living fanatic—everything we ate at home was grown in the garden, on the island, or imported but still organic. As far as she was concerned, drinking alcohol was akin to swallowing paint, or maybe bleach. But these were my course-mates, the people I'd be spending the next three years alongside. It was important to bond with them, to do what they did.

And they were potential friends, too. Jasper was kind, as was the blond girl. And Alyssa, with her contagious enthusiasm and the funny little remark she'd made about Jasper offering to get me a drink. I needed some friends.

So I smiled. "Sure," I said. "I'd love to."

Twenty minutes later, we'd gathered around two tables pulled together in a pub just off campus called the Six Swans. It was an old pub, dark inside with a sticky carpet, and the lacquered wooden surface of the table was scratched from the bottoms of hundreds of glasses. Three soggy beer mats had been stacked up in the middle as an afterthought.

Thanks to my complete lack of experience in pubs and with alcohol, I didn't know what to order. Jasper ordered a bottle of fruity cider, as did the girl with curly blond hair—whose name, I learned, was Sadie.

Alyssa ordered a gin and lemonade. The bartender turned to me, one eyebrow raised, as I debated what to order. Half of me was tempted to just ask for a Diet Coke. That way, when my parents spotted my location and undoubtedly asked me about it, I could insist I hadn't drunk alcohol.

But then again, the other half of me said, *they'll already be annoyed you're in a pub. You may as well.* So I ordered the same as Alyssa.

When I took my first cautious sip, once we were back at the table, I was pleasantly surprised. It was aromatic and bubbly and delicious, and it wasn't long before I'd drained more than half the glass.

Alyssa was sitting across the table from me, and I saw her eyeing my drink. "You don't really drink, right?" she asked.

"Right," I said, wondering how she'd known.

"Maybe take it easy, then," she said. "It's kind of strong, and it'll hit you."

I very nearly scoffed, but reminded myself that she absolutely knew more about the effects of gin than I did.

And she was right. Even sitting down, as time passed I began to feel as though I was standing on the deck of the ferry, the rusted, saltwater-crusted one with the chugging engine that took us from the island to the mainland and back in the summer. The pumps at the bar and the television showing snooker, a type of pool, and the gaudy, nicotine-stained wallpaper all swayed around me, their edges moving just slightly.

"Ah," I said.

Alyssa, who'd been speaking to Sadie, heard me and laughed. "Ah," she repeated. "There it is! Do you want to go outside, get some air?"

"Sure," I said. As I stood up, my heart and my bones both felt weightless, and a smile crept onto my face. I knew this feeling wouldn't last—Mum had drummed it into me over and over again that alcohol was a depressant, that the artificial happiness would eventually wear off and I'd be lower than I ever had been before.

But, as we stepped outside into the slowly darkening evening, it didn't feel fake. I was hundreds of miles away from home, in the city, with a group of new friends waiting for me inside—people who were kind, welcoming, funny. People whom I couldn't wait to get to know better.

A boy wearing a puffer jacket approached us. "Do you have a lighter?"

I shook my head, but Alyssa reached into her pocket.

"You smoke?" I asked her once he'd lit his cigarette, thanked her, and departed.

"No," Alyssa said. "It's an old family thing. Like an heirloom. I carry it around for good luck. And, you know, situations like that."

She turned it over in her hands, the silver of it gleaming, and then put it back in her pocket. I glanced over my shoulder, back into the warm glow of the pub, where I could see our friends laughing and talking at their table. My eyes pricked with happy tears.

Alyssa smiled at me as if she somehow knew exactly what I was thinking. "Ready to go back inside?"

"Yes," I said. "Definitely."

Chapter Four

ALYSSA

"Morning, Alyssa."

"Morning, Davina," I replied. I was fifteen minutes early, and I'd strode into *Local Times* feeling on top of the world with a coffee in my hand. Yesterday had been a long day, but a satisfying one—with work, the Journalism Society meeting, and then the pub. And meeting Crystal.

I'd offered to walk Crystal home the evening before, feeling somewhat responsible for her drunkenness. She'd had a deer-in-headlights expression when we went into the pub, and the way she'd practically downed her gin and lemonade had only confirmed her inexperience.

She'd led the way to her apartment, drifting across the pavement, stumbling over cracks and occasionally straying too close and elbowing me in the ribs. It was weirdly endearing.

I'd recognized the building as soon as we reached it. Statue House was fancy—a week's rent there was more than mine for a whole month. Not that money was a problem for me. My parents had offered to pay my rent loads of times, as a sort of "making up" gesture. *Sorry we ignored you throughout your formative years; here's some cash.*

Despite all they'd spent on me growing up—good food, expensive clothes, boarding school—it felt like giving in to admit that I needed their money. Once I'd moved out, I told them I'd do it all on my own. And, so far, I had, with ad hoc shifts at the bar down the street and selling the stupid designer clothes my parents liked to buy me online.

I'd watched Crystal sloppily make her way to the lift, then gone back to my own shabby flat and fallen hard into a dreamless sleep.

I'd woken up two hours early, and decided to make the most of it for a change—I'd carefully applied some eyeliner, red lipstick, and even straightened my hair.

"You're early today."

I hung my black leather tote on the back of my chair and sat down. "I thought I'd get a head start."

"Cool," she said. She was looking at me strangely, but I wasn't sure why.

I didn't have time to dwell on it, because by the time I'd logged into my account and checked my emails, it was time for the morning meeting. I trailed Davina into the conference room, my notebook tucked against my chest. It was hot. The sun beamed through the glass, and the effect was like being inside a greenhouse.

Bradley was in his usual spot. "I'll keep this quick," he said, loosening his tie. "It's bloody warm in here."

His gaze fell on me and, once again, he looked unimpressed. He folded his arms, his hipster glasses so low on the bridge of his nose that his watery eyes glared at me over the rims.

I desperately wanted to ask him what his problem was, but I said nothing, only smiled a closed-lipped smile as I took a seat next to Davina.

Once we were all seated, Bradley launched into the day's plans. A senior politician was visiting a factory that made parts for wind turbines. A primary school was doing a charity walk to raise money for a pupil who needed a new motorized wheelchair. The police were making a statement at a local station about a stabbing. Bradley handed out stories to everyone, but by the time he'd finished I noticed that nothing had been assigned to me.

"Bradley?" I ventured. "Sorry, I think you might have missed me. Am I just writing up copy today?"

"I need you to stay behind for a bit," Bradley said. Then, louder, to everyone else, "Okay! Let's get on with it."

As the rest of the team filtered out to start their assignments, I noticed a face I hadn't seen before.

Bradley stood up and closed the door. "Alyssa," he said as he sat back down, "this is Sophia from HR."

HR?

"Hi, Alyssa," Sophia said. She looked perfectly friendly, but very corporate—not a blond highlighted hair out of place, and wearing a pale gray suit jacket that matched her trousers.

"Hi," I said. "Am I in trouble?"

"Not necessarily," Bradley said, answering before Sophia could. "I just wanted to have a quick word. Sophia's here to make sure that I explain things correctly, and that you understand."

"Okay," I said slowly. I looked from Bradley to Sophia and back again, waiting for one of them to speak.

"This meeting has been planned for a few weeks now," Bradley began. He pinched the bridge of his nose and briefly closed his eyes as if the words themselves pained him. "Alyssa, can you tell me why you're dressed like Davina today?"

"What do you mean?"

"Davina always wears black," he said. "She paints her nails black, and she wears red lipstick."

I glanced down at my black turtleneck, my jeans, my loafers. "So nobody else is allowed to wear black? Or red lipstick?"

Bradley frowned at me. "It's not just that. You've brought the same bag as hers to work today, too."

Sophia listened, jotting down notes as he spoke. I wondered what she was thinking. Probably that this was a massive waste of her time.

I shrugged. "I thought it looked spacious. Useful. That's all."

Bradley glanced at Sophia, and I could tell that he chose his next words carefully. "For the last month," he said, "you've dressed like Jessica in Sales. You've styled your hair like her, dressed in the exact same clothes down to the brand, and you've worn the same makeup."

I grew hot. Had it been that obvious? I *liked* Jessica—she was sweet. She had an elegant wardrobe, the kind that was 90 percent beige linen trousers and sheer blouses and designer ballet flats. With her last bonus, she'd bought a satchel worth more than some people's cars. I'd counted myself lucky to find a fake of it in a charity shop.

"The month before that," Bradley continued, "you dressed like Tamara."

Tamara wore clean white trainers with day dresses: ankle-length floral affairs that were perfect for long days of reporting during the summer. Of course I'd gone out and bought some outfits that were similar.

"And today, you're dressed just like Davina. Can you see where I'm going with this?" Bradley asked.

I stayed silent.

"Maybe you haven't realized what you've been doing," he said, more gently this time. "But your behavior has been making other members of the team uncomfortable. If it doesn't stop, I'm going to be forced to terminate our agreement."

That's why Sophia was here.

"I'm sorry," I said hollowly. "I didn't realize."

Bradley nodded, but I could tell that he didn't believe me from the remaining tightness around his eyes, the way they flashed like flint at me. "You can go," he said. "I'll finish up here with Sophia."

"But, Bradley," I said, "you still haven't given me a story."

"I want you to go out and look for something yourself today," he said. "Talk to people. Listen to conversations. If you don't find anything, you can help Davina when you get back."

He didn't even look at me as he spoke. I'd been unceremoniously dismissed.

I left the conference room on trembling legs, and headed back to my desk. My new black leather tote bag hung cheerily next to Davina's, both sets of straps hooked over the backs of our chairs.

"Hi," I said to her as I approached.

Her gaze didn't stray from her PC screen. "Hi."

"Bradley's asked me to go out and about today," I said. "And talk to people. But he said I can help you when I get back."

She didn't smile, still didn't look at me. "Great."

I could feel goosebumps prickling my arms, the atmosphere was so frosty. I didn't say anything else, just grabbed my bag and made myself scarce, my heart thumping.

In the lift, I stared at myself in the mirror. My straightened hair, my bitten lips painted red. Why was I *like* this? I rubbed my mouth with the back of my hand, leaving the pale skin there smeared with crimson.

I was out in the city for three hours. I'd never done this before, just gone out to find a story—there'd always been an event, a press release, *something*. But I was determined to make it work.

As Bradley had instructed, I listened to scraps of conversation as I walked along the streets, sat on a bench beside a busy thoroughfare to watch people coming and going, fiddling with my lighter all the while. It was smooth in my palm, warmed by my skin: my talisman. I observed as passersby texted, talked, jogged, held hands with toddlers, ate sandwiches, and I still had no idea what I was looking for. I hoped I would recognize it when—if—I saw it.

Eventually, once I'd started walking again, I came upon a small protest near a council office. Ten to fifteen students held up signs demanding the council investigate the pollution filtering into the river.

Jackpot.

I chatted with several of them, dutifully taking down notes, and snapped a few pictures on my phone of them holding their placards. END POLLUTION NOW, one read, with a painting of a pipe leaking green sludge into blue water. Another had a drawing of several unhappy fish, and read PROTECT OUR WILDLIFE. The third in the picture was simple lettering in urgent red marker: SAVE THE RIVER—SAVE OUR CITY!

To ensure fairness, I decided to contact the council's press office and ask for a statement before we went ahead and published anything—that is, if Bradley deemed it worthy.

My footsteps were lighter as I took the scenic route back to the office, but I still stopped on my way to buy a coffee. I wasn't sure if I could face Bradley or Davina without a fortifying fix of caffeine.

When I got back upstairs, surprisingly little of the cold atmosphere from earlier had lingered. Davina even smiled at me as I sat back down, shoved my tote out of sight beneath my desk, and started to type up my notes. I'd written up maybe a quarter of them when Bradley spotted me and beckoned me to the conference room.

"So," he said, his stubby fingers steepled on the table in front of him in a way that I imagined made him feel far more powerful than he actually was. "Tell me what you got."

I described the students and their cause, the pictures I'd taken, my plan to contact the council.

Bradley listened without saying a word, but I didn't let him intimidate me. I couldn't. I kept talking until I'd finished and, once I had, he nodded. "It's not headline material, but it's something. It's local; it'll get people talking. Write it up for tomorrow, will you?"

It's something. Practically glowing praise from Bradley.

I took myself back to my desk, and set about finishing my notes. At least I'd proved myself, had aced Bradley's test, if that's what it had been. I'd shown him that I was worth the time he'd invested in me—I could find a story, even if it wasn't necessarily one that would change the world. One day, though, I *would* find that story. That would show them all.

Chapter Five

CRYSTAL

My head was throbbing, and when I opened my eyelids a crack the midday sun filtering in through the window made me wince. I remembered most of my time at the pub with the Journalism Society, but the details became fuzzier toward the end of the night—unfocused, with gaps like a glitchy video game. There were blurred snapshots of faces and flashes of laughter, somebody ordering more drinks. A second gin for me. A tray of shots that I'd declined.

Suddenly, I remembered Alyssa had walked me home. I'd definitely stumbled into her once or twice, and I remembered talking a lot. I pressed my face into the pillow, mortified. I hoped I hadn't told her about my parents, or about Lexie.

My parents. Oh, no.

I reached out to the bedside table, relieved to find my phone there. I grabbed it with clumsy fingers, fumbled, and it fell onto my sheets face down. I turned it over cautiously, as if it might come alive and bite me. The screen lit up, and it was filled with notifications.

I held my breath as I swiped through them. A lot were from Instagram, but that wasn't unusual. Some from my channel. A few emails—university stuff, yet another PR company desperate to send me some free clothes. Whatever.

And then I saw them, the notifications I'd been dreading, and my stomach plummeted down three floors and hit the ground with a thud. Two missed calls and five texts from Mum. I was in trouble.

I opened the messages, feeling sick.

I can see you're on campus! Let me know what you think. Love you. xxx

Still on campus? I didn't think you had any lectures today! xxx

I think your main priority today should be a "first day at university" vlog. Move in day, plus your first lecture? Campus tour? Plenty of options.

Please let me know when you're back. It's getting late.

Crystal, please respond.

How could I play this? I couldn't text back; that wasn't enough. No. I'd have to ring her.

I wouldn't tell her I'd been drinking. At least not on my very first full day in the city. She'd consider it a moral failure, a weakness on my part that had allowed me to become vulnerable to peer pressure. And I needed her to stay on my side, to be willing to let me stay here.

Mum had never wanted me to go to university. She'd insisted I had everything I needed to be successful at home. And when she'd finally relented, after months of badgering, she made it clear that she wanted me to study business or marketing—something that would actively benefit the 24/7 moneymaking opportunity that was our family's life. I'd argued that learning about things like visual storytelling and how to produce effective digital journalism would also make me a stronger asset to the channel. I'd won, but she hadn't been happy about it.

So, instead of telling the truth, I decided, I would use my very good excuse: the Journalism Society. I still had the email with the details of the meeting as evidence if she demanded it. And even though she'd undoubtedly seen my location on the map, maybe she'd understand why I'd gone to the pub if I told her about that. Maybe.

Mum picked up on the third ring.

"Hello, darling. You didn't reply to any of my texts last night." She sounded perfectly friendly, which was how I knew she was furious.

"I know," I said. "I'm so sorry. I made some new friends, and I lost track of time."

"Well, at least I knew you were home safe." She sniffed. "That's why I insisted on that app. Your father thought it was overkill, but I said to him, *You don't know how dangerous a big city can be for a young girl, James*."

"I'm really sorry," I said again.

"Where were you with these new friends of yours, then?"

This, too, was calculated. Mum was hoping that I'd lie. This was a game of cat and mouse we'd played for a long time, Mum asking me questions she already knew the answers to, trying to catch me out.

"We were at the Students' Union," I explained. "I went to a Journalism Society meeting. I thought it'd be good to meet some people on my course, and they arrange visits to television studios and stuff. And then we went to a pub."

I heard her intake of breath, ready to launch into a list of reasons why I shouldn't have been at a pub, but I kept talking to try to smooth over the conflict before it started. "It was close to campus, and the others wanted to go there. I only had soft drinks, though. Obviously."

Could she hear the slight slur as I spoke? Would she pin the tiredness in my voice down to a hangover? She'd been hungover before, I suspected—when she was younger, before she decided to disapprove of everything that could possibly be described as "fun."

"As long as you were only drinking soft drinks," she said, relenting slightly. "I'd prefer it if you didn't make a habit of going to places like that, though. Stick to the Students' Union. I'm sure it's far more respectable."

The leftover Freshers' Week posters with the neon lettering blaring from every surface about karaoke nights, fancy dress parties, and £2 shots didn't suggest respectability to me, but I decided not to bring that up. The less Mum knew about the realities of my new life, the better. The more I ever-so-slightly bent the truth or omitted the grittier details, the more I could fictionalize the videos she insisted I film—create the perfect university life for myself, the life that she wanted for me. Or, rather, the life that *she* wanted to promote to our hordes of followers.

"You're probably right," I said. "I'll do my best."

"Good," Mum said. Her tone was brisk now, businesslike. "Did you see my other text, the one about your content?"

"I did," I said. "I sent you a video before I went out yesterday."

"I know. It was short."

"I didn't have very much to say."

Mum sighed. "You're a clever girl," she said curtly. "You need to *find* something to say. Wasn't that the whole point of you going to university, to expand your horizons? Film something today, please."

"I will," I said. "I've got my first lecture later."

"Well, then," Mum said, in a completely different, brighter, tone. "That'll give you something to talk about, won't it? We need the engagement, sweetheart. There's no *At Home with the Shaws* without likes and shares, and it's tough out there at the moment. There's lots of competition."

"I know, Mum."

"Good. Then I'll let you go, lovely, and get back to your studying or whatever it is you're doing."

I lay there in my tangled sheets, and stared up at the ceiling. "Okay. Thanks, Mum. Love you."

"Love you, too, sweetheart."

The line clicked. I didn't move, a bead of anxious sweat rolling down my temple and onto my pillow. Beside me, my phone buzzed again.

I didn't want to look at it, but I knew I had to. Mum wouldn't be impressed if I ignored her after just speaking to her. It was probably something content-related. Or else an article about a missing or murdered girl—something to put me off going to pubs. But it wasn't Mum.

Hi! It's Alyssa, in case you haven't got my number saved. We swapped them last night. Do you want to meet at the SU before our lecture this afternoon? I can show you where to go. x

I was smiling before I'd even finished reading the text, and relief poured into my veins like cool water.

Hi Alyssa! That'd be amazing. What time?

I finish work at 5. Lecture's at 6. Say 5:30? x

I'd been so worried about not fitting in, about having missed the crucial early period where friendships bloomed and solidified. And Alyssa had been here the whole time, ready to welcome me. I typed a quick message back.

Thank you so much!

Buoyed by the fact that I now had a plan for the day, I dragged myself out of bed and into the shower. Afterward, wrapped in a soft new towel with my wet hair dripping onto my shoulders, I inspected the fridge for breakfast—or, rather, lunch.

Unfortunately, the sight of pretty much everything in there made me gag. Maybe Mum had been right, and alcohol was poison. Or I was just *very* hungover.

I made myself a couple of slices of toast and ate them slowly, in tiny bites, and retreated back to bed.

I was almost proud of myself for completing this rite of passage, for ignoring my mum's strict rules and actually experiencing something—even if the end result was a stomach that lurched like a rolling sea and a headache that reverberated through my skull with every blink.

By the time I was ready to leave at five, I was feeling more excited than fragile.

Several tall glasses of water and a couple of painkillers had fought off my headache, and I'd made myself a bowl of pasta with cheese mid-afternoon.

I'd tried not to overthink my appearance, but it hadn't been easy. First impressions counted. And I was going to stand out, no matter what I did. If somebody happened to recognize me . . . it went without saying that I'd draw attention.

It was still sunny but cooler outside than it had been the previous couple of days, so I shrugged on a comfy pink sweatshirt with an appliqué dolphin on the front (yet another freebie from a brand Mum worked with) and a pair of jeans. I applied my mascara and some lipstick the same shade as the jumper, and then selected my jewelry: a dainty gold bracelet and a pair of matching small hoop earrings that I'd been sent from an Italian company in exchange for a grid post.

Feeling (mostly) prepared for whatever lay ahead, I set off.

Another reason I was glad I'd gone to the Journalism Society meeting was that I already knew the way to the Students' Union. It didn't take me long to get there, but Alyssa was waiting for me when I arrived.

I spotted her from a distance, her dark hair standing out against the brightly colored posters pasted to the wall behind her. She was wearing an all-black outfit made up of a turtleneck, jeans, and shiny loafers, and she looked incredibly cool.

"Hey," she said when she saw me, with a red-lipsticked smile.

"Hi," I said. "Thanks so much for meeting me. I was so sure I'd get lost."

Alyssa pushed off the wall with her elbows, moving to walk beside me. "Don't worry about it."

"And thank you for last night, too." I gave her a sideways glance. "I remember talking to you, but I have *no* idea what about."

Alyssa laughed. "It's okay. You were talking about the island you're from, mostly."

"Oh, right. Good."

"It sounds lovely," she said, and I couldn't discern anything from her tone that suggested sarcasm.

"It's gorgeous," I said. "It's not always fun being cut off from the mainland, though. Especially in the winter."

"You did mention that, actually," Alyssa said. "Something about your sister?"

So I *had* talked about Lexie. We'd been cut off from the mainland the last winter she was alive. She'd had a nasty flare-up, but the ferries weren't running and the wind was too strong to fly. I'd spent days sitting by her bed, my legs cramping and eyes burning, praying to anyone who might be listening—every god, any god—to please, *please* just make her better. My prayers had gone unanswered.

"Yeah," I said. "She died."

"I'm sorry," Alyssa said softly. She didn't ask anything else, and I was absurdly grateful that she'd just accepted what I'd said, understood that it was all I was going to say.

We walked in a companionable silence beneath an archway and into a large, well-lit courtyard, an open space between the university buildings. Benches were set up around the edges alongside skinny saplings, their sparse leaves already scattered on the ground.

Just ahead of us was an old-looking building with a red-brick façade. I followed Alyssa through a set of glass double doors, and inside it reminded me a bit of Statue House: surprisingly warm and modern.

There were no lifts, and Alyssa showed me toward the stairwell.

"So, why'd you want to study journalism?" I asked as I followed her up the first flight.

"I want to be a journalist," Alyssa said. "I like telling stories. At *Local Times*, I'm at the bottom of the ladder so I never get anything great to write about. But once we graduate I want to do big things—uncover scandals, dig up hidden truths. I want to make the world a better place." She smiled. "What about you?"

"My parents are professional influencers," I began. "They're family vloggers. My mum started it all when I was a kid, and it sort of became their full-time job. My full-time job."

By now, I was growing a bit breathless. Alyssa paused on the landing and I waited, wanting to gauge her reaction.

"You're an influencer?" she said. "That's so cool!"

Okay. So far, so good.

"I guess I am, yeah. I've been in videos since I was tiny. I'm pretty sure my first steps are even on the channel somewhere! Anyway, I've grown up being on camera, editing videos, stuff like that—and I want to use those skills to go in a new direction."

"That makes total sense," she said with a nod. "Honestly? Good for you. Doing your own thing can be so hard."

She continued up the stairs until we reached the third-floor landing. There, a door opened onto a long hallway.

"This way," Alyssa said. Roughly halfway along the corridor, we reached a partly open door. She glanced at me. "Ready?"

"I think so."

Alyssa grinned. "You'll be fine," she said, then pushed open the door the rest of the way. I followed her inside, bracing myself.

The lecture theater wasn't like I'd imagined, a grand room with tiered wooden seating and a scholarly atmosphere. No stray dust motes floated in beams of sunlight pouring through tall windows, and no blackboard sat at the front of the room, covered in squiggly chalk equations. This was just an ordinary classroom, albeit a light and airy one. They'd clearly spent a lot of money when they refurbished this building.

White tables were set up in a bracket shape around the edges of the room, the gap at the front leaving space for a desk with a computer and a screen that was fixed to the wall. A projector hung from the ceiling.

And scattered across the bracket, lounging carelessly on the tables, were my fellow journalism students. I recognized a few people from the Journalism Society meeting: Sadie, Jasper, and a few others whose faces were familiar, but whose names I didn't know.

Alyssa greeted a few people, and then took a seat at one of the tables beside Sadie. I sat at the table next to them, hoping I didn't look too clingy.

"News quiz!"

All heads turned to the front of the room. A petite, light-haired woman was standing in the open doorway, a mischievous smile on her face. I got the impression she'd rushed here from somewhere else—her cheeks were pink with effort, and loose strands of hair floated around her face. The rest was tied back in a chignon.

She came into the room and stood behind the desk, observing us. "Did you hear what I said, everyone?"

There were groans, and the people who weren't in chairs already moved to sit down.

I glanced at Alyssa, and mouthed, "News quiz?"

"It's a quiz on current events," she whispered back. "It counts toward your final grade."

I hadn't looked at the news in a while, which suddenly felt like an oversight considering the degree I'd chosen to study.

The woman smiled over at me. "You must be Crystal," she said kindly. "Don't worry. I won't hold this score against you."

After our lecture, when most people had left, somebody from the Journalism Society suggested the pub. Again.

The group was halfway out the door when Alyssa hung back and turned to me, one eyebrow raised questioningly.

"I think I'll skip it," I said. "I'm not feeling so great after yesterday."

I was still a bit hungover, my painkillers finally wearing off, and my mum's irritation was fresh in my mind.

"You know, pubs serve non-alcoholic drinks, too," Alyssa said. "Loads of people at the pub where I work just order a lemonade or whatever."

"I know," I said, a bit put out that she thought I didn't know that, even if yesterday had been my first time at a pub. "It's more the . . . pub environment, two nights in a row. My parents are pretty strict."

Alyssa frowned. "Just don't tell them."

"That wouldn't work."

"Why not?"

I looked away. "They installed an app on my phone which shares my location with them."

Alyssa looked lost for words.

I could feel myself growing defensive, my hackles rising. "I grew up on an island with one town, and I've barely ever been to a city. They just want me to be safe. That's all."

"No, no," Alyssa said. "I get that." She sighed. "Look, I'm not going to tell you what to do. Come to the pub, or don't—it's up to you. But at the end of the day, you're an adult. You get to make your own decisions when you're here. This is your university experience, not theirs."

Alyssa was right—of course she was right—but I didn't know how to explain to her that it just wasn't that simple.

When I didn't reply, Alyssa smiled at me sympathetically. "Don't worry about it. I'm going to go with these guys, but I'll see you around, okay? And text me if you need anything—or if you just want to get a coffee."

"Thanks," I said. "I'd really like that."

I lingered behind until she caught up with the others and I was left alone in the room.

I knew that I'd have to break away from my parents eventually, escape from the thumb that they had me wedged under. But when I did, my life—or, at least, my life as I knew it—would implode. And I couldn't let that happen. Not yet.

There was something I had to do first.

Chapter Six

ALYSSA

Although I'd said to Crystal and the others I'd go to the pub, by the time we made it outside I'd changed my mind. I was still somewhat drained from my day at *Local Times*, and I just wanted to be alone.

The autumn evening light was revitalizing and I decided to walk back to the flat, enjoy the fading sun on my face, and hope it improved my mood.

As I walked, I thought about Crystal. Her relationship with her parents seemed complicated, which was something I could understand—although for the exact opposite reason. Rather than being controlling or overbearing, my parents weren't remotely interested in me. When I was growing up, they couldn't care less about where I was or who I was with, which is why they'd shipped me off to boarding school—and that obviously hadn't ended well.

The flat was empty when I got back, the key juddering in the lock and the entryway cold and dark. I took advantage of the freedom by borrowing one of Niamh's coffee pods and half a tray of ice cubes from the shared freezer and making myself a big iced coffee. I rooted through my designated cupboard, retrieved a half-eaten bar of chocolate studded with hazelnuts, then retreated to my room. The perfect cure for a bad day.

I got under the covers, and stared up at my skylight. Above me, I could see a thick layer of deep-gray clouds approaching, signaling rain.

I thought about Bradley, about Davina and her black clothes and her red lipstick, about *Local Times* as a whole. Was this even what

I wanted to do? Was I really passionate about it, in the way I'd described to Crystal, or had that been an unintentional lie? The words had come out, yes, but had I really *felt* them, deep in my chest?

I could see myself reporting on the same stories—minor local dramas, regional politics, community fundraisers—in five years, in ten years. The thought made me miserable. Maybe, if I was lucky, I could become Bradley, with the job title, the salary, and the option to take all my bitterness out on my underlings just to cope with the disappointment.

I opened my laptop. The browser was already open to my watch list, a series of videos I'd seen a hundred times or more, ready and waiting for me.

Comfort. That's what I needed.

I pressed play and let myself drift off, relaxing to the sound of familiar voices and the light patter of rain on the glass of the skylight.

I saw Crystal again the following day. We met up at the Students' Union as we had the day before so Crystal could follow me to the lecture hall.

This lecture hall was *actually* a lecture hall, unlike yesterday's classroom. It was beside the library, and had been part of the medical school before the university decided to gravitate more toward the arts and humanities and the medical school moved to its own brand-new building on the other side of the city.

"Apparently the Journalism Society's going to set up this volunteer radio station," I told her as we strolled there, unhurried. After a night of drizzle, the sun had returned and it made the leaves and buildings around us glow golden. "Want to give it a go?"

I'd seen the radio station mentioned on one of Jasper's social media accounts. I didn't follow him on any of them—I didn't want to give him the satisfaction of knowing I was interested in what he had to say—but I did check occasionally. He was a chronic over-sharer, posting his thoughts multiple times an hour—not that any of them were really worth sharing. It was all stuff like I thought Marmite was veggie/vegan, so what's the deal with Vegemite?? and Just took the bins out in Ellie's unicorn slipper boots and someone shouted SLAY at me.

On and on they went, detailing moments from his day and other random, pointless observations. But his most recent post had actually caught my attention.

> Guess what fellow students?? #JournoSoc is setting up the uni's first EVER radio station! #VolunteersWanted #GetInTouch

It had given me a wonderful idea.

I didn't necessarily need to volunteer at Jasper's radio station (since I was already volunteering with an *actual* news organization) but it seemed like something Crystal might be interested in. She'd said that she wanted to use her skillset to go in a new direction, and radio was completely new. This could be a good way for us to spend more time together—and, if things went well, hopefully become friends.

Maybe even best friends.

Now, Crystal frowned at me. "What, to be a presenter? I don't think so."

"Why not?"

"I don't think I'm the right type of person to present anything."

It was my turn to frown.

Crystal met my gaze for barely half a second before she laughed, her teeth glinting. "Okay, fair enough. Maybe I am. But I've never done radio before!"

"Exactly! It's something new to try," I said. "Besides, you've been in loads of videos, haven't you? Radio's just your voice."

"But it's live!"

"Not necessarily," I said. "You can pre-record stuff. I looked into it."

"Do you want to do it?" Crystal asked. Her wide eyes had never looked more blue, like twin pools, and I had the sudden urge to sink into them, to submerge myself and never return.

I shrugged. "I mean, I've got *Local Times*," I said. "I just wanted to see if *you* wanted to, so you could get some practical experience. If you did, I'd do it with you."

Crystal was quiet for a moment, and I knew she was considering it. "I suppose we could find out some more about it," she said. "Who's running it?"

"Jasper. We can ask him about it when we go in."

"Good idea," she said. Her cheeks had flushed, just slightly, and I grinned.

Crystal rolled her eyes, but she was smiling.

I held the door as I led the way into the lecture hall. Behind me, I heard Crystal's sharp intake of breath, and smiled as smugly as if I'd built the place with my own hands. An old operating theater, it had the creepy, Victorian medical school look: tiered seating in a circle, facing toward the middle where an operating table had once stood. It had been replaced long ago with a desk and a blackboard, and then, more recently, a smart board on the wall behind.

I'd learned during our first lecture here that our cohort wasn't big enough to fill the room, meaning we all gathered in loose groups around the circle. I led Crystal over to Sadie and Jasper, who were sitting together with some of the others: Zoe, Rowan, Ravi, Polly. I'd known Rowan the longest—they were a freelance photographer for *Local Times*, and although we'd never spoken we'd smiled at each other on the first day of the course, both glad to see a familiar face.

"Hey," Jasper said warmly when he saw us. "We were just talking about you."

I suspected he didn't mean me, but played into it anyway, putting a hand to my chest. "I'm flattered, Jasper, but you're just not my type."

There was some laughter, and Ravi nudged Jasper affectionately.

"Told you, mate," he said, and Jasper winced, as if the elbow in the ribs actually hadn't been all that friendly.

"I was talking to Crystal," Jasper said, louder this time. "We were wondering if you wanted to volunteer at the radio station with us?"

"Who's us?" I asked.

"Oh, me, Ravi, Zoe—basically all of us here."

"Alyssa did tell me about it," Crystal said. "I definitely want to know more—I guess I just don't want to commit to anything while I still have my catch-up assignments to do?"

"That's okay!" Jasper said, at the same time as Sadie said, "And your vlog stuff, too."

Crystal seemed to visibly shrink. "Yeah," she said. "Right."

"Yes!" Jasper said. "I can't believe you didn't tell us at the pub the other night! You've basically got a ready-made audience of thousands for whatever you want to do. It's awesome!"

"Well—"

Crystal was interrupted by a loud clap from the front of the theater. Our lecturer, Dominic, had arrived. In his forties, with graying red hair and a habit of leaving just one too many of the top buttons of his shirt undone, I found him a bit off-putting, a bit sleazy. While he had plenty of experience, and had already delivered some interesting lectures on his subject—law and ethics in the media—he'd had some controversial moments in his career. He shared in our first lecture that he'd briefly been a paparazzo, followed by a stint as a tabloid journalist. I even remembered his biggest scoop—an exposé revealing all sorts of sordid secrets about a family on television.

I turned to Crystal to share this, but she was already staring at him, completely rapt. Did she already know who he was? Surely not. And, even if she did, why would she be looking at him like he'd hung the moon?

"Good morning, everyone," Dominic said, with his characteristic cheerfulness. "Any reason you're all sitting up there in the gods? This isn't an operating theater anymore, you know. You're not going to get splashed with gore!"

There was a scattering of uncertain laughter.

Dominic shook his head at us. "I'll leave you as you are for now, since you're all settled. But next week, I want at least *some* of you sitting down here with me. Okay?"

"Okay," we all said in a monotone.

"Now, I know we don't always do this," Dominic said. "Since we're all adults here. But I've been asked to take a register today, just for some attendance figures. When I call out your name, just say 'here'—like you would have at school. Sadie Abbot?"

"Here!" Sadie piped up.

The register went on, enlightening me as to the surnames of the rest of the group—Jasper Humphries, Ravi King, Rowan Lennox, Zoe Sullivan, and Polly Underwood. And, of course, Crystal Shaw.

"Crystal Shaw?" Dominic repeated, looking up at our group with interest after Crystal had confirmed her attendance. "Of *At Home with the Shaws*?"

Crystal nodded. "Yes," she said, barely audible. I could feel everyone's eyes on us, and I knew that Crystal would, too.

He looked at her for a second longer, with some kind of searching gaze that I couldn't quite translate, and then moved on with the final few names. Beside me, I could feel the tension pouring off Crystal, like the heat haze wavering over a tarmac road on a hot day.

"Are you okay?" I murmured.

"Fine," she whispered back, but her teeth were gritted. I had the feeling she didn't like being ambushed with her role as a social media star.

The rest of the lecture continued without drama, and we left together. It occurred to me that the Journalism Society was becoming quite the close-knit group.

"Does anyone want to go for a coffee?" Ravi asked. "Or some food? That new ramen place on Trafalgar Street's supposed to be really good."

"It's amazing," Rowan said. "I'll come."

Ravi pointed at them, delighted. "*Yes*, Rowan! Anyone else?"

"Sure," Polly said, followed by an affirmative nod from Zoe.

"Crystal?" I asked.

She looked drawn, tired. "I think I'm just going to go home," she said, with a small, apologetic smile. "Next time, though?"

"But we need to talk about the radio station stuff," I said.

"There's not *that* much to go over," Jasper said, and I resisted the urge to glower at him. "We're meeting in the new radio studio at the SU tomorrow at ten. We'll do a bit of training then, talk through roles and maybe a rota, if you want to come along?"

"Okay," Crystal said. "Sounds good. Thanks, Jasper. I'll be there."

A warm feeling filled my chest. I was already looking forward to seeing her tomorrow; I was starting to enjoy having her as a friend. And if we got to spend more time together volunteering, maybe we'd become closer. Maybe we'd actually become good friends.

Although volunteering did mean she'd be spending just as much time with Jasper and the others, and while I wasn't jealous of Rowan or Zoe or any of the rest of them, I didn't like the thought of Jasper muscling in on our friendship, what with his floppy hair and tendency to make Crystal blush.

"Amazing," Jasper said now, just as I said, "Cool!"

I glared at him, but he didn't seem to notice. Neither did Crystal.

"See you guys tomorrow, then," she said.

We watched her leave.

"God," Zoe said. "It's so tragic, isn't it?"

"What is?" I asked.

"Her *life*. Spending her whole childhood being filmed for likes? That's just so sad."

"She doesn't seem sad," Jasper said.

I could still see Crystal in the distance as she walked through throngs of students, her light hair standing out. Her back was slightly hunched, as if against the cold.

"Yes," I said. "She does."

Chapter Seven

CRYSTAL

The invitation to go for coffee or for something to eat had been kind, but I couldn't face the rest of the group right now. Not after that.

Part of me was furious at the way that man—Dominic, the former tabloid reporter—had acknowledged my parents' channel so casually. The Journalism Society group had only just found out, and that was bad enough—never mind the rest of the cohort. I had visions of them all going home, back to their rented flats and student accommodation blocks and house shares, all looking up *At Home with the Shaws* and scrolling through my life, taking in all my highs and lows, taking in Lexie's illness and what had happened to her.

It made me feel raw like an exposed nerve.

Statue House wasn't far from campus, and I was glad. I stopped at the mini supermarket down the street and stocked up on a few bits: bread, tins of soup, milk, and some chocolate to help me feel better. I wanted a home-cooked meal, like mince or dumplings or a pie with the pastry just the way Mum made it, with buttery mashed potatoes made from the ones Oliver and Opal had dug up in the garden.

Despite everything, I missed my family. I didn't regret my decision to come to London, to try to live a life that was more than analytics and views and subscribers, but the separation from them felt like a wound. I told myself it would heal, eventually. I just had to give it time.

As I made my way back to my apartment, I considered Alyssa's proposal about volunteering for the radio station. I liked the Journalism Society, especially Jasper and Alyssa, and it seemed like a good opportunity to spend more time with them, to really solidify our friendship. Plus, maybe Alyssa had been right, and radio could be a new way to use my skills.

And then there was my other reason, my secret ulterior motive. The true reason I'd wanted to join the Journalism Society.

Back in my apartment, as I heated up a bowl of soup in the microwave, I allowed my mind to drift toward it, skirting around its edge.

I was looking to make a connection.

Alyssa's position at *Local Times*, even if it was a low-ranking one, was valuable—and, more importantly, I was sure she'd be willing to help me. But now there was Dominic, too. I'd blanched at the way he'd made me a spectacle in front of the class. He was awful, but I knew his history and there was no denying that he could be useful. He'd definitely know the right people and the right publications to approach. The question was, could I trust him? Could I trust anyone?

Once I'd finished my soup and rinsed the bowl, I changed into my pajamas and made myself a cup of tea. I got into bed, bundled myself up in my duvet, and sipped the tea slowly, savoring the warmth. Everything would come in time.

I woke up a couple of hours later, my empty mug on the bedside table. The room was dim, and outside the sky had darkened and it had begun to rain. I could hear the cars on the street, the rush of their tires in the wet as they sped by. The shadows of raindrops rolled across the floor.

At first, I wondered what had woken me—and then my phone buzzed again. Mum.

Hi lovely! Opal's asking if she can video call you. xxx

Now, if you're free. xxx

When I first saw Mum's name flash up, I'd groaned aloud. I couldn't be bothered with any more passive-aggressive comments about my content, or lack of it. But when I'd read Opal's name, warmth lit me up inside.

I texted back to say it was fine, then quickly brushed my hair, flicked on a light, and applied some tinted lip balm. I ran a fingertip under my eyes, removing any stray flecks of mascara, then started the video call. I held the phone up, and smiled.

Seconds later, Opal's face filled the screen. "Crystal!"

I laughed. "Hi! Move back a bit; I can only see your nostrils."

She did, giggling. She gave me a wave with her other hand, and I noticed her fingernails had been painted rainbow colors and then nibbled away. Typical Opal.

"That's better," I told her. "How's everything at home? How are you?"

Opal sighed. "I'm good. Miss you, though."

"I miss you, too. I'll be home soon, remember? For Christmas."

"You're *definitely* coming home for Christmas?" The hope in her big blue eyes just about broke my heart.

"I am," I said. "As long as the ferries are still running and the planes are still flying! So cross your fingers the weather's not too bad in December, okay?"

Opal held up her crossed fingers to the camera, grinning. Her smile faded slightly. "I asked Mum if we could wait till you come home to put all the Christmas decorations up, so we could do it all together, but she said we have so much to film this year they're going up early."

"Never mind. It was sweet of you to ask. Just send me some pictures instead."

"I will!" she said. The screen jerked slightly, and her tone changed—whiny and put out. "Oliver, get off! It's my turn."

My little brother's face crept into view, his forehead and eyes pressing against Opal's cheek. My siblings looked very alike, owing to them being twins, but they weren't identical. They both had blue eyes—we all did—but Oliver had darker hair. Lexie's had been dark, too, like Mum's. Mine was closer to blond, like Opal's and Dad's.

"Hey, Oliver!" I said.

"Hi, Crystal," he said, nudging his way in beside Opal. "Do you like London?"

"I think so. I'm still getting used to it."

"Is it super busy? Are there loads of cars?"

Opal scoffed. "Duh. It's a city."

"Be nice," I said to her, and she grinned cheekily. Then, to Oliver, I added, "It's really busy, loads of cars. There are lights on all night, and I can see them whenever I look out of my window."

"No stars though?"

I shook my head. "No stars."

"And what's *university* like?" Opal drew out the word, savoring it. She loved school, and was already dreaming of the day she could follow in my footsteps.

"It's good," I said. "Interesting. I'm meeting lots of new people. I've had some lectures. And there's a radio station that I might do some volunteering with."

"Mum!" Opal yelled. "Did you hear that? Crystal's going to be on the radio!"

"Opal!" I hissed, but it was too late. Mum had come through.

She took the phone from Opal, who huffed. "You're going to be on the radio?" she asked, her face looming in on the screen. "Which station?"

"It's not a real radio station," I said. "It's the one in the Students' Union. I'm just going there tomorrow to find out some more about volunteering on it."

Mum sniffed contemptuously, and I knew she had more to say—and not necessarily about the radio station, either. "Oliver, Opal? Say goodbye to your sister. I need to talk to her for a minute."

I heard a chorus of "bye!" and there came the sound of the door closing. Then silence.

"I know you want to fully embed yourself in university life," Mum said, in a very different, far more disapproving tone. "But please don't forget that you have responsibilities to us, your family."

"I haven't!" I protested.

"Crystal, you haven't sent us a video in two days."

"Not a lot's happened."

"It's been interesting. You've met lots of new people. You've been to some lectures." I realized, with a sinking feeling, that she was repeating what I'd told Opal just minutes ago. Did she listen in to all our conversations? "That sounds like plenty of potential content to me," Mum finished triumphantly.

I sighed. "You're right. Sorry, Mum. It's just been really busy."

"I want you to film something tonight," she said. "Post it on your feeds, and we'll share it." Her expression turned from stony to sympathetic. "I know it's a big change for you, sweetheart. University's a lot of pressure. You'll adapt soon, I promise. But we still need you. We need the likes and the shares—it's our income."

I was used to living under pressure—being partly responsible for my parents' financial situation, for example—but I decided against saying that aloud. "I know," I said. "I'll film something tonight, and then a longer update tomorrow, too."

"That would be perfect," she said. "Thank you, petal."

She smiled into the camera. Our relationship was complicated to say the least, but I still missed her. I missed the sea salt and lavender scent of her perfume, the tightness of her hugs, the waxy print her lipstick would leave on my cheek when she kissed me. I wondered if she missed me in the same way. Was that why she was looking at me like that, so intently?

And then she said, lips pursing, "Before you film anything, though, put on a bit of makeup, won't you? Poor thing, you look *exhausted*."

The following morning, I filmed a grudging #GRWM and forwarded it to my mum. The previous night I'd also filmed a quick video—after applying a swathe of concealer and refreshing my eye makeup—that I'd titled "UNI CATCH UP <3."

In the catchup, I'd talked about how much I'd enjoyed my first lectures, how beautiful the buildings on campus were, and how strange it was being in a busy city after living on the island for my whole life. I carefully left out any mention of the pub, my hangover, and the occasional feelings of loneliness. I had to create an image, a lifestyle, an aesthetic that people could aspire to, even if it wasn't entirely true. Because who would want to watch the truth?

Mum hadn't given me her approval for either of them yet, but I'd pre-prepared an array of hashtags and two emoji-filled captions that didn't reflect my actual feelings in the slightest. Those were the opposite of my cheerful update—I was irritated with Mum, upset she cared more about missed potential content than whether I was settling in at university and enjoying myself.

And while she hadn't technically forced me to film anything—she never had—the unspoken threats were always there. They might stop sending me money (the money that I'd helped earn), decide to exclude me from the family, or even air out the situation to hundreds of thousands of followers who practically worshipped my parents. No, fighting it wasn't worth it. Not yet, anyway.

I put on my wireless headphones, smoothed down my hair, and forced a smile at myself in the mirror. Then I switched on a mood-boosting playlist, slipped my phone into the pocket of my pink wool coat, and left the apartment behind. When my phone buzzed a while later, I ignored it. Mum's approval could wait a little longer.

The radio station was more of a radio cupboard. It had been constructed inside an old storage closet, and we all had to squeeze in tight, our elbows in each other's ribs, while Jasper went over how to use the equipment.

"This is the mixing console," he explained, gesturing to the big desk in front of us. “You’ll have your headphones on; this here is your microphone, and this is the fader for when you’re speaking. When it’s up, like this”—he moved a slider toward the top of the desk—“you can see that the microphone icon on the screen, there, turns red. That means you’re live.” He turned to us expectantly. “See? Easy peasy.”

“How do you know all this?” Polly asked.

“I did volunteer shifts on hospital radio for a while,” Jasper replied. “It runs all day and night, basically, online—like ours will. But it also plays in the wards and waiting rooms. It’s just to make people smile a bit when they’re having a hard time.”

“That’s so lovely,” Rowan said, and there were murmurs of agreement. I found myself warming even more to Jasper.

“So, yeah,” Jasper said with a self-conscious shrug and a smile. “That’s pretty much all there is to it. We’re not expecting the station to be live all day every day, so we don’t have to fill, like, twenty-four hours, seven days a week with shows. But if you’ve ever wanted to try hosting your own show, this is your chance.”

“I could host something sporty,” Polly said thoughtfully. “Looking at the university’s sports teams, their performance, their latest scores. Interview some of the future stars, maybe?”

“Sounds good,” Jasper said. “I like it.”

“What about local news?” Alyssa asked. “Could we do news bulletins? It’d be great experience.”

“I don’t see why not,” Jasper said. “Obviously, we’d have to abide by the same rules and regulations that actual radio stations have to when it comes to news, but we’re learning about all that anyway.”

Alyssa was right—it would be great experience. I’d never done anything like that before: reporting on real news, real stories. I’d only ever talked about myself. Suddenly, it seemed unbearably vain.

“I could do that with you, Alyssa,” I said. “If you want.”

"Really?" she asked, flashing me a huge smile. "That'd be amazing. Let's do it!"

"Yes!" Jasper said, practically bouncing up and down in his excitement. "We've got our sports host, our dynamic reporting duo . . . anyone else?"

"Are you going to host anything, Jasper?" Zoe asked.

"I want to," he said. "I'm still brainstorming ideas."

"You could always do some stuff with us," I offered. "In the meantime."

Jasper glanced between me and Alyssa. "Are you sure?"

I wasn't sure if it was just a trick of the light, but Alyssa's face seemed to fall. "Sure," she said. "That'd be fun."

"Okay," Jasper said, his gaze fixed on me. "That'd be great, then. Thanks."

Alyssa leaned toward me and whispered as Jasper continued talking to the others about potential shows. "We could start today, if you wanted. Like, now."

"Now?" I repeated.

"Yeah," she said. "Why not? Have you got anything better to do?"

I did not.

"It'd be good to get some practice in on a day when we don't have any lectures," she added. "And it's not like we need any specialist equipment."

This part, Jasper overheard. "That's true," he said. "If you're recording outside of the studio, you can just use your phone. It's good enough quality, as long as you're out of the wind."

"Well, why don't we do a practice run?" Alyssa asked me. "Record each other, do some pretend interviews? Try and get the hang of it, while Jasper's busy."

"I'm not busy," Jasper said, but Alyssa didn't seem to hear him—and he was quickly distracted by Rowan, who had a question about the headphones.

"Yeah, okay," I said. "Let's do a practice run."

Alyssa's answering smile was startling in its brightness. "Okay. Break for lunch, then we'll get started?"

We ate as a group at the campus coffee shop, then Jasper and the others headed back to the studio to practice with the equipment. He didn't seem too happy about it, looking at Alyssa and me longingly instead. But I didn't take pity on him and invite him with us. I felt mean about it, but I couldn't. He was the only one who knew how any of the equipment worked; the team needed him. So Alyssa and I left him behind and headed out into the city.

"It'll be good to get some experience recording where it's busy," Alyssa decided. "That way, if we're doing interviews somewhere crowded we know how to do it."

"Good idea," I agreed. "But how do we even find a story?"

"At *Local Times* a lot of them come from press releases," Alyssa explained. "Big news, like crime and stuff. Then there's local community groups, things like that. Basically, if people are passionate about something or angry about something, it's pretty likely they'll want to talk to you—to help get their message out there."

"Okay," I said. "And we'll do that? Get their message out there?"

Alyssa shrugged. "We'll try. I mean, the radio station doesn't have a lot of reach but . . . we could set up social media accounts, maybe. Post their stories on there, too. You'd be good at that!"

Maybe Alyssa was right. I knew what worked and what didn't, at least until whichever platform it was switched up its algorithm again. For the first time since we'd discussed volunteering for the radio station, I felt actual excitement. Maybe presenting a radio show wasn't a potential future career for me—but reporting news on social media could be. It might be the exact pivot I'd hoped for, a way to use my skills in a more valuable way.

By now, we were a good distance from campus, lost in the maze of city streets. It was a maze to me, at least; Alyssa seemed perfectly confident walking along, as if she knew exactly where she was going. There was a green space across the road from us, a little park dotted with benches and trees, their changing leaves every shade of fire in the autumn sun. Without consulting each other, we crossed at a crosswalk and sat on a bench, side by side.

"In memory of June," I read aloud from the plaque. "This was her favorite spot."

I understood why June had liked it. Facing away from the city's tallest buildings, with trees and a thick hedge blocking the view on the other side, it was almost easy to imagine I was anywhere else—in the countryside, maybe. Even at home.

"Do you miss home?" Alyssa asked me then, as if she could read my mind.

"A bit," I said. "Some parts of it. Do you?"

"Oh, I am home," Alyssa said. "Kind of. I grew up in the suburbs here."

"Wow. What was that like?"

"It was wonderful," she said. Then her expression grew sad. "When I was younger, anyway. My parents don't really care about me so much now I'm older and more independent. Especially now I've moved out. I really miss us being close like we used to be."

"That must be hard."

"It is," Alyssa said. "We used to have so much fun. This one time, when I was a kid, we were at the beach. It was supposed to be sunny, but clouds came over and it got all cold and dark when we'd only been there for an hour. My dad insisted it was time to give up, go home, but my sister and I pleaded and begged until we finally convinced him. Mum stayed with us while he went to get some blankets from the car, and he bought us hot chocolates from this cute little coffee van in the car park. There's a video of us, wrapped in these huge blankets on the sand, smiling fit to burst with our cups of hot chocolate."

Alyssa's words stirred something in me, but I wasn't sure what. A flash of something. A reminder of one of my own memories, maybe. I pushed it away. "I didn't know you had a sister," I said instead.

"We're not really on speaking terms."

"I'm sorry."

"Don't be," Alyssa said gently. "Your sister's dead."

Her words dripped with sympathy, and I allowed it to wash over me.

"I miss her," I said eventually. "We were only kids when she died. She was older than me. I always wonder what she'd be doing now, where she'd be."

"Where would she be?"

"I think she'd be traveling," I said. "She always wanted to get off the island, see the world—even when she was tiny. She wanted to be an explorer. We had this globe in our bedroom that glowed in the dark, and at night sometimes she'd turn it on and she'd whisper to me all the names of the countries she knew. And the landmarks, too—the Great Wall of China, the Colosseum. Although she couldn't say Colosseum. I think it was the *Colossal-eum*." I smiled at the memory, laughed a little, even as a tear slipped down my cheek.

"She sounds fun," Alyssa said wistfully.

I wondered if she was thinking about her own sister. "She was," I said. "And it's horrid to think that she never got the chance to see it, the Colosseum. She never got the chance to see any of those landmarks. Not a single one. Sometimes, it feels like I have to do all these things because she can't. Go to university, *do* something with my life. Because she would've done something with hers."

"I'm sure she'd be proud of you either way," Alyssa said. "No matter what you did."

"I hope so," I said. "I hope she'd approve of all this."

All this. All this meant my decision to leave the island to go to university, my choice to study journalism, my new friendships with Alyssa and the others.

And then there was the other thing—the thing I hadn't told

Alyssa or anyone about yet, the thing I needed help with. I wanted to just blurt it out, but I didn't want to ambush her. I had to take my time, weigh up my options. I had to talk to Alyssa, find out more about *Local Times*. And I would speak to Dominic, too, as much as the idea sickened me.

I had to make sure that it was done correctly, that as many people as possible listened to me—so that when my parents inevitably denied everything, nobody would even care.

Chapter Eight

ALYSSA

It was nice, just letting Crystal talk. I listened as she told me about Lexie, imagining what it would be like to have a sister just like her—fun-loving, adventurous. Being an only child sucked.

"Do you want to practice some interviews?" Crystal asked, changing the subject.

I decided she'd shared enough, so I didn't call her out on it. "Okay," I said. "We don't have to actually ask each other questions or anything, though—it's just to get the hang of the app."

We took out our phones, and I showed Crystal the app I planned to use, one that Bradley had recommended to me on my first day at *Local Times*: a simple, pre-installed voice recorder. Crystal had the same one.

"So what you do," I explained, "is hold this end, the bottom end, away from you. You can get mic muffs—these sponge-type things—which you put over the top as a buffer against the wind, your breath on the mic, that kind of thing. You hold it about here . . ." I held my phone roughly arm's length from her chin. "And then you tilt it back toward yourself if you want to record yourself speaking." I demonstrated. "Like this."

"Seems like you don't need the practice," Crystal said wryly.

"I've only done it once or twice," I said. "For *Local Times*. They don't use the audio for anything, not like radio, but it's good to have it to refer back to sometimes. My shorthand isn't great."

Crystal held out her phone as I'd instructed, the microphone pointing toward herself. "Alyssa Hayes," she said seriously. "What is your go-to coffee order?"

She tilted the microphone back toward me.

For a second I was taken aback, wondering how she knew my surname. Obviously, I was curious about Crystal—but was she curious about me, too? Had she looked me up? Not that there was much to find. And then I remembered Dominic's lecture, the one where he'd taken the register. *Of course.* Something a bit like disappointment sat heavily in my chest.

I considered. "A large latte with a flavored syrup," I said. "Either caramel or vanilla."

Crystal nodded sagely, as if I'd shared a very good answer to an important question. "And, if I may, a follow-up," she said. "Black coffee. Thoughts?"

"Disgusting."

"Fascinating." A smile was starting to break through her attempt at being a serious journalist. "Thank you for sharing that essential information."

"You're so welcome," I said. "Now it's my turn. Watch and learn." I brandished my phone like a weapon. "First of all, could you please give us your full name, just for the recording?"

Crystal's eyes lit up. She hadn't thought of that. "Crystal Shaw," she said.

"Perfect," I said. "So, Crystal—"

Beside her on the bench, Crystal's phone buzzed. Then again. I glanced at it.

"It's fine," she said, flipping it face down. "It's probably just my mum. Go on."

"So, Crystal," I repeated, trying to get back into the role. "What was your first impression of the Journalism Society?"

"Welcoming," Crystal said. "People were very kind, easy to talk to."

"And Jasper?" I asked, wiggling my eyebrows. "What was your first impression of him?"

She laughed. "I'm not answering that!"

"Why not? He's never going to hear it."

She shook her head at me, still smiling. "Fine. I thought he was a *little* bit overenthusiastic when he offered to get me a coffee. But I like him. I think he's cute." She leaned back. "And if you play him this recording, I will kick you in the head."

I looked her up and down. "Like you could reach."

"I absolutely *could* reach!"

"What are you? Five foot two?"

Crystal's jaw dropped in mock outrage. "How dare you! Just because *you're* so tall."

"I'm a very respectable, and pretty average, five foot six." Crystal rolled her eyes at me, grinning, and I realized that this was it. This was what I'd always wanted. *This* was a real friendship—somebody to have a serious conversation with, to open up to and *be* opened up to, and then to learn together, and mess around with.

Sitting together, Crystal's hair shining white in the sunlight and just the grass and trees in front of us, we could have been the only people in the world, if it wasn't for the cars and buses speeding past on the busy road behind us. And for Crystal's phone, which was still buzzing.

"Don't you ever get tired of that?" I asked her, nodding toward it.

She sighed. "Always."

"Why don't you turn it off?"

"Because then my mum would panic," she said. "The last thing I need is her coming here to try and find me. Or, God forbid, uploading a 'Crystal is missing' video to the channel."

I couldn't tell whether she was joking or not. "It's nice that she cares so much," I said. "That she wants to talk to you all the time."

"It's exhausting," Crystal said. "Sometimes, I wish she'd leave me alone. Even just for a day."

Unbidden irritation crept into my veins. How dare she brush off that kind of love? That kind of singular attention from a parent? She had no idea what it was like to have parents who weren't obsessed with you, who didn't want to know your every move. Parents who didn't want to know any of your moves at all, who checked in with a perfunctory text once a week—but only when they remembered, when they didn't have anything better to do.

"Maybe she'll calm down the longer you're at uni," I said.

"Hopefully," Crystal said. She looked at her phone, and sighed again. "Shall we head back now? I think I get the idea of how it all works."

"Okay," I said. "Maybe we can get Jasper to show us how to edit it on the software and get it playing in the studio or something?"

I was hoping she'd take the bait, laugh and tell me that Jasper was never going to hear that clip, no way!

But she didn't pick up on it. "That'd be great," she said, still looking at her phone screen, a troubled crease between her eyebrows.

She wasn't even listening to me. We'd had such a lovely time—or so I'd thought—and now this? I bit my lip so I didn't say something I'd regret later. Why was she paying more attention to her phone, to her mum whose love she was apparently happy to push away, than to me? It was bad enough that she seemed unbothered by her parents' love, their commitment to giving her the life she deserved, but somehow I was worth even *less* attention than they were.

I tried a different tactic. "You know," I said carefully, "I've really enjoyed this—just us two, working together. Don't you think the others can be a bit of a . . . buzzkill sometimes? And I know they meet up without us, too. They don't invite us places all the time."

I didn't know if this was true. But it didn't matter—Crystal still wasn't listening.

"I'm sorry," she said then, looking up at me. "I just can't concentrate on anything else. Look at this."

She held out her phone. The screen was filled with notifications, every single one from her mum aside from a solitary text from Opal, Crystal's younger sister. The lack of space at the bottom of the screen suggested if she scrolled down there'd be tons more.

"It's okay," I said. "I get it."

I *wished* I got it. Why didn't she understand how lucky she was?

We walked back to the campus, both of us quiet, lost in our thoughts.

"Hey," Crystal said when we were just a street or two away. "Actually, can we finish this up tomorrow? After our seminar?"

I was startled. "Why?"

"I'm just—I'm kind of exhausted," she admitted, with a self-deprecating little laugh. "I'm feeling pretty drained from the past few days."

"Oh. Okay, yeah," I said, stumbling over the words. Even though I was irritated with Crystal, I still wanted us to be friends, to be her best friend. And her dismissal stung. Didn't she enjoy being with me? Wasn't I helpful, showing her how to use the app?

"Seriously," Crystal said. "I've had a lovely time, and it's been super educational. I'm just so tired."

"No, no, of course," I said. "I totally get it. It's such a huge adjustment, right? It feels like we've never stopped since we got here."

"Exactly," she said, looking at me gratefully. "Thanks so much for understanding. Maybe we could grab a coffee tomorrow, after, and get Jasper to show us the software stuff?"

"Maybe. As long as he isn't busy."

"Well," she said. "We can ask him at our next lecture. Or I'll text him!"

She had his phone number? How had that happened? *When* had that happened? My mood went from bad to worse.

"Sounds good," I said, forcing myself to sound normal, to smile.

Apparently, it worked, because Crystal threw her arms around me in a completely unexpected hug. "Amazing," she said. "See you tomorrow, okay? Have a good rest of your day."

"You too," I said, a little stunned.

I turned back the way we'd come, heading toward my flat. I wasn't sure how to feel—I was still annoyed at her, and at Jasper for his apparent audacity, but I liked her, too. I liked her so much. She was so sweet, and kind, and pretty—she was everything I wanted to be. But she also *had* everything I wanted, too, and she didn't even appreciate it. It was complicated.

Back at the flat, I said a cursory hello to my flatmates (they were huddled up watching an old episode of *The Great British Bake Off*—exciting adults, we were not) and went into my room.

My laptop was still on my bed where I'd left it, and I changed into a soft pair of joggers and a T-shirt before allowing myself to open it up, to indulge myself. It was nearly out of power. I plugged it into the wall and set it on my bedside table. I needed something comfortable tonight; something familiar, like a favorite old jumper.

I opened the website and scrolled through the list of videos, wondering which one would be the perfect antidote to my glum mood and tonight's inevitable insomnia. I saw a title, and smiled. I'd watched this one before, more times than I could count. I clicked on it.

Lettering appeared on the screen in a white bubbly font: "A Day at the Beach."

I laid my head on my pillow as a woman appeared on the screen, smiling fondly with perfect white teeth. There was an empty beach, ironclad clouds in the distance, a brisk breeze. And the ending: two small girls, wrapped in blankets and coated with sand, each of them clutching a paper cup of hot chocolate and steam rising up toward their flushed, glowing faces.

My eyes were heavy. I clicked replay, and the title reappeared onscreen again, those familiar bubble letters. I wanted the video to play forever; I wanted to crawl inside it, to live inside that day, that memory. Even if it wasn't my own.

I let the sound of the girls' laughter lull me to sleep.

Chapter Nine

CRYSTAL

My stomach churned with guilt for abandoning Alyssa, but there was no way I could focus on the goings-on in the studio when Mum was in one of these moods. It took me straight back to my childhood, that grating, walking-on-eggshells atmosphere that would permeate the house whenever she and my dad had had an argument—usually about money.

I wanted to stay out, to make friends—it was one of the main reasons I'd come to university, after all. I wanted to put myself first, but every time I saw Mum's name flash up on my screen, the preview of yet another passive-aggressive text, my heart sank and my skin prickled and I just wanted to be alone.

I started to calm down once I was back inside Statue House, safely locked away in my apartment. It was beginning to feel like a safe place, my own space—one that nobody else could touch. Not even my mum.

I filled a glass with water from the tap, and sipped it slowly until I could feel my heart rate decreasing. Then I sat down on the edge of my bed, and read each notification one by one, in the order they were sent.

> I've watched the videos you sent, and I think we can make some improvements! Do you have time today? xxx

> I'd like something uploaded today, so please get back to me ASAP. xxx

Hello? xxx

Crystal. Answer me, please.

Video-calling you to discuss at 7 p.m. No excuses.

Anxiety-induced nausea rose in my throat, acrid and burning. I couldn't escape my fate—a video call *would* be happening, whether I wanted one or not—but I could try to do some damage control before I had to see her face-to-face.

Sorry, Mum! I was at a training session for the radio thing I told you about. No phones allowed in the studio, and then it was on airplane mode because I was using it for recording. Video call sounds good. x

Were my excuses believable? Yes. But would *Mum* believe them? That, I wasn't sure about. I flopped back onto my bed, already bracing myself for 7 p.m.

Mum was in her pajamas when she video-called me, but she didn't look any less beautiful. She always looked elegant, like a film star—even when she was in a quilted coat and wellies in the garden or, like now, wearing a simple white flannel pajama set with her hair pulled back from her face.

"Hello, darling," she said, then immediately launched into a monologue about a school project Oliver and Opal were doing that had been causing chaos.

I nodded along, wondering when she'd actually address the reason she'd insisted on calling me, until eventually she ran out of steam. Then, she looked at me sorrowfully and let out a long, drawn-out sigh.

"I watched the videos you sent, Crystal," she said. "Why do you sound so happy in them?"

She spoke in a deceptively calm way, but her eyes glittered.

This wasn't what I'd expected. "I—what?"

"You're so *happy* in those videos you've filmed. Do you want the world to know how much you love being away from us all?"

"Mum, I—"

She ignored me. "You want the world to see you hundreds of miles away, gallivanting around London without a care in the world? Is that it?"

"No!" I protested. "That's not it at all. I promise, Mum. I was just . . . excited."

"You were excited," she repeated, her voice utterly devoid of emotion.

"Yes," I said. "I thought my—*our* followers would want to see that, you know? The real emotion of it all. It's my first day at university—I *should* be excited, right? Excited and nervous?"

I could see that my words were placating her, that furious gleam in her eyes beginning to fade. A decade's worth of learning exactly what to say and when to say it had paid off.

"I've been talking to your father," she said. "And he agrees with me that we need something different."

"Different how?"

"It's unsatisfying as a viewer to watch you go to university and immediately be happy," she explained. "We pride ourselves on the wonderful home life you and your siblings have. Our home is idyllic; we emphasize slow, clean living and natural foods. It just doesn't make sense for you, as a character in our brand's story, to leave this lifestyle and immediately thrive."

Ah, of course. Our brand's story.

In conversations like this, I wasn't Crystal Shaw, daughter, with hopes, dreams, and plans of her own. I was Crystal Shaw, of *At Home with the Shaws*, the bookish older sister of the cutie-pie twins.

I read, cleaned, gardened, and experimented with makeup and hair styling—but only light makeup and pretty, girly hairstyles. Nothing too "grown up." Sometimes, I was surprised that Mum didn't try to make me wear floral dresses or have my hair in plaits like I used to when I was six. Anything to stop me from becoming an adult, to prevent their beloved followers from losing interest in me.

"So should I make something up?"

"It isn't making something up, necessarily," Mum corrected, clipped. "It's adapting the truth to tell a more engaging story. I'm sure, deep down, you felt odd when you first arrived in the city—alone, small, frightened. We're just going to extend those feelings for a while for the sake of the brand, to create a story that people will want to follow. We want them to come on your journey with you."

I didn't want anybody on my journey. It was *my* journey, and mine alone.

Besides, I would never admit it to her, but I felt less alone in the city than I had on the island. It was beautiful there, yes—but here I could truly be myself. On the island, I was acting a part. All the time.

"What if I talk about feeling homesick? I could cry a bit."

"Don't overdo it," Mum said. "I don't want people saying I'm an irresponsible parent for letting you move there."

Ah, yes. Mum's two top priorities, I thought bitterly. *The brand and her reputation.*

And her reputation was sure to be tarnished when I'd completed my plan. No, not just tarnished—it would be beyond tarnished. It would be decimated. Destroyed. She'd never monetize a video again.

My cold sense of satisfaction at the thought meant it was far easier to smile and agree with her. Just for a little bit longer. "Okay. Maybe I'll just choke up a little, talk about how much I miss you and Dad and the twins."

"Please emphasize that," Mum said. "The twins are missing you something rotten, and it'd look callous if you didn't feel the same."

I heard the unspoken warning behind her words: miss them while you have the chance, because you know how abruptly a sibling can be torn away from you. And once they're gone, no amount of missing them will ever bring them back.

I didn't have to pretend to miss Oliver and Opal, though—I missed them like I'd probably miss a hand or a foot, something that you took for granted. Something that would always be there until suddenly it wasn't.

Like Lexie.

The thought of the twins filled me with gritty determination. They were why I was here—everything I had planned was for them. I just had to find the best way to carry it out. And to do that, I had to stay on the right side of Mum. For now, at least.

So I smiled, and promised her I'd re-record the videos and do my best to appear a little more subdued and anxious.

Once we'd ended the video call (with a promise to speak again "soon," as if she'd ever let me have a single day of peace), I set up my phone on my go-to tripod and adjusted my lamp for the best lighting. I practiced a watery smile, and hit record.

"Hi, everyone," I began. "If you've been following *At Home with the Shaws* over the past couple of weeks, you'll know I've been getting ready to go to university on the mainland. Which is where I am, right now." I waved my hands around in a gesture encompassing my surroundings: the studio, the city outside its walls. "Honestly? I want to be all happy and excited for you guys, but, well . . . it's been tough."

A few minutes later, after lamenting the lack of home comforts like sea air and evening board games with the twins and Mum's delicious cooking, I ended the recording. The second it stopped, I couldn't help but smile. It was a load of rubbish, obviously, but Mum was going to eat it *up*. Her followers would, too.

It was so strange that all we seemed to do online as a family was *lie*.

But then, wasn't that the whole point? Nobody tuned in to watch influencers telling the truth about themselves and their lives unless it was at least a little bit exaggerated. Wasn't that the whole point of "story time" videos, of shopping hauls, of videos relaying gossip and rumors and scandal? We had to create something to talk about, and make sure that that "something" was us. Even if there was nothing going on at all in our lives, we'd find a scrap to dramatize—from a lavender athleisure set we'd been paid to review that was INCREDIBLE, to a new restaurant we'd tried that served THE BEST truffle parmesan fries. Everything was new, fresh, and exciting—even if it wasn't entirely real.

I wondered if anybody would ever be interested in me for me. If I wasn't Crystal Shaw of *At Home with the Shaws*, if I was just Crystal, would anybody care about me or what I thought? I had to believe that they would. What else did I have?

My phone vibrated, and I groaned. I didn't even want to look at it—surely such a quick response from Mum could only be criticism, and I didn't think I could handle that right now. I'd probably end up tossing my phone out of the window with frustration.

But it wasn't. It was a text from Jasper. I was surprised to see his name flash up.

> Hey! Sorry to miss you this afternoon. Happy to go over the rest of the studio stuff whenever you're next free/ if you're still interested? No probs if not tho, just let me know what you think! J :)

I couldn't help it; a silly little smile spread across my face. Alyssa would have absolutely made fun of me for it. But Jasper was texting me! A *boy* was texting me.

And, okay, he probably didn't think of me like that. I didn't even know if I thought of *him* like that, but I did like him. He was sweet, if a little overenthusiastic, and he had great hair. It was a start, and I felt guilty for leaving him hanging.

Hey! So sorry, really had to rush off otherwise I would've explained & said bye! That'd be great.

No worries! Maybe after our next lecture? No pressure, though! How're you finding it here?

I'm starting to settle in, I think! Really enjoying it.

Good! Let me know if there's anything you need any help with or whatever, always happy to. :)

I will! Thanks so much.

A little glow lit up my chest and I lay back on my bed, smiling. Jasper clearly cared about the real Crystal, not the carefully edited online fabrication. And so did Alyssa.

Why not the rest of the world?

Chapter Ten

ALYSSA

I didn't see or hear from Crystal again until our next lecture, which was two days later, and it felt like an age. I'd spent the majority of both days in bed, obsessively watching video after video of people who were happier than I was. That was, admittedly, one of the negatives of social media—everybody was always happier than I was.

I was more cheerful the morning of our lecture though, excited at the prospect of seeing Crystal again. My long brown coat, a new purchase ready for the onset of winter, flapped in a rising wind, crisp fallen leaves, and assorted detritus dancing around my black boots as I strode through the cobbled city streets toward campus. The campus was in an older part of the city, and I liked to pretend sometimes that the rest of it—the cars and the shopping centers and the high-rise buildings—didn't exist. I loved the city, loved the life and the din of it, but I also loved the quiet dustiness of the old buildings. The university library, for example—I adored its towering shelves of books and the shafts of light, cathedral-like, that poured in through its arched windows.

Everything in my life had always been new, new, new. Metal and plastic and silver-mirrored sheen, lurid and gaudy and utterly tasteless. I preferred old things to my parents' ultra-modern taste. I found junk shops and car boot sales havens of antiquity whereas my parents saw only rubbish. They'd never understood the appeal of anything historical, and they didn't like the Cradlewell University campus—named for the former village that had been absorbed into the city sprawl decades earlier. The only bit of the campus they'd approved of the one time they visited was the Students' Union, and that was because it was 90 percent glass.

I still had a bit of time to kill before the lecture, so I made my way to my favorite spot in the library, in a lamp-lit corner, and texted Crystal.

Here early! At the library if you want to meet up. x

I wasn't sure if she'd reply, considering her hasty exit the last time we'd seen each other. I hadn't texted her since—I didn't want to be clingy. If I came on too strong, it'd only be off-putting, like what had happened with Davina: her freaking out and running to Bradley because I wore the same color nail polish as her. No, Crystal and I would soon be best friends no matter what; it was written in the stars.

Leaving my phone open to wait for Crystal's reply, I pulled out my laptop. About 80 percent battery. I'd forgotten to charge it before I left the flat; I was relieved it had been plugged in and sitting on my bedside table for most of the past forty-eight hours. I usually preferred to hand-write my notes, but Tony, our lecturer for Practices of Broadcasting, talked at the speed of sound—which meant a *lot* of notes.

Maybe I should have warned Crystal. She'd only brought a notebook and pen last time. But then, I didn't want to double text . . .

On the table in front of me, my phone buzzed. When I saw Crystal's name on the screen, I let out a sigh of relief. I wouldn't need to double text after all.

Amazing! I'll be there in 10–15, just about to leave.

If you have a laptop, you should bring it. Tony talks fast, and it's hard to keep up by hand! I learned the hard way last time. x

The screen lit up seconds later.

Good idea! Thanks so much.

We had thirty minutes until the lecture, and if Crystal arrived in fifteen minutes maximum, we'd still have fifteen minutes to catch up, to become even closer than we already were.

It was only ten minutes later when she found me, her cheeks pink and her hair windblown. The light strands framed her flushed face beautifully, and I found myself wondering whether I, too, might suit that shade of blond.

"Hey!" she said cheerily. "Thanks for the tip about the laptop. I was literally just about to leave, so I'm so glad you texted."

I shrugged. "No worries," I said. "Are you ready for two hours of Tony?"

Crystal peered at me. "I don't know. Am I?"

"You're going to need a coffee," I said. "I know that much. Why don't we go via Black's?"

I'd hoped she'd ask what Black's was, so I could remind her that I'd already told her about it, but she only nodded.

I gathered my things and set off out of the library, down the stone steps, with Crystal at my heels. I wondered what she'd been up to for the past two days, why she'd disappeared so hurriedly after our radio training. I wondered if she'd been with Jasper, and the thought brought up a hot rush of jealousy. It wasn't that I didn't like him, or the others on our course. I liked all of them. But none of them had what Crystal had, that magnetism, that sheen that said *I'm going to be somebody, and if you're my friend I'll bring you with me*. I didn't think Crystal even knew she had it.

When we got to the coffee shop there was a queue three or four deep, and Crystal glanced anxiously at her phone.

"We're in the same lecture hall as last time," I said. "It's only a minute away. We're not going to be late."

"It's not that," Crystal said, biting her lip.

"What is it?"

"My mum."

"Oh, right," I said. Inside, I thought, *This, again?*

Something in my reaction, the intake of my breath, perhaps, must have tipped her off to my frustration.

"I don't mean to sound ungrateful," she said, backtracking slightly. "It's just . . . it's a difficult relationship."

Difficult. That, I understood. My mum wasn't interested in me whatsoever, but she was difficult—an enjoyer of awkward silences, a purveyor of stilted responses and pursed lips. Maybe I needed to be more sympathetic. I didn't know what Crystal's life was really like, even if it looked and sounded perfect.

"You don't sound ungrateful," I said, and she immediately brightened.

By now, we'd moved to the front of the queue. I ordered a sticky toffee latte, my favorite drink from the autumn menu, and Crystal ordered a caramel latte, size large, with an extra shot of espresso.

"That'll keep you awake," I said lightly. "Between the caffeine and the sugar."

"That's the plan," she said. "I didn't get much sleep last night."

We waited in companionable silence at the end of the counter once we'd paid, watching other students and customers coming and going. Every time the door opened, it brought in with it a gust of crisp autumnal air and, with the undertone of roasting beans and someone's musky perfume, the place smelled magical.

Once we'd got our drinks (Crystal chirping "thanks!" at the harried barista while I nodded my gratitude) we walked together to the lecture theater.

"Journo squad!" cried a voice from behind us. "Wait up!"

I kept walking, very deliberately, but Crystal stopped and looked over her shoulder. Her expression broke into a smile—one wider than she'd ever given me. "Jasper! Hey."

"Hey," he said. He'd broken into a jog, and was a little out of breath as he reached us. He pushed his infuriating fringe out of his eyes, a gesture that I knew made hearts melt. Including Crystal's, apparently.

"You didn't have to run!" she said. "We've still got a few minutes. We just stopped for coffee."

Jasper held up a travel mug. It was silver, with a thermal rubber band, and it looked expensive. "Great minds. Did you go to that place I texted you about?"

Crystal opened her mouth to reply, but I got in there first.

"I didn't know you two were texting," I said pleasantly.

They both glanced at each other guiltily, like children who thought they were about to get into trouble.

"We haven't been texting a lot," Jasper said.

"Only for the last couple of days," Crystal said at the same time.

I shrugged. "Whatever," I said lightly, trying to show how little I cared. I *did* care, though—I couldn't lose Crystal to someone like Jasper, with all his prom king perfection. She was *my* friend.

Crystal flashed me a dazzling smile, and I let my jealousy dissipate. I tried to think about it all more reasonably. Yes, Jasper was kind—but he wasn't me. They weren't kindred spirits like Crystal and I were.

Even so, something niggled at me, and it continued to do so through the lecture—all of us frantically typing away on our keyboards, the sound of our fingers hitting the keys a racket in the otherwise quiet room. Tony spoke as quickly as I'd promised, making jokes as he veered from topic to topic. Tony had also worked at *Local Times*, more than a decade ago now, and I'd hoped that, at some point, I could connect with him over it. Maybe he'd have some tips for surviving the more insufferable people like Bradley.

Once Tony had finished the lecture and answered some questions from the group, we all started to pack up our things.

"Hey, Lyss," Crystal said. "Do you want to come and do some radio training stuff?"

Something in my chest warmed at the nickname, thrown out so casually. Crystal *did* like me. Maybe she even felt the same way, saw the possibilities that I did—that we could be best friends, practically soulmates.

Jasper was hovering by the door, textbook clutched to his chest like a teddy bear, his face hopeful. I wanted, more than anything, to go with her. But I had an article to finish off for a shift at *Local Times* the following day—and I could hardly get on Bradley's bad side now, after the stupid nail polish debacle.

"It's okay," I said. I nodded toward Jasper, who immediately glanced up toward the ceiling, focusing intently on something in the corner. "I think Jasper's keen on it, though."

"Another day, then?" Crystal said. She leaned in for a hug, and I could smell the perfume she was wearing: it was sweet, sugary. "We should go for breakfast or something. Tomorrow?"

"That would be nice," I said. As I spoke, Jasper hitched his bag up higher onto his shoulder. I took the hint. "Okay, well, have fun! See you on Wednesday, right, Jasper? That's our next session?"

"Yeah," Jasper said, his smile unfairly dazzling. "See you Wednesday."

I let them go, then followed them out a minute or so later. By the time I'd made it outside, they'd gone.

I trudged home, one hand in my pocket as I ran my fingertips over the solid, smooth edges of my lighter. I was bitter at having to bail on potential plans with Crystal to do anything for Bradley. I decided that, after I'd finished the draft, I would have a lazy night. I wanted to conserve my energy for dealing with Bradley's bullshit. And Davina's. Maybe I was going to be hauled into another meeting tomorrow, this time about my hair color or the music I was listening to, something equally as pointless as the last one.

Back at the flat, I made myself a coffee with another one of Niamh's pods and crammed myself into the seat at my tiny desk. It was wedged between the skylight and a beam (a perk of being in the attic room—*not*) and opened my laptop.

Before I started, though, I decided to check on my favorite channel.

And yes—there was a new update! Several days early. I leaned forward, resting my chin on my hand, as I clicked play, eager to see what was going on with the happy family.

Marjorie was talking today, recording on her phone as she walked around the garden. The few trees around her were nearly bare, the last golden leaves only just hanging on, and I could see mountains behind her in the distance, hazy in low clouds. Marjorie was exactly the kind of mother I wished I had—she was playful and attentive, used phrases like "slow living" and "gentle parenting." She wore floral dresses and soft jumpers and sandals or walking boots, grew vegetables in the garden, and cooked hearty meals. She was never passive-aggressive; she never ignored her children; she never had better things to do than spend time with them. Sometimes, when I watched these videos, it was easy to imagine that I was part of her family.

"I know a lot of you have been following us since before Lexie passed away," she said, her expression taking on a mournful look, a wrinkle forming between her eyebrows—the same one that Crystal had, actually, but more set in. "Which means you've watched our little Crystal grow up. She's eighteen now, can you believe it? I can't, sometimes. Anyway, Crystal's moved away to go to university in the big city, which means she'll be featuring on this account a little bit less. Luckily, you'll be able to follow her university journey on her very own channel! She'll be posting the usual content she posts on her Instagram—reviews, makeup tutorials, all of that—as well as regular updates about her university experience. How exciting! So if you miss seeing Crystal, make sure you give her a follow. I'll pop the link in the caption. And look out for our Christmas video, when the Shaw family will be reunited! I think it's going to be an emotional one. Anyway, on to today's topic—clean eating! What is it, and how can you make sure *your* family are eating clean like ours?"

I'd lost interest in Marjorie. The mention of Crystal's university channel had set off an excited little alarm in my mind—had she mentioned *me*?

I'd been trying to separate the Crystal who I knew from the Crystal I'd watched grow up. She was the reason I'd chosen this university, after all. When her mum had mentioned in a video she was applying here, I couldn't believe my luck. Of course I'd made this university my first choice. I couldn't wait to meet her.

Crystal was like a sister to me. And in person, just like I'd hoped, she was quickly becoming my best friend. But it did upset me the way she talked about her family, somctimes—especially her mum. Every time she complained about the way she'd grown up, my picture-perfect image of her cracked just a little bit more.

I switched over to Crystal's new channel, which already had several thousand subscribers. There was one video, which had been uploaded the previous evening.

In it, Crystal—pretty but paler than she had been earlier today, with visible dark circles under her eyes—chatted about her first day at university only in the vaguest of terms. She described the campus—the beautiful library, the old stone buildings—and then the apartment she lived in, at which point she faltered.

"I'm so used to being at home, in a busy household with my parents and the twins, that it all feels very quiet here. The only background noise is the cars outside, which isn't a thing on the island." She laughed at herself. "We have cars, of course, but we're not near a main road. And even on a main road, there's about five cars an hour, if that. So the city's *very* different. I'm starting to make friends, I think, but honestly? It's pretty lonely, and I'm really missing home. I miss Oliver and Opal, and my parents. I miss sitting around the table at mealtimes, the big old scratched one you'll have seen in our most recent house tour video, when everyone's talking over each other and it's total chaos but it's so lovely, too. Right now, I'm eating my meals sitting in my apartment, and they're from the microwave. Nothing like

Mum's cooking." To my surprise, she wiped her eyes. They were reddening, a little wet around the edges. "I'm just homesick, I guess. It'll wear off eventually, I'm sure. And I'll be back home for Christmas, so it's not all tragic. And I'm sure I'll make friends. A friend. Eventually." She smiled bravely. "Okay, guys, that's it for today, I think. I'll keep you updated, and let you all know how I'm settling in. Love you all, and as always don't forget to like, share, and tell your friends!"

The video ended with a little credits screen, directing me to Crystal's other accounts and her parents' channel. I stared at the screen until it went black, my reflection appearing as a blur.

Homesick? Missing sitting around the table? Missing Oliver and Opal, and her parents? The same parents she was irritated with for checking up on her? She missed her mum's cooking, but couldn't stand to see a notification from her appear on her phone?

Her hypocrisy infuriated me. Crystal had no idea. She had no idea what it meant to have parents who cared about you, who were invested in you and your future. Whose absence you actually felt when they weren't with you. And here she was, pretending like she was grateful for it, like every notification on her phone didn't fill her with disdain.

She didn't deserve them.

She didn't deserve her family, the life and fame she'd been gifted.

I deserved them.

Chapter Eleven

CRYSTAL

We were only a short way down the hallway when I stopped. We were outside Dominic's office, and there was no time like the present.

"Hey, Jasper, is it okay if I meet you at the SU? I need to ask Dominic about something, and he's got his office hours now."

"Oh! Yeah, of course," he said. "Want me to wait for you?"

I shook my head. "I'll catch up. I won't be long, anyway."

Jasper smiled. "Sure. Take your time. I'll go and set up the studio, and I'll see you in a bit, yeah?"

I watched him go, and tried to keep from looking too fondly after him.

Once he'd left, I knocked on the office door cautiously, the first far quieter than I'd intended and the second a demanding rat-a-tat, which more than made up for my first meek knock.

"Come in!" a voice inside called, and I opened the door, peeking my head around it.

The lecturers didn't have their own office unless they were a senior lecturer—a professor or a program leader—and so Dominic shared his office with two others. Neither of them were there, a coffee-stained mug and an unlocked PC the only signs they'd been there recently at all. Dominic was at his desk, with a half-eaten muffin and a mug of something steaming beside him.

He swiveled his chair around, and seemed surprised to see that it was me, his gingery eyebrows rising even as he smiled. "Hey, Crystal!"

"Hi," I said. Now that I was here, I was beginning to regret my decision.

"Please, take a seat," he said. "What can I do for you?"

I did as instructed, my hands clasped in my lap. Almost without realizing, I picked at my fingernails, the dry skin around their edges: a well-ingrained nervous habit. "I was wondering if I could ask you a bit about your career," I said eventually. "Specifically . . . the influencer exposé."

"Ah," Dominic said, leaning back in his seat. "Struck a chord, did it?" I stared at him, shocked, and he hurriedly continued, "I just meant I know you're from an influencer background. That's all."

"Oh, yeah," I said, calming down. "I guess I just wondered how you did it, how you found out all that stuff. When these people all look so perfect on the surface."

"Interested in becoming a tabloid journo?"

I barely resisted the urge to pull a face. "I don't think so," I said, instead. "I'm more just curious about the research aspect."

"It's the same as any investigative journalism," he said. "It starts with a source, a snippet of information. And you follow that trail as far as you can. In my case, it was a whistleblower."

"What kind of whistleblower?"

Dominic eyed me. "The parent of a fellow student at the kids' fancy private school. Said that the influencer kid had told *their* kid all sorts of stuff—some things that made it into the article, others I'd prefer not to repeat."

"What made you decide it'd be a story? Like, at what point when you were talking to them did you think it was something to actually investigate?"

Dominic considered this. "I wanted to investigate because I believed it was very much in the public interest."

"Did you think about going to the police first?"

"When you're covering a story like this, it is important to think about the legal and ethical side of things, yes. I spoke with my editors, and we decided to inform the police of the allegations, *and* ask the family for a statement once they'd been made aware of them, too. But in my opinion, the world needed to know what was happening to those children. I knew there'd be an outcry if I covered the story. So I did." Dominic shrugged. "Look, that family were practically celebrities. They had multiple TV series with new contracts being written up; they had book deals—all featuring their happy, smiley kids. And behind the scenes it was an entirely different story. Their fans deserved to know the truth."

Dominic was right; it had been an entirely different story. The influencer parents had been responsible for a variety of crimes and general misdeeds—from neglecting their children to gambling away their television earnings. Dominic's exposé had ended their careers. Their children had been sent to live with relatives, and when they were eventually allowed to return home under the watchful eye of social services they were no longer forced to perform for the camera. *That* was what Oliver and Opal deserved. Freedom.

But for Dominic, it sounded like it was all about the outcry, and therefore the clicks and attention and headlines. It wasn't about stopping monsters, or about the kids themselves.

Was he the right person to tell my story? For some reason, I didn't think so. And I had to trust my gut.

Dominic was watching me. "Is there anything else I can help you with, research-wise?" he asked.

I shook my head. "No, thanks. That was really helpful. Really informative. Thanks so much."

"No problem," he said. "And hey, Crystal—don't forget, I'm here for anything you need, okay? Anything."

The way he said it wasn't leering, pushing the edges of professional boundaries. It was sincere, a promise, his expression terribly earnest. He knew something. Or, at the very least, he suspected.

I smiled at him as disarmingly as I could. "Thank you," I said, and stood up. "If I think of anything, I'll let you know."

"Make sure you do," he said.

I slipped out of the door as he turned back to his PC.

Okay, I thought. *So it's going to be plan B.* Like the influencer family Dominic had exposed, my parents were demanding, controlling, and often cruel. Online, they displayed a façade of perfection. My goal was to strip it away, to expose them for what they really were: liars.

What I was doing was, in a way, incredibly ironic—because my mum had done the same thing many, many times. Across the family influencer industry, there was sometimes a sense of kinship, of unity—of sisterhood between the mums, friendship between the kids. But, despite how much she fawned over other accounts and engaged with their content, there was no solidarity to be found in her behavior. My mum was a saboteur, committed to the downfall of those whom she saw as her rivals—*our* rivals.

Over the last few years, from an anonymous email account, she'd sent false tips to every major media organization I could think of. I'd seen the emails, scrolled through them. And I'd been appalled. They weren't just nasty—they were potentially life-ruining. Allegations of domestic violence, of tax avoidance and evasion, even child abuse—from suggestions of emotional abuse to parents forcing their children to have cosmetic surgery.

And then it had all blown up, though no one knew it was my mother who'd caused it. One of the other families, the Birches, was investigated. Their kids were even taken away while the police looked into it, presumably because of all the damning details in the complaint—details Mum only knew because of their videos through the years, innocent moments that she deliberately twisted to sound problematic. They got their kids back in the end, but they'd lost their audience, their sponsors, and it wasn't long before their channel was wiped and they disappeared from the internet altogether. I figured they'd realized it must have been an obsessed follower who'd turned them in and distorted things, so they'd put a pin in it entirely. And

Mum's hypocrisy infuriated me because, despite outward appearances and Mum's obsession with other influencing families, Oliver and Opal hadn't exactly grown up in a house filled with love and happiness.

There was the residual grief from Lexie's passing, of course, the death of a sister they never knew, but there was also the heavy focus on the channel. My parents loved the twins, but they also shouted at them, bombarded them with commands, and insisted they follow stupid rules designed to ensure that the Shaw family appeared perfect at all times—or else.

I'd struggled with it, and I knew that they were struggling, too. I had to bring it to an end.

The problem was, I couldn't do this—couldn't expose my parents—on my own. Look at Mum's efforts: hundreds of emails, sent over a period of years, and only one family she'd targeted had ever been seriously looked into. If I emailed any of these organizations, there was a significant chance they'd think it was just more of the same sort of spam and never reply at all.

I needed somebody to help me. Somebody with media contacts who could get me through the door. I'd hoped Dominic might be that person, but—although he seemed trustworthy enough—I'd seen the glitter in his eyes as he recalled his glory days, the scoop that had, albeit temporarily, made him a household name. I didn't want my story to become all about him, another thing for him to boast about to future first-year students in his lectures. It had to be handled properly.

I needed somebody I could trust, who wasn't out for fame and glory, who wasn't out for themselves. Two names sprang to mind: Jasper and Alyssa.

Jasper could be a real possibility; he was kind, keen to help others—as he'd proven with his eagerness to get us all involved in the radio station—and he was dedicated to becoming a news reporter. Alyssa, however, had the bonus of ready-made connections at *Local Times*.

As I walked across the quad to the Students' Union, passing huddles of students in knitwear with paper cups of hot coffee and tea and the odd cold pint of something or other, I decided that this would be Jasper's audition—unknown to him, naturally. If we continued to get on well, if I thought I could work with him, then maybe he'd be the person I was looking for.

I pushed open the radio studio door to find him sitting in the seat behind the desk, sliding faders up and down as he spoke into the microphone. The red ON AIR sign was off, and I knew he was just testing them out, practicing.

"One . . . two . . . three," he said, adjusting something on the microphone. The big, chunky headphones he was wearing looked like coconut halves. "Four . . . five . . . six . . ."

He smiled up at me as I took a seat on the black plastic sofa on the other side of the desk. "Won't be a sec," he said, and started pressing assorted buttons.

I watched him, intrigued, and by the time he removed his headphones it felt like I already knew a lot more about the workings of the mixer than when I'd had my first session here with the group.

"Sorry about that," he said. "Polly was in here earlier recording some stuff for her sports show, and she faffed around with the settings so much she got herself completely confused." He grinned. "And obviously I'm the only one who could fix it."

"Obviously."

"How's your news stuff with Alyssa going?"

"We haven't done too much yet," I said, deciding not to tell him about my swift exit on our practice day. "I think we've both been a bit busy."

"Well, I've got a new idea for a show," Jasper said, "if you fancied helping me out instead?"

"What's it about?"

"Okay, are you ready? It's good. It's really good. I was thinking . . . local crime."

I waited a second, unsure I'd heard him correctly. "Local crime?"

"Mhm," he said. "I had a look at the *Local Times* coverage after Alyssa was talking about it—you know, to see what she's been working on lately. And there's so many crimes, recent ones and old ones, too, that are so interesting. I thought I could maybe do a show about those."

I squirmed. "The *Local Times* coverage is just the facts, right? Basically bullet points. Wouldn't that be a bit boring to listen to?"

"Well, yeah," Jasper said. "I'll go through the same facts of the case, just with more spin, you know? We'll make it more exciting."

"Wouldn't that be a bit exploitative, though?"

"Maybe." Jasper shrugged. "But true crime is *such* a hit right now. I think it'd be really good for us."

I didn't say anything.

Jasper watched me. "I get it," he said, softer. "Is this because of what happened to your sister?"

I stiffened. "What do you mean?"

"You know, people putting their noses where they shouldn't? Is that why you don't like the idea?"

"Not exactly," I said. "It just weirds me out a bit. Like, I think being a victim or knowing a victim of a crime is probably really traumatic, you know? It's not just 'content.'" I made quotation marks with my fingers. "It's someone's life."

Jasper did seem to be listening to me, but when I'd finished he just shrugged again. "I find it interesting," he said. "So I guess we'll have to agree to disagree. Although I assume this means you don't want to help me?"

"Yeah," I said. "Sorry. Maybe I'm not the right person for that one. Thanks for the invitation, though."

"No problem."

We continued with the training session, Jasper encouraging me to take the hot seat and practice reading a script he'd prepared, an old news bulletin.

Afterward, when I'd mostly got the hang of which buttons to press and when I needed to press them, he leaned back on the sofa. "So," he said, running his fingers through his hair. "Now you know what you're doing, do you want to go and get a drink?"

"Actually, I think I should head back," I said. "I want to go over my notes from this morning. I'm pretty sure I missed half of what Tony was saying because I was too busy typing it all up."

It was a weak excuse, but Jasper didn't call me out on it. He just smiled. "No worries," he said. "Another time?"

"Definitely," I said. "Another time."

I left him in the studio with a wave, and set off back to Statue House.

I considered texting Alyssa, wondering whether she wanted to go for that coffee we'd spoken about, but I assumed she had better things to do. She was probably at *Local Times*, writing copy and making connections to further her career. While here I was, avoiding one of the few potential connections I could use because I didn't love the way he talked about true crime.

I wrapped my coat tighter around myself as a cold wind hit, my eyes watering and head down against the gust. It wasn't that I *disagreed* with true crime, necessarily—I understood the importance of it, of covering it and analyzing it and making sure that all the victims were remembered. But, lately, it seemed that there was a lack of sensitivity around it when it came to podcasts and videos and blogs—vicious muggings and shootings and slashings all melted down into easily digestible nuggets, framed either side with quips and jokes.

And that's not to mention the sponsors—they'd be mid-conversation about a serial killer who brutally mutilated his victims, and suddenly a different voice would pipe up to talk about the merits of their brand's little blue pills. *Please.*

It was the lack of ethics, of respect. *That* was what bothered me.

Maybe Jasper had been right, and some of it *was* related to my feelings about Lexie. Grieving in public, on a huge platform, hadn't been fun—even though I'd been young enough to be blessedly unaware of most of it. Being filmed in the midst of my grief, though . . . that I'd been aware of, and that had been painful. I remembered feeling exposed and vulnerable even though I wasn't required to do much but be in the background or off to the side while Mum poured out her feelings to her followers. Maybe it was the other people involved in true crime that I felt this sympathy for, as well as the victims—the friends and relatives, the colleagues. All forced to ignore it as their loved one's story was played out for an audience again and again, always ending in the same terrible way.

I crossed the road at the traffic lights, Statue House in the near distance. A group of pigeons squabbled over crumbs on the pavement, and I stepped around them gingerly. They were different from the birds I was familiar with on the island, wild and distant; the city pigeons were disconcertingly streetwise, and I didn't want to inadvertently start a turf war with a flock of them.

Back in the warmth of my apartment, I kicked off my shoes and got comfortable on my bed, then opened up my parents' channel. I scrolled through the videos. A video had been uploaded a couple of days previously, but aside from that there was nothing new to me—I could probably recite the title of every video just from memory. But as I hit play on a couple, I tried to look at them through fresh eyes. Through a *collaborator's* eyes.

Because, by a process of elimination, I had my prospective collaborator.

The person to help me would be Alyssa.

Chapter Twelve

ALYSSA

My *Local Times* shifts over the previous couple of weeks had continued without anything unusual—no strange assignments, fewer glares from Bradley. Even Davina and I were back on relatively good terms; she'd actually smiled at me once when I brought her a coffee from downstairs. But, unfortunately, the peace wasn't to last.

I arrived at *Local Times* at 8:51 a.m. and had only made it halfway to my desk before Bradley spotted me.

"Alyssa!" he said. "A word?"

He waited until I'd nodded, then disappeared back into the conference room and closed the door. I resisted the urge to roll my eyes at his theatrics—I could still see him through the glass.

I dumped my bag on my desk and spun around, almost bumping into Davina who was carrying a mug of what looked like green tea back from the kitchen.

"Hey," I said, and she gave me a small red-lipsticked smile.

"Morning."

"Everything okay?"

She nodded as she sat down, placing her mug on a white coaster with the words *Drink up your positivi-tea!* printed on it in hot pink. I wondered who had bought it for her. Clearly, they didn't know her very well.

"Bradley's called me in again," I said. "Any ideas?"

She shook her head, but she didn't look at me. That was not a good sign.

My stomach now having dropped into my shoes, I gave in and

approached the conference room. I could see that Sophia from HR was sitting beside him, and they were having what looked like an in-depth conversation, Bradley's hands flapping around like trapped birds. He clasped them together on the table as I knocked on the door and opened it, presumably once again trying to look intimidating.

"Alyssa," he said. "Please, take a seat. I'm sure you remember Sophia?"

"Yes," I said. "Hi."

She nodded and smiled at me, but didn't say anything.

There was an uncomfortable silence. I looked at Bradley, waiting for him to speak, and he looked back at me, seemingly waiting for me to give in.

"Why am I here?" I asked. I didn't want to give Bradley what he wanted, and it was worse when I spoke, the smug little smile that played on his lips.

"Unfortunately, Alyssa, we've had another complaint," he said.

I glanced sideways through the glass, where Davina was apparently making a concerted effort not to look my way. Bradley followed my gaze. "It wasn't from Davina," he said. "For the record."

I frowned. "Who was it from, then?"

"It doesn't matter," Sophia interjected. "They didn't give us permission to share that with you."

Bradley looked at her, and nodded. "Quite right," he said.

I folded my arms. "What was the complaint about?"

"Mimicking," Bradley said.

"You mean, dressing similarly to somebody? *Again?*"

"It's not that, Alyssa," Bradley said with a sigh. "If it was *just* that, we might be able to overlook it. But, unfortunately, we're told a colleague believes you're making a deliberate effort to intimidate them through your behavior."

"That's not true!" I burst out. "Whatever it is, it's a coincidence. I swear!"

"While that may be the case," Bradley said, "we've already

discussed what would happen if somebody were to make a similar complaint about you within a short period of time. And that means we've been left without a choice."

I waited for the bomb to drop, to erupt, to tear apart the life I'd built for myself, the position I'd fought for. I was expecting it, but when it came it still took my breath away.

"We're going to have to let you go, Alyssa," Sophia finished for him.

I allowed myself a couple of deep breaths, to take this in, and then I stood up. "Fine," I said. "But just so you know, this is ridiculous. First it's because I have the same bag and color nail polish—*nail polish*, by the way—as someone else here, and now there's been *another* complaint and you won't even tell me who made it? This is a witch hunt. You just don't want me here."

"Alyssa," Bradley said, and I was gratified to see that he looked startled, the yellowing whites of his eyes visible in his shock. "That isn't true."

"You haven't wanted me here since the start," I said. "You've always hated me being here. Always giving me the rubbish assignments, always glaring at me. Even Davina noticed it."

Sophia glanced between us.

"Well," I continued. "Now you're getting what you wanted. And I'd say, *Hey, send my check in the post*—but I don't even get paid. You're firing me, and I've been working for free! How's that for ironic?"

I didn't wait for either of them to respond. I barged out of the conference room, the bang of the metal door handle against the wall pleasing. Heads appeared over the tops of cubicles, from around corners, as I stormed over to my desk. I pulled on my coat, and picked up my bag.

"Is that it?" Davina asked, looking at me from her seat.

"That's it," I said, breathing heavily. "I'm done. I've been 'let go.'"

Bradley watched me from the doorway of the conference room, Sophia hovering behind him.

"I never complained about you, by the way," Davina said. "Not last time, and not this time, either. I don't know who it was."

"Whatever," I said tiredly. "It doesn't matter now, does it?"

"I knew he was going to do something," she continued. "I just didn't know what. I'm sorry to see you go."

"Thanks, Davina. It's been great working with you." I raised my voice. "Not so much anyone else."

Bradley didn't move, just stood there with his arms folded, stony-faced. I took out my access pass and placed it on my desk. Or what had been my desk. It wasn't mine anymore. Somebody else would sit here, some eager little idiot keen to work for free just like I had been. Maybe Bradley would hate them, too. I hoped so. If he did, it would mean that all this wasn't just about me. That it wasn't personal.

"Right," I said. "Bye, Davina."

"Bye, Alyssa," she said. "I'm sure we'll see each other around."

I nodded, tried to smile. I didn't look back as I walked to the door, as the frosted glass closed behind me, shutting me out and everybody else in.

What was I supposed to do now?

I had a full day to myself, and nothing to fill it. It was barely nine thirty by the time I'd been spat out onto the pavement, the guy on Reception looking at me sorrowfully as if he understood what had happened upstairs. He probably did—I'd bet money on Bradley having pre-emptively called down and warned him not to let me back in.

I shoved my way out of the revolving doors and onto the street. It was colder now that we were nearing the end of November, the previously golden trees now bare and wet, the flagstones littered with their leaves, the gutters clogged. For old times' sake—since I doubted I'd visit this part of the city anywhere near as regularly when I wasn't working at *Local Times*—I popped into the coffee shop and ordered an indulgent drink: a mint hot chocolate, topped with cream, with green and brown sprinkles.

I sipped it, savoring the rich flavor combined with the cooling sensation of the mint as I walked back toward my flat. A city native, I was adept at dodging the people who seemed to appear from all angles: a delivery person carrying parcels, a woman running in gym leggings and chunky trainers, a man with an armful of orange shopping bags all labeled "Louis Vuitton." As always, I wondered about them, who they were and where they were going. I wondered if they'd had happy childhoods, if they'd grown up feeling lonely like me, and if they'd ever managed to repair that feeling, the emptiness that always seemed to linger. I wondered, if they had, how they'd done it—and if they could offer me any tips.

Halfway back to the flat, I realized I didn't want to go there. Another full day holed up there by myself—or worse, with a flatmate or two—wasn't a pleasant prospect. I didn't have any assignments I should be working on or any books I wanted to borrow, so the library wasn't appealing (even if the smell of old books, worn binding, furniture polish, and coffee was). I didn't want to go to the radio studio, either—I couldn't face Jasper, his inevitable smugness when he asked about *Local Times* and I had to admit they'd let me go. Everybody would find out eventually; every journalist and journalism student in this city seemed to know each other by a maximum of two degrees of separation. What would Bradley tell people about me? How would it affect my job hunt after graduation? Three years would be a blink of an eye when it came to stories about the weird girl who'd been in for work experience and copied everybody's style.

My thoughts swirling with anxiety, all I knew was that I didn't want to be alone. And there was only one person I wanted to see.

Hi! If you're not busy, do you fancy breakfast? Or coffee?

It didn't take long for Crystal to text back.

I was literally just going to text you! Coffee would be amazing.

Instead of turning left, back toward the flat, I smiled to myself and kept walking as I typed my reply.

Have you been to the Rose & Crown Coffee Bar?

Hers came seconds later.

Not yet, but that sounds good to me!

I was pleased with how well things were going between me and Crystal. We'd been going to lectures together and grabbing coffee, doing those little things that real friends at university do, getting closer all the while. I considered giving her directions to the Rose & Crown, but I knew she'd have Maps. Besides, I didn't want to be patronizing—this was her home now, too.

I wondered whether the city was beginning to *feel* like home yet, or if she longed for the salt air and mountains of the island, that idyllic upbringing I'd idolized since my own childhood. For years after first stumbling across *At Home with the Shaws*, I'd curled up in my dark bedroom, my loneliness a physical ache in my chest, and watched those videos—and, finally, felt like I belonged somewhere.

I'd pretend that Marjorie and James were my parents, that Crystal was my sister, that my own distant parents were nothing but temporary caretakers. I'd imagine I'd been stolen away, that they were desperate for me to return. And that one day, I would.

When I first found the channel as a kid, they were still grieving for Lexie. She'd only been gone a year or two and they were still healing, waiting for Oliver and Opal—who didn't even exist yet—to bring a newfound happiness into their lives. I'd gone back through their archive over the years, watched all the videos—from Lexie's birth to her first Christmas, from when Crystal was born to her first steps. Marjorie talked about Lexie a lot, and eventually it became almost as if I'd known her and lost her, too. They were my family.

I got to the Rose & Crown before Crystal, and picked a table toward the back of the café. I'd noticed that most people liked to sit toward the front, where the diamond-paned glass left shadows on the tables and you could see the street outside, but I preferred the depths—warmer, a bit shadowed, the air rich with the smell of ground coffee and the cinnamon buns baking in the kitchen.

It had been a pub, once, until hard times meant it had fallen into a state of disrepair. The coffee was still served from behind the old bar, and antique painted mirrors hung on the walls bearing advertisements for long-ago brands: ale and cigarettes, beer and cigars. It still retained some of the warm, sticky air of an old pub, but the coffee was delicious, the baked goods were fantastic, and the seats were comfortable. It was one of the neighborhood's best-kept secrets.

I ordered my second seasonal coffee of the day—sea-salted caramel—and a slice of carrot cake, which came still warm from the oven. I was lifting a forkful to my lips when I spotted Crystal standing in the doorway.

I gave her a little wave.

Her face lit up, and she made a beeline for me. "Hi," she said, throwing her bag onto the seat beside her, looking around. "How did you know I love old buildings that have been turned into something new? I did a whole video about that once! I'm so glad you suggested this."

"Me, too," I said. "I've had the *worst* morning."

"Likewise," she said. "I'll get something to drink, and we can talk all about it? Inhale some sugar and caffeine, vent a bit, and make ourselves feel better?"

I laughed. "Absolutely," I said.

How wrong I was, thinking I might feel better after this.

Chapter Thirteen

CRYSTAL

Alyssa really *had* had a terrible morning.

Once I'd brought my coffee back to the corner booth, along with what might have been the world's stickiest chocolate brownie, she launched into her story.

"Wait, wait," I said, after she'd explained the details. "They gave you a warning for wearing the same nail polish as somebody else? And today they didn't even give you a proper reason?"

"That's right," she said. Her eyes were alight with dignified fury, the joy of sharing it.

"That's unbelievable," I said, shaking my head. "How is that even fair?"

"It's not," Alyssa said. "They wouldn't tell me who made the complaint, either. I get it, but still, it's frustrating. The first time, I reckon it was Davina—even if she said it wasn't her. But she seemed surprised this time. I think Bradley just wanted to get rid of me."

"Why would he want to do that?"

"He doesn't like me," Alyssa said darkly. She shrugged, and I was surprised to see her face shutter along with the motion; it was like she'd slammed a door to herself closed, any openness in her expression completely vanishing. *Teach me how to do that,* I wanted to say. *Show me how to be unreadable.*

"I'm really sorry," I said. "I don't know how anybody couldn't like you."

Alyssa brightened at that, her closed, empty expression receding like clouds revealing sunshine. She lifted her coffee mug to her lips, and even from where I was sitting I could smell the caramel. I took a bite of my brownie, and groaned.

"This is so good," I said, and Alyssa smiled as proudly as if she'd baked it herself. As I chewed, I took in our eclectic surroundings: the bar turned coffee counter, the diamond patterns on the window glass, the old landscape oil paintings and the Tiffany-style stained-glass lamps. "How did you even find this place?"

"I used to come into the city by myself a lot when I was younger," she said. "It was really cold one day, and I was looking for somewhere to sit for a bit, get warm. I was in the park over the road, and I saw the sign, so I thought, *Okay, why not?* And I came in, and just fell in love. It helps that the food and drink are so amazing. They do cocktails, too."

"Really?" I asked. "Have you had one?"

"One or two," Alyssa replied. "They do an unbelievable salted caramel espresso martini."

"We're going to have to come back here for one of those!" I said, momentarily forgetting about the complicated relationship (courtesy of my mother) that I had with alcohol.

"Definitely."

The smooth silkiness of the coffee, the comfortable surroundings and the rich velvet of the brownie alongside Alyssa's dramatic story had more or less distracted me from my own day, and a stone lodged in my throat when I remembered why I'd agreed to come here in the first place. What I'd come to ask Alyssa to do.

"Actually, while we're here, I wanted to talk to you about something," I said. "It's a bit . . . sensitive."

"Of course," Alyssa said warmly. "Anything."

"Thank you. I knew I could trust you."

A hint too flattering, maybe, but I wanted Alyssa to know that she was the only person who could help me.

She leaned forward, frowning. "What's going on?"

"You already know that my sister died," I began slowly. "And, by now, I think you already know about my parents and *At Home with the Shaws*."

Alyssa nodded.

"Well, when Lexie fell ill, my parents—my mum, mostly—sort of focused on her journey on the vlog. It got them a lot of attention. And I mean, a *lot*. It's what really launched the vlog, made it into what it is today. And when Lexie died, they got . . . stuck."

I could practically see the cogs in Alyssa's brain turning, sparks of electricity behind her eyes. "Stuck?" she repeated.

"Yes. The vlog . . . it was like a coping mechanism, almost, as well as their job. They didn't know what to do without it. They couldn't stop it, but they didn't have Lexie to focus on anymore. So they moved their focus onto me." Old fury long gone cold lodged hard in my chest like a stone. "And now it's Oliver and Opal."

"What are you saying?" Alyssa asked gently.

"This . . . this *vlog*. It's been more or less my whole life. I barely remember a time before it, when we could cook a meal or celebrate a birthday or even just go to the beach without having to perform for thousands of strangers. I'm exhausted; I feel like a *shell*. And it feels like I'm still trapped. I don't want—" My voice cracked. "I can't let this happen to Oliver and Opal. Their entire *lives* are online, Alyssa. It has to stop."

"What are you going to do?"

"I want to expose them," I said. "I want to pitch an article or an opinion piece to a publication. A big one. I want to talk about growing up as an influencer, the pressure of being perfect. I want to talk about how it's ruined my life." I took a deep breath. This was it. The scandal. "And I want to tell the world about how my mother is trying to take down every other vlogging family we know. She's been lying, spreading rumors, and sending horrible false accusations to the press for *years* now—all so that we come out on top. It has to stop. If it doesn't, somebody's going to get hurt."

Alyssa considered this for a few seconds, my words hanging in the air between us. "Crystal," she said finally. "Why did you tell me this?"

I reached out, and took one of her cold hands in mine as I fixed her with a pleading look. "Because," I said. "I need your help to do it."

Chapter Fourteen

ALYSSA

My mind was reeling when I got back to the flat.

"Alyssa," Niamh said, appearing from the kitchen, her arms folded. "Have you been stealing my coffee pods?"

I pushed past her, heading for the stairs. "Not now, Niamh."

"Can you at least replace them?" she called, following me into the hallway. "There's loads gone."

"I only have the vanilla ones," I said over my shoulder. "But yeah, fine, I'll replace them. Go after Toby for the others. He's been taking all the mocha ones."

Behind me, I heard Niamh huff, and she disappeared back into the living room, presumably to lie in wait for an unsuspecting Toby.

I hung up my coat, kicked off my shoes, and emptied my bag onto my desk like a robot, putting my *Local Times* shift essentials away without even thinking about it. An unexpected emotion started to rise up in me, like the tide creeping up a beach: anger.

Why didn't Crystal appreciate how lucky she was? All she did was complain about her life, about her parents—how they'd gifted her fame, how they were constantly in touch with her, how they wanted so much to be involved in her life. She was so ungrateful, intent on dismissing their love and care at every turn.

They'd given her everything, and this was how she planned to repay them: by telling the world how awful they were. And she'd asked for *my* help to do it.

"Please," she'd said, after she'd explained what she wanted me to do. "There's no one else I'd trust. You don't have to answer me now. Just . . . think about it?"

"I will," I'd said, as my insides twisted. "I'll think about it."

She'd quickly changed the subject then, bringing our conversation back around to *Local Times*, Bradley, and what I planned to do next—but my mind stayed with her request, turning the thought over and over like a worry stone. After a while, she must've known that I was distracted, and delicately made her exit.

Once she'd gone, I'd finished my coffee and headed back to the flat, which brought me to where I was now: cross-legged on my bed, simmering with a mix of jealousy and injustice.

Usually, when I was plagued by such strong feelings, I'd navigate my way to an *At Home with the Shaws* video. I'd let myself fall into their lives, pretending their idyllic routine—the luxurious island home, the fresh vegetables from the garden, the adorable hand-knit clothes—was my own. But today, everything I watched filled me with increasing fury.

A bedroom redecorating video. Crystal aged around ten, baby-faced; Oliver and Opal aged three or four. All of them in cutesy patterned boiler suits, splashed and spotted with paint, giggling and grinning from ear to ear.

A gardening day a year or so earlier. Oliver and Opal toddlers still in matching straw sun hats and dungarees, their hands caked with soil from helping their mum plant flowers. Crystal uncharacteristically mussed: bare knees dirty below the stained hem of her sundress, her white ankle socks lopsided and streaked with mud, yet smiling fit to burst.

Looking at their happiness, their harmony, I found it hard to believe that what Crystal had told me was the truth. First, there was what she'd said about how she'd hated growing up on camera. And yet she looked so comfortable in those videos, so relaxed. So happy. And then there was what she'd said about her mum, the lies she'd supposedly spread, taking other families down to grow the Shaws' success. Even if that was true, how did Crystal *know* that what her mum had told the press were lies? What if she'd had information that Crystal simply didn't have? Was Crystal really willing to take a chance on that? Had she even considered it?

Crystal was still grieving, I knew; maybe this was her way of coping with it, desperately searching for somebody to blame for her unhappiness? I sympathized with her, but I couldn't let it be her parents, her little brother and sister. I couldn't let Crystal tear her family apart.

There was only one thing I could do. I had to help her, but in my own way; I had to thwart every plan, spoil every idea she had to "expose" her parents for who she seemed to believe they were. I had to keep her quiet.

Maybe, one day, Crystal would tell her family about this, about what I'd done for them—how I'd helped her through her grief and stopped her from doing something she'd surely come to regret.

And maybe, just maybe, they'd be so grateful that they'd welcome me in. They'd let me be part of their family once and for all.

I picked up my phone, and texted Crystal before I could change my mind.

Hey. I'm in. x

Although we jumped right into brainstorming ideas, each more wild than the last, we couldn't decide on a plan. A couple of weeks passed by as we debated and discarded different options, and soon it was nearly Christmas. In just a few days, term would be ending and most of us would be leaving Cradlewell's leafy campus for at least two weeks, if not longer.

"Are you going home for Christmas?" I asked Crystal. We were in the library, racing toward our final deadline of the year. We'd been in the library a lot, lately. Our course-mates seemed to view essay-writing as a team sport, huddling at tables in the library with their laptops, copious paper cups of coffee, and a lot of chocolate. I generally preferred the solitude of the flat when I needed to concentrate, but I was keen to stay close to Crystal. I worried that if she sensed any reluctance on my part, she'd involve somebody else in her plan—and they might actually help her carry it out. No, I had to be the best possible friend to Crystal. And so I went to the pre-Christmas library meet-ups and coffee catch-ups, wrote essays in their company. The strange part was, I found myself actually enjoying it.

"I am," Crystal said now. "Are you?"

"Definitely," I said, although I wasn't sure if I was. My parents hadn't been in touch about it.

"Will your sister be there?"

I blinked at her for a half second before remembering my lie. "Hopefully," I said.

"You know what we need?" Sadie said from the table to my right, saving me from any more questions. "A night out at the Apple Club."

"Absolutely not," Zoe said.

"Come *on*," Sadie whined. "We're officially done for the year after we hand this final essay in! We have to celebrate."

"Can't we celebrate by sleeping, though?" Zoe asked. "Or with, like . . . cake?"

Rowan perked up. "I second cake."

"You're all *boring*," Polly said, although her grin showed she was joking. She attended every sports social, even the ones that weren't football-related, and so was strongly on Team Sadie when it came to a group visit to a nightclub.

"I don't drink," Ravi reminded us. "So I absolutely will *not* be carrying any of you home if you are drunk."

Sadie nodded. "Fair enough. But you won't be carrying any of us home anyway. We'll share taxis, make it cheaper!" She turned to Crystal. "Crystal?"

Crystal's eyes were on me. "I don't know . . ."

"I'll come," I said, already half-regretting the words as soon as I said them. "Clubbing doesn't necessarily mean getting *drunk*, right?"

"It does not," Ravi agreed. "It's all about the dancing for me." He started to dance in his seat, shimmying his shoulders.

"Unfortunately," Jasper said, "a lot of us need a drink to be able to do *that* with confidence."

"So who have we got?" Sadie asked, speaking over him with an eye roll. "Me, Polly, Ravi, Alyssa . . ."

"And me," Jasper said tiredly.

"I'll come," Zoe added.

Rowan sighed good-naturedly. "I suppose I'm in, too, then," they said. "I'm not being left out."

"Oh, why not?" Crystal said. "If we're all going."

Sadie clapped her hands, unfazed by the "Shhh!" signs taped up around the library. "Yay! Okay, awesome. Shall we all go home and get ready, then? Meet at the doors at, say . . . ten?"

Crystal's eyes widened. I could imagine what she was thinking, the words emerging like thought bubbles from the top of her head: *Ten o'clock? That's bedtime!*

For some reason, I almost wanted to sneer at her. *We're not on your little island anymore. We may be at the edge of the city, but it's still the city. Things happen at night; people go places—drink and dance and fall in love and break up and laugh and cry and scream, all in the glittering dark.*

"Ten's perfect," I said, speaking for all of us.

Gradually, we all dispersed: Ravi and Jasper together, Rowan and Sadie, Polly and Zoe.

Crystal, however, stayed still as a statue until everyone else had gone, unmoving in her seat. "Is this a good idea?" she asked me. "Going out? Shouldn't we be, you know . . . focusing on our plan?"

I'd had a feeling this was coming, and I was prepared.

"There's not much point in starting now," I told her. "We're all going home soon, and we'll be apart. We can start properly next term—start fresh, at the beginning of the year." Crystal still looked unsure, so I persisted. "Look, any big story that comes out now's just going to get buried under all the Christmas headlines. This deserves proper coverage. We'll give it the best chance of going viral if we wait until the new year."

Going viral. Crystal's language.

"I guess," she said.

"Is this still about your mum? The location tracker thing?"

She glanced up at me, caught. "A bit," she said. "I'm trying not to care as much. I'm an adult. I can do what I want."

"Exactly," I said encouragingly. "You can. And, like Ravi said—you don't have to drink. He won't be. I probably won't drink much, either."

"I don't know if my mum will believe that," Crystal admitted. "That I'm in a club and not drinking."

"So what?" I said. "You'll know the truth. You could even film some content after and send it to her, show how sober you are."

Crystal seemed to recoil from the idea at first, but then her eyes widened. "A sober night out with Crystal Shaw!" she said. "That is exactly the kind of thing my parents would love."

"Really?"

"Yeah! They're all about 'sensible teens' and 'family values.'" She made air quotes with her fingers. Her nail polish was a shimmery pink. I wondered if it'd suit me. "They'd be all for it, if it was for my channel. If you guys are all okay with me filming, of course."

"I don't have a problem with it," I said. "You'll have to check with the others, though."

"Yeah, yeah," she said. "Of course." She stood up, stretched. "I suppose I'd better get going, if I want to get ready in time. Unless—do you want to come to my place?"

I stared at her. "What?"

"You can get ready at Statue House, with me," she said. "We're about the same size, I reckon. You can borrow an outfit, some makeup if you want? It'd save you going all the way back to yours."

I thought about my room at the flat. My flatmates. I didn't want to go back there.

"Okay," I said. "That'd be really nice! As long as you don't mind."

"I wouldn't have offered if I minded," Crystal said. "Come on, let's go. We've got a couple of hours, but it'll fly. And we'll have to actually *get* to the club. Do you know where it is?"

"I do," I said. "I've been there before."

A night out best left unmentioned: I was sixteen, using a friend's ID. I'd drunk too many bottles of cheap, fruity alcohol at £3 a pop and got vomit in my hair in the ladies' loos. My so-called "friends" had left me alone, and I'd been kicked out by a doorman who'd spotted me and decided I was far too drunk to be there. He wasn't wrong.

This didn't seem like the kind of thing that'd appeal to Crystal. It hadn't appealed to me, either. I briefly hoped the doorman who'd unceremoniously chucked me out that night wouldn't remember me, but then shook away the thought. Of course he wouldn't; I was one face in thousands.

Crystal seemed to be trying to read my expression, but when our eyes met she shrugged. "Cool," she said. "You can show me the ropes, then."

It was dark outside when we left the library, and damp. The campus was lit up by streetlights, their glow reflecting on the wet ground in amber streaks. The earlier drizzle had stopped, but the few fallen leaves still scattered were wet and slippery underfoot.

"It won't be long till it snows," Crystal said. She turned to me. "We do *get* snow here, right?"

"Sometimes. Only if it's really cold, though."

"We get snow every year on the island," Crystal said dreamily. "You see it on the tops of the mountains from October onward, pretty much. And sometimes it lasts till April, or even later."

I resisted the urge to say *I know*. I'd seen it in the backgrounds of her videos, the mountains and hills tall and purplish, coated with a layer of pristine white snow like icing on a cake.

"Sounds beautiful," I said instead, and Crystal smiled as if I'd paid her a compliment.

Chapter Fifteen

CRYSTAL

It wasn't long until we got to Statue House. I caught Alyssa tilting her head back as we got to the entrance, looking up at the building. I wondered what her flat was like—probably nothing like this, in all its purpose-built luxury.

Inside, I showed her to the lift which swooshed us up to my floor in just a few seconds. On the landing, I took out my keys just as the door beside mine opened and a face peered out.

"Crystal! I thought that was you," Hayley said. "Wait there one sec!"

The door half closed, and I shrugged at Alyssa. "My neighbor, Hayley," I explained.

A moment later, Hayley reappeared. Her brown hair was messy, and she was smiling wildly. She held out a clear plastic Tupperware. "Brownies!" she announced. Then she added quickly, "Not weed ones. I promise! Just regular old chocolate."

I took it. "Thank you so much," I said. "That's so lovely."

Hayley beamed. "I'll leave you both to it," she said. "I just wanted to grab you while I could. I know you're always busy." She turned her gaze to Alyssa. "Lovely to meet you!"

"You, too," Alyssa said.

Hayley disappeared back inside her own apartment, and I smiled at Alyssa. I put the keys, which I was still clutching in the hand that wasn't holding the Tupperware, into my door and pushed it open with a flourish. I watched Alyssa's gaze flit around the room, taking everything in.

I saw it from her perspective, the huge arched window on the far wall with a view of the city, lights outside stretching and spreading as rain slid down the glass. My queen-sized bed in the far corner and my kitchen along one wall. I kept it clean, but I realized now that it was strangely impersonal. There weren't any photographs anywhere, any rugs or cushions or throw blankets, no magnets on the fridge. The only personal touches I'd made were my bedding and a small pile of books on the desk. I set the brownies down on the counter in my kitchenette, pulled my laptop from my bag, and placed it beside the plastic tub, then turned to Alyssa, assessing her reaction.

"It's lovely," she said. "Very minimalist."

"I know I haven't decorated much."

"No," she said. "I like it. My flat's totally cluttered—I've got clothes and books everywhere, and loads of trinkets that get all dusty. This is like a clean slate." She looked around a bit more. "Doesn't it get lonely? Being by yourself all of the time?"

I shrugged. "I have the Journalism Society."

I didn't want to admit to Alyssa that that wasn't enough. Our timetable was sparse, and days could go by without a lecture or a seminar, or some kind of extracurricular Journalism Society activity.

She seemed to know how I was feeling even without me saying. "Maybe we should do more radio stuff," she suggested. "Now that I'm not with *Local Times* anymore. We could do that news reporting show we said we'd do—it'd get you out a bit more."

"That and our *other* project," I agreed. "That would be a good excuse, actually, wouldn't it? Say we're doing a radio program, when actually—"

"We could do the radio stuff, too," Alyssa pointed out. "It doesn't have to be an 'either or' kind of thing. Then you'd actually have something to show your parents."

I considered this, but as I did my gaze caught the clock on the wall. We were running late already. "Okay," I said. "If we still want to go, we'd better get sorted—we haven't got that long. *Do* you still want to go?"

"I do."

"If you do," I said, somewhat reluctantly, "then I do, too."

"Great."

I heaved myself up from where I'd been perched on the edge of my bed. "I guess I'll go and put some makeup on," I said. "Make yourself a coffee or something if you want. There's a jar of instant in the cupboard. And see if there's anything you want to wear in my wardrobe."

Alyssa looked down at herself. "What about my clothes? We can't exactly take them with us."

"Leave them here." I shrugged. "You can come back and get them. Or I'll drop them off at some point. Whatever."

I opened the wardrobe door to show her. I had a capsule wardrobe, everything carefully chosen in shades of beige and pink and light blue and cream to match perfectly. I wondered if Alyssa had guessed that Mum had chosen this color scheme, had bought me these clothes. Most of them still had the tags on, revealing the frankly insane prices she'd paid for some of the designer pieces.

I moved some of the pastel-hued clothing aside to reveal a sprinkling of denim, net and sequins in black and silver and gold. *My* choices.

I took them out, one by one, so Alyssa could get a good look. Black denim jeans, a see-through tiered net dress, a tight sparkly silver top with straps, a shimmery gold satin shirt that tied at the waist. None of these were like anything I'd worn before.

Alyssa reached out and stroked the gold shirt. "This is gorgeous."

"I like that one," I said. "There's loads of stuff in that drawer, too."

Alyssa opened the drawer I was gesturing to. It was packed with clothes, a mix of dungarees and bikinis and baseball caps, socks and T-shirts and shorts.

"I'll give you some privacy," I said, and disappeared into the bathroom.

Once I'd closed the door behind me, I faced the mirror, unzipped my makeup bag, and gave myself a new face. I didn't want subtle makeup for tonight—I wanted to look like somebody else. A city girl, not an island dweller.

Once I'd finished, my makeup glowed in the dim light: highlighted cheekbones, sparkly pink eyeshadow, fluttery eyelashes coated liberally with mascara. The lipstick I'd chosen had a shimmer to it, so my lips appeared to give off tiny fragments of starlight.

When I emerged from the bathroom, Alyssa was still looking through the drawer.

"Those are my freebies," I said, in answer to her unspoken question. "The stuff PR companies send, or stuff I'm sponsored to post. I don't wear a lot of it—some of it's pretty impractical."

Alyssa raised her eyebrows as she held up a tiny, low-cut crop top. If I put it on, it would barely cover my bra. "This doesn't seem like something your mum would like, judging from the rest of your wardrobe."

"She doesn't mind if she's being paid," I said. "She only minds when it's my choice to wear something skimpy, apparently. Anyway," I said, in a far cheerier tone. "I can't wear that to a club. Or can I?"

Alyssa eyed it. "It's way too cold for that," she said. "What about the gold shirt?"

"I think you should wear that."

"You think?"

"Absolutely. Gold's your color."

"I didn't think I had a color," Alyssa said. "Okay. Thanks so much!"

"I've got some gold eyeshadow in my makeup bag, too," I said. "It's pink and fluffy, on the side of the sink. There's some Charlotte Tilbury stuff, foundation and concealer, and there's a brand-new mascara in there, too, that you can use. For hygiene and stuff."

"Amazing, thank you," she said. "Do you know what you're going to wear, if not a crop top?"

"Jeans," I replied. "And a dress."

Alyssa looked puzzled, and I laughed. "It'll make sense. You'll see. Now, come on, get in there. We haven't got long."

She disappeared into the bathroom. By the time she came out, I was dressed.

"What do you think?" I asked, doing a little twirl.

I'd teamed my silver strappy top and black jeans with a pair of black Dr. Martens, and then I'd layered the see-through dress over the rest of the outfit—a gauzy covering that looked vaguely gothic and that, I felt, added intrigue. I'd never dressed like this before, like how I wanted to dress, and it was freeing. It was elegance with a little bit of edge, the materials flattering and juxtaposing.

"You look awesome," she said. "I mean . . . not awesome. I don't know. Great?"

I smiled. "A bit different than from my usual look, right?"

"Right. What do you think your mum will make of it, in your video?"

"I'd like to think she'd appreciate me finding my own style," I said. "But I think she'll be more annoyed that my color palette isn't on brand."

"Well, pastels aren't club appropriate."

"That might be a good title for the video," I quipped, and Alyssa laughed.

She disappeared into the bathroom with an armful of clothes, and came back out wearing the gold shirt with the black jeans she'd already been wearing. They worked well together. I held up a pair of gold heels, which she looked at doubtfully. "I think I'll stick to my boots," she said.

I nodded. "Good idea. They'll be way comfier than these." I studied the heels. "Another PR product. I haven't worn them out yet—I tried them on and they gave me blisters pretty much immediately."

"I don't know why women's clothes and shoes have to be so uncomfortable," Alyssa said. "So many things are tight or restricting or made out of a horrible material—something itchy, or practically translucent, or both. And then some of the shoes are just plain *painful.* I don't get it."

"Me neither," I said. "I think it's something to do with making us suffer."

Alyssa blinked at me.

"You know, there's this whole moral thing with having to suffer to be pure, to be good? Apparently, there's nothing more important for a woman to be than *good.*" I snorted.

"Well," Alyssa said. "Just for tonight, why don't we be the opposite?"

"Bad?"

"Not bad," she said thoughtfully. "Let's not be anything. Let's just be us."

A smile crept across my face. "I think I could handle that."

Chapter Sixteen

ALYSSA

Our taxi arrived ten minutes later.

Crystal didn't have any alcohol in her flat for us to drink before we left, of course (she regretfully told me she'd long since trashed the contents of the mini bar), but that didn't matter. We were giddy with freedom, with the restraints we'd decided, just for tonight, to cast off.

From the back of the taxi, the city was a kaleidoscope of light and color: car headlights and the lights still on in office buildings, streetlights, people in their Christmas party clothes—sequins and sparkles, velvet and satin, bright jewel tones.

"How far away are we?" Crystal asked, craning to look at the driver's GPS.

"A couple of minutes," I said.

She bounced in her seat. "I'm so excited!"

The driver started to indicate and pulled over at the side of the road. People milled back and forth along the pavement: students like us, and groups in their twenties and early thirties.

We thanked the driver—the fare already paid on the app—and closed the door.

"Okay," Crystal said. "What now?"

The club was through an arched alleyway. People were gathered there, smoking and talking, and we walked single file past them to the main door. It was nondescript, just black, with a doorman standing outside. He was surprisingly short for a doorman, and looked friendly.

"IDs please, ladies," he said.

Mine was tucked into my back pocket, and I brandished it like

I once would have my *Local Times* pass. The memory of how proud I'd been when I first received that pass really stung now that I'd been forced to return it.

Crystal, meanwhile, presented her passport.

"Your passport?" I said. "Is that the only ID you've got?"

"Yeah," she said. "There was no point in learning to drive on the island, so I never got a provisional."

"Best keep an eye on it, then," the doorman said after he'd checked it and given us the nod of approval. "Those things cost a fortune to replace."

Crystal tucked her passport back into the little silver clutch bag she was carrying and zipped it up carefully, as if losing it wasn't something she'd considered.

The doorman stepped aside, and in we went.

Immediately through the double doors was a small flight of steps, but I paused to let Crystal take in the room around us. An old brick warehouse, the Apple Club was far bigger inside than it looked from the outside. With a black floor, walls, and ceiling, studded with strobe lights and spinning disco balls, it was like being inside a giant cave—one that was filled to the brim with people. As we descended the stairs and entered the crowd, the tension started to leave my shoulders and I settled in, finding my rhythm among the gyrating bodies.

I felt something cold touch my hand, and realized just before I pulled it away that it was Crystal, wrapping her chilled fingers around my own, fixing herself to me.

When I glanced up at her, from our interlocking fingers, she gave me an embarrassed smile. "I don't want to lose you."

I had to ask her to repeat what she'd said, and she shouted to be heard over the music, which was pounding a pulsing, entrancing beat. The strobe lights moved in time with the bass and so did the crowd, swaying almost as one. I held on to Crystal's hand and used it to pull her through the throngs of people toward the bar.

It was surprisingly less cramped at the bar, as people bought their drinks and moved back to the dance floor. Crystal blew out her cheeks, her hair sticking to the side of her face. "Wow," she said. "I knew it'd be busy, but I didn't think it'd be *this* busy. Or this hot!"

She was right; it *was* hot, the heat of hundreds of bodies exerting themselves in the enclosed space. I knew that the black walls would be wet with breath, with sweat, and fought the urge to shudder. I had to play it cool, look like I knew what I was doing—because Crystal definitely didn't.

"Do you want a drink?" I asked her and she nodded. "If you want non-alcoholic, there's lemonade or Coke or . . ." I stood on my tiptoes to see the selection of drinks they had in the fridges at the back. "I think they've got zero percent cider and stuff, too."

"Lemonade's fine," Crystal said. "But hey, I'll get these. What do you want?"

I debated something alcoholic, but I wanted to be clear-headed. "I'll have the same. Thanks, Crystal. I'll get the next lot."

"Don't worry about it. It won't be a very expensive night if we're drinking lemonades the whole time, will it?" she said, and turned toward the bar, trying to get the bartender's attention.

As she waited, I looked around for a familiar face in the pulsating crowd. In observing Crystal's excitement, I'd forgotten that we were supposed to meet the others at the doors. Luckily, they hadn't waited long—there was Sadie near a speaker in the corner, with Polly beside her, the two of them doing a round of shots. Rowan and Zoe looked on, laughing, and Ravi stood beside them sipping a Coke. And there, a few feet away, was Jasper, chatting to somebody facing away from us. A girl.

"Here!" Crystal thrust my drink at me and I took it.

"Thanks," I said. My lemonade was in a clear plastic cup with two half-melted ice cubes and a striped paper straw. It looked a bit sad.

Crystal eyed her own drink. "You get the impression they don't like serving plain lemonade," she said, "from the weird look they gave me. Wonder why?"

"They think you've snuck your own alcohol in," I said. "People do it, to make nights out cheaper. They bring a flask, or a little bottle of something in their bag, or tucked up their sleeves."

"Well, this bag is tiny—and I don't even have long sleeves!" Crystal said, offended, and I had to laugh.

"The others are over there," I said, lifting my drink in their direction. "And Jasper is . . . well, I think he's too busy to talk to us."

Crystal looked where I was indicating, and her expression darkened, just a little. Was Crystal *jealous*? As we watched, Jasper leaned in. Even from this distance, in the dark and surrounded by flashing strobe lights, I saw his lips brush her neck.

Crystal was staring as if there were nobody else in the room but her, Jasper, and the girl whose neck he was kissing.

When she finally managed to tear her gaze away, she met mine. "It's fine," she said. "We're not that close, anyway."

This was news to me. "What happened?"

"When I went to do the radio stuff, he was talking about the show he'd finally come up with," Crystal said. "A true crime show. Actually, he was inspired by *your* stuff, your articles for *Local Times*—the crimes you'd covered. Except I got the impression he wanted to sensationalize them a bit."

"You'd need to, for a full podcast episode," I pointed out. "Most of my articles were just reporting the facts we got from the hearing or sentencing or whatever. It's like a thousand words, max."

"That's what I said to him," she said. "He didn't seem to care. He *wanted* to do it, sensationalize stuff."

I glanced over at Jasper again with newfound irritation. How dare he try to build an audience using information *I'd* put together? How dare he use the worst—or even final—moments of someone's life to make himself look good?

He was still talking to the girl, holding her hand. I could see her face now, and she was laughing, throwing her head back.

"It's *Hayley*!"

"What?" I asked. "You know her?"

"She's my neighbor! The one you just met," Crystal said.

Maybe Crystal wasn't quite over her budding crush on Jasper—or maybe it was just the idea of somebody she knew being with him that rankled. Either way, she was done watching.

"Come on," she said, taking my hand so that I sloshed some of my drink on my borrowed gold shirt. "Screw Jasper, I want to go and see the others."

And suddenly it was me being pulled through the crowd, towed by the hand in Crystal's wake. Where had this sudden confidence come from? Was this transformation because of Jasper? I supposed that jealousy was a powerful thing—something that I knew firsthand.

Sadie spotted us first, shrieked, and elbowed the others. Polly, who was mid-shot, choked and looked less than impressed.

"Thanks for that, Sadie," she said wryly. "I never would've seen our friends standing right in front of us if you hadn't elbowed me."

Our friends. The phrase warmed me.

Crystal, I could tell, wasn't feeling the same welcoming sensation. Her eyes flashed at Jasper and Hayley, her lips a tight grimace.

Sadie rolled her eyes in Polly's direction, and reached over to a tray propped on a chest-height wall. Behind it, I remembered, was a door leading down a flight of stairs to the toilets. The tray still had several filled shot glasses on it: strange things, with an inner and an outer layer.

"What is it?" Crystal asked, at the same time as I said, "Jägerbombs? Really?"

"They were three for a fiver," Polly explained. "So we got twelve."

"Naturally," I said.

Crystal was eyeing the shots with what seemed to be a mixture of suspicion and interest. "Can I have one?"

"I thought you weren't going to be drinking tonight?" I said. Luckily, Crystal didn't hear me. *You're not her mother,* I reminded myself. *She can drink if she wants to.*

"Sure," Sadie was saying. "Go for it! They're for us to share."

Crystal picked up a Jägerbomb, braced herself, and then downed it in one smooth movement. I was impressed that she didn't cough and splutter—I hated shots, and presumably this was Crystal's very first one. The group gave her a round of applause.

"Look at her go!" a familiar voice said, and I turned to see Jasper. The girl he'd been with, Hayley, was nowhere to be seen. "Crystal," he said, laughing. "Are you sure you've never done this before?"

Crystal smiled at him, but it was tight. "I think I'd remember," she said. Her tone was sweet, but there was an underlying chilliness to it that seemed to take Jasper aback.

"I guess you would," he said, turning to talk to Ravi instead, gesticulating with his hands, and Ravi started to laugh. He slapped Jasper on the back in a "laddish" kind of way, and my lip curled.

"What's up with those two?" I said to Rowan.

They rolled their eyes. "Being annoying," they said. "Jasper's rebounding, apparently."

"Rebounding?" This surprised me. "From a relationship?"

"A crush, I think. Jasper messed it up with a girl he liked, apparently. Ravi's convincing him that getting out there is the only way forward."

I snorted. "And what do you think?"

"I think both of them are idiots. But I am enjoying watching Jasper try to flirt."

"He's doing a bit more than try, I think," I said, mostly to myself.

The girl that Jasper had messed it up with *had* to be Crystal. From what she'd said, she hadn't been receptive to his true crime radio show plan—and she'd made that known. Would that qualify? I thought so.

I decided not to share this newfound knowledge with Crystal. I was more than happy to let Jasper make a fool of himself in front of her. And I wanted Crystal to need *me*—not him.

What if, I thought with a sudden stroke of horror, *she decides I'm not the right person to help her? Will she ask Jasper instead?* No—surely not. Not if she thought he had the potential to sensationalize what had happened to her, what had happened to her sister. But . . . if the project didn't work out between the two of us, if we didn't manage to achieve what Crystal wanted, Jasper might well be her second choice after me.

I couldn't let that happen. I had to be careful, so she couldn't possibly suspect me of sabotaging her project. I had to stay close, to be supportive. Because if she went to Jasper, who I knew would be more than eager to help, it would ruin everything. *He* would ruin everything.

While I'd been lost in my thoughts, Crystal had done two more shots—what was she trying to prove, and who was she trying to prove it to?—and started dancing with Zoe and Polly. Beside them, Sadie was talking to a girl, taller than her and athletic-looking, and was looking up into her eyes like they held all the stars in the sky.

I sipped some more of my lemonade, which was going flat—Crystal's was drained, the plastic cup abandoned with the empty shot glasses on the tray—and then joined them. The girls shimmied their shoulders. Polly showed off some intricate footwork, which I suspected had been somehow transported from her football training. Rowan joined us, and they and Polly danced together.

Crystal, her cheeks so pink I could tell they were flushed even in the multicolored strobe lighting, took my hands in hers. Her palms were clammy, and she held my fingers loosely as she spun me round, laughing.

"This is what it's going to be like," Crystal said to me.

"What?" I said. "This is what *what's* going to be like?"

"This is what it's going to be like," she repeated giddily, "when it's all over. When we've told everyone everything."

Did she really think that? That she could potentially destroy her family, their perfect life, *her* life and everything would go back to normal? Did she truly think that her life afterward would be drinking, dancing, friends, and nightclubs?

I didn't say anything, though, just nodded and smiled. She squeezed my hand harder, then pulled away, turning to the others to dance with them, too.

Crystal's utterly clueless happiness, her hopefulness, only solidified my resolve to stop her. I had to prevent this from happening, for her sake.

And for mine.

Chapter Seventeen

CRYSTAL

I'd never had so much fun in all my life.

I'd been terrified to go to a club—a real actual club, not just a pub—but now that I was here, I was in my element. Dancing with my new friends beneath the multicolored strobe lights, the bass thumping deep in my chest, I'd never felt more myself. I even *looked* like me, the kind of me that Mum never would have approved of back on the island—a translucent dress thrown over jeans I'd ripped with a pair of kitchen scissors, my hair wild around my face as if I was underwater. My demure, natural makeup had been replaced with sparkly eyeshadow and glossy lips. Somebody had thrown a handful of glitter at some point, and it had stuck to my sweaty skin.

Everything was a blur, the rush of the alcohol and adrenaline and happiness fizzing and overflowing as Zoe took my hand, and then Polly, and as a group we twirled and laughed and tripped over each other's feet. And then Alyssa's hands were in mine instead and we spun in a giddy circle.

I laughed aloud, joyous, as realization set in.

"This is what it's going to be like," I told Alyssa.

Alyssa frowned at me, her face lit up by a streak of green and then red. "What?" she asked. She hadn't heard me.

"This is what it's going to be like," I said, "when it's all over! When we've told everyone everything."

My mum's cruelty, her lies, her backstabbing—once it was all out in the open, this is what my life would be like. I wouldn't spend my days and nights feeling like a cartoon character with an anvil hanging over my head, just waiting for the rope to break, for my mum to snap. I would be free.

Alyssa smiled at me, and I knew she understood.

It was only the following morning that I remembered I'd planned to make a video at the club. I swiped through my photos, hoping for—at the bare minimum—some still images that I could maybe add a quirky caption to. No luck. There were only three pictures in total: a blurry picture of the dirty club floor that was probably accidental, one of a tray of shots (not the first tray, but possibly the second . . . or the third) and one of Alyssa, doing a peace sign and grinning at the camera. I smiled when I saw it, remembering our dancing and laughing together, the sense of freedom that permeated the warm, smoky air.

I'd been disappointed to see Jasper flirting with Hayley, and then annoyed when Alyssa told me she'd heard Hayley at the bar telling someone that I was her "bitchy neighbor" who was "too famous and stuck up to hang out." It had really hurt my feelings, actually—I'd always been nice to Hayley when I'd seen her around, and I'd been really grateful for the brownies.

Now I definitely didn't want to be friends with her. And now that I knew Jasper's judgment was absolutely no good, I was especially glad I hadn't decided to involve him in my project. But despite that, our group had sung until our voices were hoarse, and twirled on the dance floor, and I had a really good friend to do the fun stuff and the hard stuff with.

I'd had so much fun that I'd forgotten what lay ahead: Christmas.

Christmas in our family was less a religious or festive celebration, and more a non-stop content train. Followers always engaged with our socials and the vlog in the run-up to Christmas—manically liking and sharing videos with hashtags like #giftideas, #toyreviews, and #decorinspo—which meant more income. As far as my parents were concerned, the festive season was for churning out as much #magical content as possible and raking in the money.

The whole thing had left me feeling a bit cynical about Christmas as a whole. Whenever I caught wind of a cutesy social media trend, like matching patterned pajamas or hot chocolate stations with multiple flavors, it just made me wonder who had started it and if or how they were benefiting from it now. Because of the pressure of making everything so perfect, I hadn't enjoyed a Christmas since before Lexie died, and I often wondered if I would ever enjoy one again.

Reluctantly, and significantly slower than usual due to another hangover, I showered and dressed, ready to venture into the city center. I had one day left before I headed back to the island, and I'd been so caught up in my deadlines I hadn't even considered buying Christmas presents.

For the first time, I ventured to the nearest Tube station, tapped in with my phone, and waited for a train to whisk me into the touristy part of the city, the one with the department stores and the iconic landmarks. I'd already decided I wasn't going to stay long—even though I'd lived in the city for a few months, the thought of festive season crowds was overwhelming.

When I emerged from the tunnels a few stops and a Tube change later, I had to stop and stare. Grumpy people pushed past me on either side, muttering in their irritation, but I couldn't bring myself to care. Oxford Street was sparkling. Lights in all colors of the rainbow glittered above me in the shapes of dangling stars and angels with their wings outstretched, and every shop window was packed with Christmas trees and fake snow. One or two were even adorned with enormous ribbons in shades of scarlet like giant presents.

I thought back to the island, to our tiny town's harbor and the way it was decorated at this time of year: the stacks of lobster pots with string lights wrapped around them, the steamy windows of the tearoom and the gift shops with their artificial Christmas trees and paper decorations, and of course the tractor parade, each one decked out with tinsel and driven by a local fisherman or farmer sporting a fake—or occasionally authentic—Santa beard. This here was on another level. It was nothing less than a spectacle.

I consulted the list I'd written, mostly ideas for gifts and where I could purchase them. Oliver and Opal were definitely too old for toys (how had *that* happened?) but I knew Opal loved making friendship bracelets, and Oliver was into collecting little model cars. That was relatively straightforward. I searched on my Maps for directions to the nearest toy shop, and fifteen minutes later I was back on the pavement with a branded paper bag and a significantly lighter bank account.

I popped in and out of a couple of department stores, browsing their displays of gift ideas for men and women, but nothing seemed like a good fit for Mum and Dad. They weren't necessarily difficult to please—the twins still gave them handmade gifts—but I wanted to get them something unique, something they couldn't get back home. The quicker I could get into their good books over Christmas, the better.

Eventually, I settled on a miniature luxury skincare set and a silk scarf for Mum, and some cologne and a thick, woolly hat for Dad. The last step was retrieving some wrapping paper and tape, and then I lugged everything back onto the Tube and home.

By the time I got back to Statue House, I was boiling hot despite the cold outside. I stripped my fleecy layers down to my T-shirt and began to wrap the gifts. I even put on some Christmas music to try to feel festive, to embrace the sparkle and happiness of the season. But my feelings from earlier had returned, the Christmas spirit Oxford Street had brought me dissipating. All I could think about was what lay in store for me when I was back on the island—the family pictures that had to be *just* right, having to wait until our Christmas dinner was practically cold so that Mum could take pictures of us pretending to enjoy it before we could actually eat it. I remembered one time, just before Christmas, when Mum had decided to redecorate the twins' room. It had been a fraught, days-long experience—a sponsor had sent a paint color that Mum hated but was obligated to use anyway, and she stormed through the house wielding paintbrushes and rollers like weapons. The twins donned paint-spattered overalls every morning in tears, because they hated the color too and they were sick and tired of being filmed painting the same patch of wall over and over because Mum was desperate to get the perfect shot of them doing it.

A lot of our family experiences, presented so positively on the vlog, were like that. And the more I thought about it, the idea of leaving my university life, friends, and independence behind to go back to that was suddenly not just uncomfortable, but unbearable.

And then I had an idea.

When I'd asked Alyssa if she was going home for Christmas, she'd been a bit subdued. And when I'd asked her whether her sister would be there, the way she'd said "hopefully" had sounded very much like she'd really wanted to say "hope not." If they didn't get on, a Christmas Day spent with her sister would probably be really awkward.

But I could invite Alyssa to come home for Christmas with me! That way, we could both avoid uncomfortable interactions with our respective difficult family members.

I decided I'd ask her first, before broaching the subject with Mum. But I didn't have many doubts about my parents—the Shaws kindly taking in one of Crystal's university friends for Christmas because she wasn't going home to her own family? That was the kind of content my parents' followers would *devour*.

And if it would make them look good, there was no way they'd refuse.

Chapter Eighteen

ALYSSA

It was four days until Christmas, and I was all alone in the flat.

Every room bore the mark of a hurried exit—crumpled paper from wrapping last-minute presents, half-open drawers, and stray socks spilled across the carpets.

The others had all locked their rooms, of course, but the flimsy old locks, made for aged keys, couldn't keep me out. I'd considered stealing something from each one like I had in the past, or maybe leaving a little mark to say *Alyssa was here*—a tiny burn somewhere, maybe, or a smear of lipstick—but then decided that it'd probably make for an unpleasant living environment when they all got back. If they didn't guess that it was me (why would they, when they'd locked their doors?) they might assume it was a burglar—and increased security on everyone's rooms was the last thing I wanted.

In the end, I left the flat as it was. Not spotless, but it wasn't my job to clean it. Not entirely my job, anyway. And my own room was perfectly clean and tidy.

I let the door swing shut behind me, listened for the telltale clunk as the lock slid itself into place, and then set off toward my parents' house.

I wasn't looking forward to spending Christmas with them. My old life was nothing compared to my new one: Crystal and socializing and Crystal and lectures and Crystal and clubbing. My Mum and Dad couldn't offer me anything that I didn't already have here. Except for parental affection, maybe, but that was unlikely to be forthcoming. They'd managed not to show they cared about me for eighteen years. Why would they start now?

My parents lived in one of the suburbs just outside the city proper, reachable on foot, by bus, or by one of the many trains that traveled underground like rumbling metal snakes.

I stepped into the mouth of the nearest Underground station, a five-minute walk away, ready to board one that would take me down, down into the deep underbelly of the city and then back up and out into the wider, leafier streets. It smelled of oil and grease and, above it all, of someone's perfume, dark yet sweet, like coffee and vanilla.

It was a short wait, only a couple of minutes, and then I was crowding onto a train with dozens of others, all of us shaking the cold from our jackets, stamping our boots, nudging each other with shopping bags and backpacks. I pushed my way to the corner of a carriage, where there was an empty seat next to a man who appeared to be either drunkenly passed out or asleep. I sat on the very edge of the seat so as not to disturb him, and then looked attentively at my phone for some kind of distraction. I didn't have any signal down here, but it didn't matter—I had downloads that would keep me busy. I found the perfect title, then hit play.

"Hello," a familiar voice said through my earphones, as if she were inside my head. "And welcome to an *extra*-special edition of *At Home with the Shaws*!"

It was an old video featuring Marjorie wearing a white, high-necked jumper dress, with sparkles threaded throughout the knit material. Her smile was a bright, berry red, her hair loosely curled. "It's time for our annual Christmas round-up video, where we'll go over all of the festive fun we've had, the gifts we've received, and thank our wonderful Christmas sponsors!" Here, she winked. "We hear they're Santa's very favorites."

I gazed out of the window as we emerged from underground, the clustered-together maze of streets in the center of the city slowly opening up, becoming wider and greener, concrete being replaced with rugged brown stone and brick. In my ear, Marjorie continued to talk, her words soothing—warm, cozy phrases like *homestyle cooking* and *wood-burning stove* and *Scandinavian knit socks* washing over me.

I paused the video as we slowed to pull in at the station closest to my parents' house. As I got up, gathering my bags, the man beside me shifted, grumbled in his sleep, but didn't wake.

I stood on the platform as the train pulled away, clickety-clacking on the tracks until I was left in relative silence. I texted Mum that I'd arrived.

I was one of only a few people on the platform, the others having just disembarked, too—sorting out children's buggies and shifting shopping bags from arm to arm, laughing with each other and chatting on phones.

After five minutes with no reply from Mum, I texted Dad. As the platform emptied, I walked out of the station and huddled under the awning of a nearby greengrocer's as it started to rain. Eventually, giving up on a response from either of my parents, I set off in the direction of the house. I trudged along glumly as the rain, which seemed to be getting heavier by the second, dripped from my hood onto my nose, ran down my cheeks, plastered my fringe to my forehead. My parents' presents might get wet—but it was their own fault if they didn't even care enough to come and pick me up.

By the time I got to their street, I was drenched. My coat had soaked through, my jeans were sticking to my legs, and even my boots were sodden. My bags weren't in a much better state, and my hands were damp and chilled as I fumbled for my house key. I let myself into the townhouse, and slammed the door pointedly behind me. But no one came running; no heads appeared from the archway into the living room; no voices inquired who was there. No one was home.

They'd known I was coming. I'd told them the night before. And, okay, they hadn't exactly been enthusiastic, but they were never enthusiastic about *anything*. Especially when it involved me. They weren't like Marjorie, who'd been posting about Crystal's homecoming for days—and she hadn't even left the city yet. Jealousy bubbled up in me, thick and viscous like honey. I felt stuck in it, a bluebottle trapped by flypaper, my footsteps slow as I ventured into the living room and flicked some lights on.

At least the Christmas decorations were up, bringing some cheer into the dimly lit space. In the huge bay window stood a Christmas tree, a real one, needles scattered about its base. I could smell pine and, beneath that, the scent of furniture polish.

I left my bags by the overstuffed velvet sofa, a deep blue to match the living room walls, and went to inspect the tree. It didn't just hold ornaments, it held memories.

Here was the salt-dough star I'd fashioned as a toddler, pressed with glitter and threaded with a red ribbon to hang it from a branch. And here, the angel I'd made out of a wooden clothes peg, with pipe cleaners for its arms and halo, a drape of white fabric and glued-on sequins for its dress. It smiled a red felt-tip pen smile, its hair scribbles of yellow. Beside that, a cross-stitched Santa, its face orange, its eyes wobbly black knots. I touched it, gently, with my fingertip and it spun on its gold string.

I wondered what the Shaws' Christmas tree looked like this year, whether it was real pine like my parents,' standing tall and proud in that big, glass window they had in their living room. I imagined the decorations they had on their tree, the way the whole family—besides Crystal, of course—had probably got together to hook each ornament onto a branch with love and care. Maybe they'd even reminisced about them—where they'd bought or crafted each one, who'd chosen or made it. Whether it was Crystal, or Oliver or Opal, or even Lexie.

Or maybe Lexie's decorations were carefully hidden away, wrapped in delicate tissue paper, to prevent damage and to hold on to the precious memories they held. But are memories more precious when they're hidden, or when they're shared?

I left the lights on as I took my things upstairs, deposited them in my bedroom, and then went into the family bathroom. It had been redecorated since the last time I was home, the azure blue hues now replaced with jungle-themed wallpaper, dark and sultry with leopards skulking around in the shadows. The combination of the new wallpaper, the tropical potted plants, and the dim lighting made me look like a lost adventurer, my hair tangled and mascara running down my cheeks.

I borrowed some of my mum's face wash to take off the smeared makeup, then rooted around in the basket where she kept her skincare products. Mum was a skincare fiend—she'd sampled what seemed like every moisturizer, serum, chemical exfoliant, or anti-aging serum that was on the market, and often tossed whatever was left my way.

I applied a pea-sized drop of hydrating serum from a tiny, green glass bottle that promised "plumper, bouncier skin in a single use" and rubbed it into my skin in smooth, circular motions.

Then I looked at myself in the mirror. My skin was glossier, but I was still the same disappointing Alyssa.

I went back into my bedroom and rifled through my old wardrobe to look for some dry clothes. I found some pajama bottoms that were slightly too big and a sweatshirt and changed, then laid the cold, wet clothes on the radiator.

Once I was more comfortable, I looked around my childhood bedroom properly. It was still more or less the same as it had been: the swirling floral wallpaper, the cream fluffy rug. Mum had chosen the design, not me. Apparently when I was going through my black-eyeliner phase, I couldn't be trusted in matters of taste, which I supposed was fair enough.

The shelves were lined with books I hadn't read in years, classics like *Little Women* and *The Secret Garden*, the covers all in pretty jewel-toned binding with gold foil text. I wondered at these previous iterations of Alyssa: the girl who loved classic novels, the grungy teenager who loved black fingernail polish and loud music. And now, the journalist.

My heart sank. Well. Not anymore.

I hadn't told Mum and Dad about my dismissal. I didn't want to explain it to them, to go into the specifics about what had happened. They'd only assume it was my fault, anyway.

Downstairs, I heard the rattle of the key in the door, followed by the sound of rustling paper and plastic bags as someone arrived home. I waited just inside my bedroom door with bated breath. And then—

"Hello? Is anyone here?"

It was Mum, her voice shrill with anxiety. She must've noticed the lights were on.

I ventured to the top of the landing. Mum was surrounded by what looked like a food shop, a loaf of bread sticking out of one brown paper bag. Her hair, usually immaculate—the opposite of my own—was slightly mussed from the rain, and she looked harried.

"Hi, Mum," I said.

She blinked up at me, her face half in shadow. "Alyssa?" she said. "What are you doing here?"

Such a warm welcome. There was no sign of affection in her voice, no indication that she'd missed me, that she was happy I was here. Because, although we'd been in the same city, we hadn't seen each other in weeks.

"I'm home for Christmas," I said.

"Right," she said. She looked at the bags on the colored tiles of the hallway floor. "I suppose you'll be wanting something to eat. I'll get this lot put away, then."

She didn't ask for my help, and I didn't offer it.

I retreated back to my bedroom, which no longer felt like my bedroom and maybe never really had, and sat on my bed, knees tucked to my chest, and unlocked my phone. There wasn't a new *At Home with the Shaws* video yet. I assumed they'd be waiting until Crystal arrived so they could celebrate her homecoming. I wondered what it was like to have parents who were actually excited to see you.

They had uploaded some highlights on their socials, though—throwbacks to the previous Christmas. The Shaws walking up their snow-covered driveway, Crystal and Oliver and Opal practically shoulder to shoulder. Opening the front door—thick, chestnut wood, arched, studded with panes of glass the size of paper napkins—to unveil a festively decorated hallway complete with a stylishly thin Christmas tree with frosted, fake snow branches. A glimpse at the living room, with the main tree covered in dozens of vintage baubles. And the last clip, the one that hurt my heart the most—Crystal beaming, *literally* beaming happiness out of her face, as she sits on the sofa with a sibling either side, all of them holding matching red mugs with mountains of whipped cream.

She wants to destroy you, I thought, as I tapped through the series of clips. *She wants to ruin all of this.* If Crystal succeeded, what would next Christmas be like? Surely not this perfect, this picturesque.

One more tap, and *At Home with the Shaws* vanished altogether, taking me to a different influencer's feed. Another lucky, lucky girl no doubt showing off her beautiful face and her beautiful home and her beautiful family.

Why wasn't I that lucky?

I lurked in my bedroom, losing myself among the pixelated evidence that everybody else was having more fun than me, until Mum called me downstairs for dinner.

I set the table in the dining room—awkwardly, as they'd shifted things around in the kitchen since I'd moved out and the cutlery was in a totally different drawer—then hovered until I finally had to break the ice.

"How's work?" I asked.

Mum, in the process of taking a dish out of the oven, glanced my way. "Work? Same old, I suppose."

Mum was the CFO of a big regional charity. Before I was born, she'd started a successful accounting firm (how she'd met my dad, who ran his own company) but had eventually sold the firm at a profit and moved on to what she described as a "far more important role for a charitable cause" when I was fifteen. I reckoned she only made the move because it was a massive pay raise and she could make excuses to stay at the fancy office after hours to avoid both me and Dad.

"So you're . . ." I wrestled with the phrasing. I didn't know enough about her job to ask any detailed questions. "Raising lots of money? Doing lots of projects?"

"Plenty of both," she said, placing the dish on the heatproof board on the kitchen island. It had a watercolor design, a green landscape with poppies and a bright blue sky.

"Cool," I said.

Mum scraped roasted vegetables, drizzled in oil, onto plates. "Tell me about university," she said. "How's your course going?"

"It's good," I said. "I'm enjoying it. Learning a lot."

"Well, that's what's important," she said. "Making friends?"

"I am," I said. "There's this girl called Crystal. Her family does online vlogging stuff—you know, *At Home with the Shaws*?"

"I can't say I'm familiar," Mum said.

"Oh," I said. "Well, anyway. She's really nice."

This was a test. I was glad Mum didn't recognize Crystal's name, didn't know how long I'd followed her and her family's online journey. I tried to keep the Shaws and my own parents separate—they were two different worlds, two parts of me that I didn't want to collide. My real life and the life I dreamed of having.

"Hello, Alyssa," Dad's deep voice said from behind me. "When did you get back?"

The expression on Mum's face tightened, everything about her immediately growing more distant.

I turned to see him standing in the kitchen doorway, and forced a smile. "Hey, Dad," I said. "I got back about two hours ago. Have you just got home?"

"I've been here all afternoon," he said gruffly. "Up in the office."

The office was on the third floor, up in the converted loft, while my bedroom was on the first. It was altogether possible that he hadn't heard me come in the front door, hadn't heard me shout "hello," hadn't heard me talking to Mum from the landing. It was also possible that he had, and that he'd chosen to ignore the two of us.

Dad spent the majority of his time in the office when he was at home. He wasn't always even working—sometimes when I lived here, I'd pop in to find him just sitting in an armchair reading, his wire-framed glasses balanced precariously on the bony bridge of his nose.

If it wasn't so tragic, it'd almost be funny. I wondered, now that I'd left, how often the living spaces in my parents' house—the kitchen, the living room, the sitting room—were left cold and empty because they were both so busy trying to avoid each other.

The meal Mum had made was delicious, the roasted vegetables perfectly crisp and the chicken breasts, which had been carefully seasoned and stuffed with soft, creamy cheese and herbs, filled with flavor. But every bite felt like I was swallowing sawdust, sticking to my tongue, in my throat.

The awkwardness in the dining room was palpable. Mum and Dad were sitting at opposite ends of their stupidly oversized dining table, with me beside Mum. The odd one out, the third wheel. The table was a light oak with glass corners, and had twelve modern chairs huddled around it, as if Mum and Dad had been planning to host dinner parties when they'd first bought it. As far as I knew, no parties—dinner or otherwise—had ever materialized in the tall city townhouse.

I felt very small in the dimly lit room, the silver chandelier in the center of the ceiling not quite bright enough to light up the far corners, parts of my parents' faces in shadow. It was claustrophobic, almost, being trapped in a small pool of light in the middle of the room with them.

And, clearly, it wasn't just me who was uncomfortable. Mum and

Dad didn't seem to know what to talk about with me there, making stilted conversation in low voices about traffic and the new coffee shop on the high street and Mum's upcoming charity ball.

I moved my food around my plate, waiting for them to finish their meals so that I could plead exhaustion and leave.

"How's university going?" Dad said, finally addressing me directly. His voice was slurred, the bottle of wine on the table half empty although no one else was drinking.

"It's good," I said.

"We've discussed this already, Richard," Mum said lightly. "She's doing well. Making friends."

"I wasn't there," Dad pointed out.

"No," Mum said. "Because you were choosing to ignore us."

Dad chose to ignore that comment, too, and continued speaking to me. "So you're settled in? Your course is going all right?"

"Yeah," I said. "It's all going well. The flat-share's good, too."

"And how's the job at the newspaper?"

They didn't know I wasn't being paid for it.

"Well," I hedged. "I . . ."

I had both their attentions now. "You haven't lost it already, have you?" Mum said. When I didn't say anything, she sighed and laid her cutlery down. "Oh, Alyssa. What happened?"

"Why didn't you tell us?" Dad asked at the same time. "What did you do?"

Mum reached over to put a calming hand on my arm, but it was too late. My embarrassment sparked into anger at his words. "I knew this would happen," I said through gritted teeth. "You always blame me for everything."

To her credit, Mum actually looked guilty. "We don't blame you for—"

"Yes, you do." My voice grew louder with every word. "I saw your face. You both immediately assumed that me losing my job was my fault!"

Dad's lips were pressed together in a thin line. "Well, you can hardly blame us."

There was a silence. It was a long moment before Mum broke it. "Richard, please—"

"No, Veronica," Dad snapped. "I'm not going to pretend like it just didn't happen."

"It's Christmas!"

"It's not bloody Christmas yet! And besides, that's no excuse!"

I stared down at my half-eaten meal, their hissed words hovering in the air around me like wasps. I was no longer hungry, the ache from earlier replaced by queasiness, a natural aversion to the thick tension in the room. "Please, may I leave the table?" I asked, raising my voice to be heard.

They both stopped berating each other and looked at me.

"You may," Mum said.

I pushed my chair back, the screech of the legs across the hardwood floor painful in the sudden quiet, and left the room. The door had barely clicked closed behind me before they started up again.

I crouched at the bottom of the stairs, half-hidden behind the banister railings, as I listened. It was the same position I'd sat in a hundred times, listening in to my parents fighting—about Dad's spending or Mum's work or about me. It was often about me.

"We've been over this," Mum was saying. "You can't treat her like a criminal every time she's home! She's our daughter."

"She is a criminal," Dad retorted.

"No charges were ever brought—"

"You know Alyssa," Dad said. "She was obsessed with that girl. Are you honestly saying you don't think she did it?"

Mum's silence was utterly damning.

Slowly, so that the floorboards didn't creak, I crept up the stairs and back into my bedroom. They wondered why I never came home to visit—this, *this* was why! They were always dragging up the past, refusing to let go of my mistakes.

And that *had* been a mistake. Nobody was hurt. It was just silly, petty behavior.

Anyway, none of that mattered. Not anymore.

I had Crystal now. I had Crystal, and I had her wonderful family who I was sure would welcome me with open arms once they'd got to know me.

Downstairs, my parents were still arguing. I climbed into bed, pulled the duvet up over my head, and inhaled the unfamiliar, artificially clean scent of a new fabric softener; it was nothing like the floral scent of my childhood that I'd been hoping for. Some things changed, and some things stayed the same.

The following morning, my parents were stern-faced and serious at the breakfast table.

I was only halfway through my morning coffee when Dad said, "We think you should stay at your flat for Christmas."

My blood ran cold with shock. "What?" I said. "But *why*? What have I done?"

"It's the atmosphere you create," Dad said, "wherever you go. It's oppressive, and we can't trust you, Alyssa. We can't trust anything you say. You've lied to us over and over again. I want you out of my house."

"Mum?"

Mum didn't look at me, her back turned as she sliced strawberries at the kitchen counter. "Your dad's right," she said. "I think it's for the best."

My jaw actually dropped. "Are you serious?"

Neither of them answered me. I tried again.

"What happened wasn't my fault! It was—"

"We all know exactly what you did," Dad spat. "So do us a favor and stop lying, for once in your life!" His voice grew louder with every word until he was shouting.

I swallowed any emotion in my voice as I said levelly, "Fine. I'll get my things and I'll go."

My parents didn't say anything as I stormed upstairs. Once I'd changed back into my now-dry clothes, I thundered back down into the hallway and out the front door.

Mum followed me, her expression moving between concern and resignation. "Here," she said, standing on the doorstep. She handed me a crisp white envelope, which I knew contained my usual Christmas present: cash. "Get yourself something nice. Some clothes, maybe. Or a haircut."

Or a haircut. Why did everything have to be a fight?

I wondered sometimes if my parents would hate me this much if I hadn't done what I did at boarding school. But even as a kid they'd never been particularly interested in me, even if back then they hadn't so clearly disliked me. Maybe I just wasn't the daughter they wanted. Maybe they'd never wanted a daughter at all.

I yanked my keys from my pocket, and slipped their house key from its keyring. "I suppose you'll want this back," I snarled, flinging it in her direction. "Since I won't be needing it anymore. Your Christmas presents are in my bedroom, by the way. You're welcome."

Mum looked anxiously from side to side, and I realized that she was checking there were no nosy neighbors observing my tantrum, whispering comments to each other behind their living room blinds. It made fury well up in me so quickly and overwhelmingly that I wanted to scream, to rip out my hair, to set the house in front of me on fire and turn my back on its blackened, collapsing walls with both my parents still inside. I wanted the neighbors to see what they'd driven me to.

I didn't say goodbye. I just looked at her without speaking, hoping that my expression relayed the toxic cocktail of emotions I was feeling—hurt, rage, abandonment, disappointment, hatred. Then I walked away.

In my pocket, my phone buzzed. It was Crystal.

Hey, I know you said a while ago you and your sister don't get on. If you don't want to go home for Christmas, do you want to come back to the island with me instead?

I'm leaving tomorrow though, sorry it's short notice!! Let me know what you think! xx

I stopped dead in my tracks. All at once, the upset, the fury, the indignation of the last day or so melted away. I no longer cared about my parents, about whether I spent Christmas with them or not. It was happening. It was *finally* happening.

I was going to meet the Shaws.

Chapter Nineteen

CRYSTAL

I couldn't describe how relieved I was when Alyssa said yes. Immediately after she'd replied, I booked her tickets for the train and the plane and forwarded them to her. And only then, when it was too late to say no, I checked that it was okay with my mum to invite her. As I'd predicted, Mum was delighted.

"Oh, the poor dear," she said, and I could imagine the concerned crease of her brows, the downturn of her lips. "And she lives *in* the city, too? That's so sad."

"She doesn't have a good relationship with her parents," I said. She'd explained, over text, that her parents continued to be distant on her latest visit and she didn't want to spend Christmas with them in their cold, lonely house.

"Well, of course she's welcome here, Crystal," Mum said. "There's always more than enough to go round. She can enjoy a big family Christmas with us."

"I think she'd love that," I said honestly.

We said our goodbyes and hung up, and then I flopped back on my bed and kicked my legs in the air, like a very excited beetle. And then I leaped back up. It was time to pack.

I carefully placed my now-wrapped Christmas presents in my suitcase, and then crammed in a couple of pairs of jeans and as many jumpers as I could fit. The island was rarely prettier than it was at this time of year, with its glowing winter sunrises and snow-dusted peaks, but it was also freezing cold. I sent Alyssa another text to warn her, and received a picture of a gargantuan pile of knitwear in response which made me laugh. Maybe this Christmas wouldn't be so bad.

I met Alyssa at the train station at seven o'clock in the morning, ready to begin our journey back to the island. It was the exact reverse of the one I'd taken to get to the city back in October, and it was strange—there was so much that I knew now that I hadn't known then. Everything was different. My parents would never see it, but I was returning to the island a different person after just a couple of months. Maybe this would even be the last time we were all together before . . .

I didn't want to dwell on that.

Throughout the train journey, we chatted and read books and shared snacks (Werther's Originals that Alyssa had brought, like a sweet grandparent) and napped. I watched Alyssa as she slept. She had a perpetual little frown, as if she couldn't quite fully relax even when she was unconscious.

A few hours later, we disembarked, took a taxi to the airport, and then boarded the island-hopper plane. Alyssa took copious photos of it—from the terminal, on the tarmac, when we were seated. There were only seven of us on there in total.

The plane taxied to the end of the runway and then sped up, the propellers fighting hard to get it off the ground. And then we were soaring into the sky.

I'd always preferred the plane to the ferry (even if the ferry was sometimes more convenient) because I got to see the landscape. I let Alyssa have the window seat, and she pressed her face up against the window, taking in the landscape below: fields stretching out, a winter gray-green, stitched together by hedgerows, drystone walls, and weaving roads. Eventually we left the mainland behind, the wobbly line of the coast dropping off behind us seemingly all at once. And then suddenly there was the island, the mountains rising up ahead, its borders surrounded by an archipelago of smaller, rockier islands.

The mountains were already coated with snow, white scattered over the lowland hills and the villages.

Alyssa's eyes were shining as she took it all in. "Where do you live?" she asked. "Can you see it from here?"

"No," I said. "The house is on the other side of the island."

Alyssa didn't seem disappointed, just kept looking out as our plane got lower, lower, and then landed with a wobble.

The airport itself was little more than a runway, a control tower, and a terminal. My parents were waiting for us inside the terminal building, which was small, white, and drafty, and was never more than half full. Oliver and Opal were holding hand-painted signs reading—in tall rainbow letters—WELCOME HOME CRYSTAL. In smaller letters, one of them had added AND ALYSSA!

As sweet as the signs were, I had no doubt that it was my mum behind them. As Alyssa and I walked toward them I could see the phone in Mum's hand, held up to film my arrival for the vlog.

I didn't want to ruin the moment for the twins, though, so I pretended the camera wasn't there, let go of my suitcase, and held my arms open wide. They dropped their signs (they'd undoubtedly be told off for this later) and ran toward me, one falling into either arm. I clutched them tightly to me, inhaling the familiar, warm scent of home, sea salt, and bubblegum. Opal wasn't allowed bubblegum, but I knew she used her pocket money to buy it at the village shop.

You're not supposed to have favorites but if I did, it would be Opal. Oliver was his dad's son—talkative, enthusiastic, always busy exploring the moors, building dams and trenches on the beach, camping in the garden, shooting at inanimate objects with a slingshot he'd made. Opal was softer, more gentle—just as keen to explore, but equally as happy reading a book. Like me. Like Lexie, although Lexie had had more of Oliver's personality, the cheekiness you couldn't help but love because of the way her dimples appeared when she grinned.

Alyssa was standing to one side, smiling as she looked on, and Opal gave her a hug, too. We headed toward my parents together, Opal hanging on to one of my arms and Oliver running ahead, jumping in the air.

Opal released me so I could hug Dad and then Mum, who'd paused filming but was still holding her phone in one hand. Its hard edge pressed up against my spine, the pressure a reminder of what I was doing, and why I was doing it.

"Good trip?" Dad asked. "Not too bumpy?"

Dad's attempts at bonding typically involved traveling, weather, and food.

"It was good," I said. "Mum, Dad, this is Alyssa."

"It's so wonderful to meet you, Alyssa," Mum said, in her special voice—the gentle, motherly one she put on for videos. "We've heard so much about you."

That was a downright lie, but it seemed to soothe Alyssa. "Hi," she said. "It's so lovely to meet you. Thank you so much for having me."

Mum glanced at Dad approvingly and I knew what she was thinking: she was a stranger to them, yes, but at least Alyssa had good manners.

"Maybe next time you should get the ferry," Mum said as we walked toward the terminal exit. "We had an icy drive over the hills to get here, and Opal was nearly travel sick. The ferry terminal's closer."

Opal looked at me with big, apologetic eyes.

"Yeah, but that'd mean changing trains like three times," I said. "And trains are always canceled at this time of year, so I'd probably end up having to get a bus to the ferry terminal."

Mum seemed surprised that I'd argued with her. In the past, I would've just nodded meekly. I had to be better at this, to show her that things hadn't changed—even if I knew they had.

"Besides," I added, knowing this would win her round, "the content wouldn't be as good."

I'd dutifully filmed my journey with Alyssa in snippets, from a blurry selfie of the two of us smiling on the train platform to the view out of the plane window. I planned to layer music over it, possibly something festive, and post the series of clips all in one as a "coming home" montage.

Mum clearly envisioned the same thing, and nodded approvingly. "I'm glad to see your mind's still in the right place."

As we followed my parents out of the terminal and across to the car park, Opal said, "By the way, we baked you a cake. Double chocolate. Do you like double chocolate, too, Alyssa?"

"I love double chocolate," Alyssa said.

"Opal," Oliver groaned. That was supposed to be a surprise!"

Opal shrugged. "Mum put the video on the channel last night," she said. "I thought Crystal probably already knew."

I hadn't already known, but I couldn't fault Opal's logic. Mum's, though, I could. What kind of person would put a surprise cake online before the person it was baked for had even glimpsed it? Answer: the kind of person who cared more about views and engagement than the person in question.

Opal's statement also surprised me. When I left, she'd still been very much enthusiastic about *At Home with the Shaws*—at least, most of the time. Yes, she'd pouted and sulked a bit when we'd had to retake the same candid shot five times, and yes, she'd been embarrassed when she and Oliver toured the local secondary school on the next island over and their peers had looked them up and down. But she'd never really shown any resistance. This was troubling, but also potentially useful.

The thoughts about their school tour reminded me that I wasn't the only one who'd had a big change this year.

"Hey," I said as we all piled into the car. "How's big school going?"

We squashed into the backseat, with Alyssa on one side, Oliver on the other, and myself in the middle with Opal on my knee. Mum glanced back at us uneasily. This disregard for safety was definitely something she wouldn't want appearing online.

I didn't mind, though, and stretched the seatbelt across both of us. Opal wriggled on my lap. "Big school?" I asked again.

"You don't have to call it that," Oliver said. "It's just school."

"Fine," I said. "Moody. How's *school* going?"

Oliver began to ramble on, about how many more people there were (eight hundred pupils from across the islands, as opposed to the local primary school which had a total student body of twenty-three), what his favorite lessons were, and who his favorite teachers were. "Mr. Jenkins is really nice, but strict if you cause trouble," he said matter-of-factly. "He told Opal off on our first—*ouch!*"

Opal's hand had suddenly become visible on his leg, and I suspected the cry of pain was from a well-timed pinch. "Shut *up*," she hissed.

Mum and Dad, who'd been having their own conversation, quietened. Dad eyed us all in the rearview mirror. "Causing trouble already, Crystal?" he asked with a grin. "You've only been back ten minutes."

"You know me," I said. "Always the troublemaker."

This was funny because I'd never been a difficult child—or teenager, for that matter. Lexie had always been the one with the sass and the attitude. Dad winked at me, shaking his head fondly, and turned his attention back to the road. Mum looked at us disapprovingly over her shoulder, but didn't say anything. Clearly, Opal had timed her interruption well and neither of them had heard what Oliver had been about to say. I was sure that whatever Opal had got into trouble for, my parents didn't know about it. Opal was the golden child, whereas I'd always been the scapegoat. It was interesting that she'd finally decided to rebel.

Despite how I felt about the island, I couldn't help but lean forward as we crunched along the gravel driveway toward the house. In one direction, the sea stretched out like a mirror. In the other, muddied farmers' fields led up to the violet mountains, their peaks crusted with snow. Alyssa's face was practically up against the window as she took it all in, and I was strangely proud that she was seeing it. *Welcome*, I wanted to say to her. *This is where I come from.*

"It was an early first snow this year," Oliver piped up. "Miss Darcy says it means we're in for a bad winter."

"That's just an old wives' tale," Mum said, more harshly than she probably meant to.

Oliver looked at me, and shrugged. He didn't seem bothered by her tone. I wondered what that must be like, for her barbs not to penetrate your skin. I felt Opal tense up.

I glanced at Alyssa, but she didn't seem to have noticed anything was off. Her gaze was still fixed on the mountains, magnificent in the low winter sun.

I could see the house properly now, up ahead, and my heart started to beat faster at the sight of it, a trembling flutter behind my ribs. Every beat said, *I'm home. I've missed it here. I don't want to be here. I want to stay here forever. I never want to see this place again.*

The first thing that people always noticed about the house—the main thing they commented on in videos—was that one entire wall was made of glass so that it had an incredible view of the sea. If it was dark, and you were standing on the beach and the curtains were open, you'd be able to see all our movements throughout the downstairs: the front door, the hallway, the living room with its wood-burning stove at one side of the house, and the sweeping, modern kitchen diner at the other. Upstairs, you might be able to see the landing, home to various doors that led off into bedrooms, bathrooms, my mum's walk-in wardrobe.

If you cared enough, you could sit there on the sand and watch us emerge one by one from our enclosed rooms. You could watch us descend the stairs, go into the kitchen, grab a smoothie, light a fire, lounge on the sofa. But, of course, you wouldn't need to be on the beach to see that. You could find all that online.

The sun had nearly set, the light reflecting off the enormous window, curiously reminiscent of my first day in the city when I'd been so struck by the boiled-sweet colors of the skyscrapers, the glossy pinks and oranges, as my taxi weaved through the traffic.

All this spun through my head, a kaleidoscope of good memories and old frustrations, as Dad parked the car and switched the engine off. We got out, Oliver and Opal skipping ahead while Alyssa, Mum, Dad, and I lingered to get our bags from the boot. Dad passed Alyssa her bag, and they started walking up the path.

As I leaned in to grab my own backpack, Mum said, "Would you like to tell me where you were the other night?" I could hear the edge in her words; it was a cold clifftop, boiling waves below, eager to swallow me up and tear me apart.

I decided to stick to the story Alyssa and I had planned. "I was filming some content."

"Content?" Mum repeated. "At a *nightclub*?"

"Yeah," I said. "It was about having a sober night out. About not giving in to peer pressure."

We reached Dad and Alyssa, waiting by the front door with Oliver and Opal. Dad had clearly overheard, and looked pleased. "You see?" he said to Mum. "I told you there'd be a reasonable explanation."

"I haven't edited the video yet," I said. "Because I need to do an overview of the night, filmed separately. I got lots of footage while we were in there, though."

Obviously, a lie. But it wouldn't be for long. Once term started again, it'd be easy enough to go on another night out and actually film it this time.

"It isn't exactly family-friendly content," Mum said. "Which you *know* is what we're all about. But I suppose it's appropriate for your own channel—your followers will be expecting more grown-up content from you at university. If you're going to post anything, it should be that. I'm sure I've suggested it before, actually."

I closed my mouth so quickly that my teeth clicked together. It was *so* like Mum to be prepared to tear my head off about some content—and then, once she'd realized it was a good idea, to take credit for it. Even though what I'd told her was utterly untrue, the injustice still smarted like a splinter wedged into my skin. I'd grown a thick skin when I'd lived here, but distance had lessened the effect. I'd forgotten what it was like to need armor.

I swallowed down my feelings, which had lodged in my throat like a fish bone, and smiled, gripping the handle on my suitcase so tightly I knew my knuckles would be white.

"Let's get these inside," I said brightly. "I can't *wait* to see the Christmas decorations."

In true Mum form, Alyssa and I weren't allowed to see how she'd decorated the interior of the house straight away. We were urged to remove our shoes and herded toward the staircase, the plush white carpet soft beneath my socked feet—my soles now more used to institutional carpeting and hard pavement—and more or less commanded to clean ourselves up (but not too much, because we still had to look travel-weary) and prepare for a video.

"Welcome to the Shaw family," I murmured to Alyssa as we reached the landing. "I hope you enjoy being on camera."

Alyssa didn't seem too perturbed by it all as I showed her to the guest room, which I was grateful for. I supposed she'd probably already suspected she'd be filmed here, and she didn't mind.

The guest room was pristine, with a view out toward the mountains. Mum had clearly made an effort to impress Alyssa, with fresh, cornflower-blue bedding and a set of soft, clean towels waiting on the dresser.

"This is lovely," Alyssa said as we entered.

"I'll let you get sorted," I said. "The bathroom's just down there, second door on the right. My room's at the end of the hallway."

"Thanks," Alyssa said. Then, as I turned to leave and give her some privacy, "Hey, Crystal?"

I turned back. "Yes?"

"I'm so glad I'm here. Thank you."

"I'm glad you're here, too," I told her. "Now get changed, before Mum throws a hissy fit."

I saw Alyssa grin as I closed the door, then went down the hall to my own room. It was just as I'd left it, which surprised me—I wouldn't have put it past Mum to turn it into a home gym or something. My window looked out on the side of the house, with a view partly of the mountains and partly down the coast, the sea a choppy, steel gray.

I did as Mum had instructed and freshened up, making sure my makeup wasn't smudged and my clothes weren't creased. Luckily, jumpers don't really need ironing, so I wasn't too rumpled from our day of traveling.

Apparently, Oliver and Opal hadn't received the same instructions—I could hear them downstairs tearing around, and then the yell and long, drawn-out whine which meant one of them had lost the game they were playing.

I was jealous of them, the twins. Sometimes, it seemed as though they were two halves of a whole—their secret games, the way they whispered into the soft shells of each other's ears. When they were tiny, they'd even had their own language, a gobbledegook of words and sounds that made no sense to anybody else. I wasn't a twin, of course, but I'd had a bond like that with Lexie. And now I had no one, and they had each other.

As if summoned by my feelings, Opal peeked her head around my door. "Knock knock," she said.

I smiled. "Hey."

That was all the invitation she needed, and she ran into the room, bouncing on the bed and knocking the pillows into disarray. She lay on her stomach, legs in the air, and I found myself realizing just how much more grown-up she looked. She didn't look like a little kid; there was a pre-teen in there, the upcoming shift in the bones of her face somehow obvious beneath her round cheeks.

I listened to the voices downstairs. And then I turned to her.

"So," I said. "What did you do at school to get into trouble?"

"Ugh," she said, rolling her eyes. "Oliver is *so* annoying. He said he wouldn't tell."

I met her gaze in the mirror. "And yet."

"Mr. Jenkins was wrong about something," she said eventually. "And then he acted like *I* was the idiot."

"What was he wrong about?"

She huffed. "We were talking about baby animals," she said. "It was an icebreaker sort of thing—you know, 'What do you think is the cutest baby animal?' As if we're all toddlers. *Anyway*, we started talking about how some of them have actual names, how they aren't just baby sheep or baby cows—you know?" Her cheeks were growing pink as she talked. "So I said, baby rabbits are called kittens, or kits. Which they are. And he just looked at me like I was a total idiot, and said, 'Don't be ridiculous, Opal—baby rabbits are called *bunnies*.' And then everyone laughed."

She sat up again, blustering with embarrassed fury. "It was so unfair that I was right, and he was wrong, and everyone was laughing at *me*. So I told him to Google it. He didn't even do it on the big screen, so everyone could see—he looked on his computer. Then, when he saw I was right, he sent me to stand outside in the corridor."

"He sent you out? Why?"

"Because I made him look stupid," Opal said, chin tilted defiantly. "He came out after a while, and told me that next time I shouldn't argue back."

I gritted my teeth. What I wanted to say was *what a prick*, but it felt inappropriate to say that to an eleven-year-old. Instead, I said, "He sounds horrible."

"He is."

"Why didn't you want Mum or Dad to know? They could speak to the school, or something."

"Yeah, right." Opal sniffed. "Be serious, Crystal. Dad probably wouldn't think it was a big deal, and Mum would end up making some kind of call-out video or something. And that would just make things worse, because everyone would see it."

She had a point. I could see it now: "OPAL PUNISHED FOR PROVING TEACHER WRONG!!!"

But something else she said niggled at me. *Everyone would see it.* "Opal," I asked. "Do people make fun of you because of the videos?"

"No," she said, but the way she said it very much sounded like she wasn't telling the whole truth. I raised my eyebrows at her, and she said, "Sometimes."

"Are you getting tired of making them?"

I tried not to sound hopeful. If Opal was being bullied because of the videos, if she was just as sick of being a social media star as I was, then maybe I wouldn't feel so bad about tearing everything apart.

"Not exactly," she said thoughtfully. "I guess I just wish everyone at school didn't have the internet."

I didn't let the disappointment show on my face. I couldn't pursue the topic, anyway—because just then, Mum called up the stairs.

"Girls! Can you hurry up, please? While we've still got some sunset?"

Opal grinned at me as I rolled my eyes.

"Come on, then," I said to her, and she hopped up off the bed. "Let's go and get Alyssa. It's showtime."

Chapter Twenty

ALYSSA

Heaven. I was in heaven.

It was the end of my first evening with the Shaws, and I was tucked up beneath the lavender-scented duvet in the guest room, clean from a dip in the whirlpool tub that lived in the family bathroom. Crystal had offered up her ensuite, but in doing so she'd apologized for the lack of a whirlpool bathtub—like it was a huge shortcoming, something I'd actually complain about.

It had been an absolutely perfect evening. After I got changed, brushed my hair, and added some tactical concealer and mascara to make myself look (and feel) more awake, Crystal knocked on my door and I followed her and Opal downstairs.

Marjorie was waiting for us and took both my hands in hers, a gesture that both surprised and warmed me. "I'm sure Crystal has told you about our little channel," she said with a chuckle, as if she was making fun of both herself and the concept of having a channel. "We make a lot of content at this time of year, and we were planning to film Crystal's homecoming, as well as opening presents and Christmas lunch—the most special moments. I completely understand if you're not comfortable with it, but would you like to—"

I spoke before she'd even finished. "I'd love to."

Marjorie looked pleased. She squeezed my hands briefly, then let go. "Wonderful," she said. "Our darling daughter, bringing her best friend home from university for Christmas. What a wonderful thing."

I smiled at Crystal, who was standing by the door with her

siblings, but she wasn't looking at me. She was looking at Opal thoughtfully, and I wondered what was going through her head.

Marjorie herded us all outside, where she instructed us to walk up the icy driveway together with the rosy sky glowing in the background. The four of us walked in a loose line, Crystal and Opal laughing about something and Oliver capering ahead in excitement, and it was odd how natural it felt, how easily I fit in with them.

Once we'd done the walk twice, each time returning to the same spot beside the car, Marjorie moved to film us from behind. After that, we were allowed back inside the house and into the living room. For the other shots, I'd been trying to coax my expression into a natural half smile, rather than the thrilled grin that was desperate to burst onto my face. This time, though, my reaction was nothing but genuine.

I'd seen inside the architectural marvel of the glass-fronted house before, of course, on the Shaws' channel. But nothing compared to being *in* it, especially at Christmastime.

The living room was a magical grotto, a winter paradise of warm lighting, snowy fur, and sparkles. It was warm, too; there was a real fire crackling away in the fireplace. As we stepped through the white-painted double doors, the luxurious pale gray carpet sank beneath my feet. In front of the enormous window, placed perfectly in the middle, was possibly the biggest Christmas tree I'd ever seen outside of a public display. It was huge, stretching nearly to the ceiling above the mezzanine above us. It gave off the fresh scent of pine, and was decorated exquisitely from top to bottom in white, silver, and blue—every shade of blue, from dark navy to baby blue to a color that looked like the light reflected off the sea.

I'd completely forgotten I was being filmed until I heard Marjorie clapping. "That was wonderful!" she declared. "Oh, Alyssa, your *face*."

"Her eyes absolutely lit up," James said with a chuckle.

"I've never seen a Christmas tree so beautiful," I said, honestly, and Marjorie clasped her hands to her chest.

"Well, aren't you a delight?" she said. "I just know our followers are going to *love* you."

We spent the rest of the night eating dinner—a rich pie with thick gravy and home-grown vegetables from the garden—and then relaxing. Marjorie put a Christmas film on, something from the eighties I remembered my mum liking. It made my heart twinge. What was Mum doing now? Did she miss me? Or was she perfectly happy, drinking a glass of Baileys and ice with her feet tucked up, watching this very same film?

The difference in this household was that I didn't have to stay utterly silent or face Dad's irritated huffing from across the room. No—here, the film was just background noise for what the Shaws called "family time," i.e. chatting and messing around.

I'd never seen Crystal so lively. It was like she'd been plugged into an electric socket, all bright eyes and gesticulating hands and laughter. Every so often, though, when her parents' eyes weren't on her, I saw that light dim, the exhaustion behind it.

It was all an act.

I couldn't imagine having to put on an act here. For the first time in a while, I felt truly myself. Marjorie and I chatted like old friends, her asking about my upbringing, my schooling, my hobbies. Naturally, I didn't disclose my *At Home with the Shaws* hobby, but I told her about the horror books I liked, and my brief stint at *Local Times*. When I explained why I'd left she shook her head in disgust.

"Clearly, they don't know a diamond when they see one," she said.

I snorted. "I reckon I'm more like a lump of coal."

I didn't mean to sound quite so self-pitying—I was intending to be funny—but Marjorie sighed with sympathy. "You're clearly a very intelligent, thoughtful girl, Alyssa," she said. "They obviously can't see talent when it's right in front of them."

I swallowed the lump in my throat. "Thank you," I croaked.

I looked around at the family, happy and comfortable, lounging across the sofa and armchairs. Outside, it was pitch black, a sudden harsh wind coming off the sea to batter at the glass, but inside was warm and beautiful. It was as if we were the central figures of a snow globe, cut off from everything and safe in our own little world. I didn't want it to end.

After a while longer, it was time for the twins to head up to bed. Crystal and I followed, tired from our day of traveling, but not before Marjorie had pulled me in for a tight, baking-scented hug.

And now, as I lay there in the Shaws' guest room, listening to the wind howling around the chimneys, I knew that being Crystal's best friend wasn't enough. I didn't just want her—I wanted her family, too. I wanted this island, this incredible house, to be my home. I wanted Marjorie and James to be my parents. I wanted Oliver and Opal and Crystal to be my siblings. I wanted them to be my family, more than anything else in the world. And I promised myself that, somehow, I would make it happen.

No matter what.

Chapter Twenty-One

CRYSTAL

I slotted back into life at home quicker than I'd expected. It was almost as if the months at university had never taken place—as though that were all some strange, idyllic dream. Alyssa's presence was the only proof that it wasn't.

It was Christmas Eve, and we'd already filmed two different videos—our homecoming the previous evening, and a Christmas Eve box reveal. Christmas Eve boxes hadn't always been a tradition in our family (Lexie and I certainly hadn't had them when we were little) but the Christmas after Oliver and Opal were born various sponsors got in touch offering to send across products to put in their Christmas Eve boxes. And so the habit stuck.

Our boxes were usually full of festive-themed freebies that we were required to smile about and hold up to the camera, our teeth shining in the Christmas tree lights and our eyes wide, ecstatic. It was almost disturbing how good Oliver and Opal were at faking their excitement. No wonder Opal had managed to keep her growing uncertainty about the channel a secret.

I was glad that the day's filming was over for now, aware we still had Christmas Day and New Year's Eve to contend with—plus some bonus "festive island activity" videos that Mum liked to upload in the lull between Christmas and the New Year.

We sat in a loose circle comparing our various #gifted items, while Dad made a start on dinner. Mum had vanished, presumably to upload and edit the footage ready to add to the schedule.

"So apparently *this* is organic," Opal said, holding up a pot of bright purple slime. "But it's in a plastic tub and it has glitter in it. Not even eco-friendly glitter. Actual glitter."

Oliver and Opal had done well, their gifts a selection of bits and pieces up-and-coming companies wanted to promote—and they'd just *love* to get the Shaw family's endorsement.

There were some lipglosses with tiny flowers inside, a circular blanket patterned like a tortilla, some hair chalk (I could see both of them using that), a night light (less likely), a water bottle bedazzling kit, and two pairs of wireless earphones that claimed to rival the market's current bestsellers.

I had received a set of bath bombs and some luxury skincare minis, which I was pretty pleased with. I made a mental note to record a video using a bath bomb for my own channel while I was still at home—Mum would demand it at some point, and my en-suite here had a better view than the one at Statue House. Within forty-eight hours, my brain had slid back into its old thoughts and rhythms. I was almost *excited* to film content.

Alyssa had received a Christmas Eve box, too. I pictured Mum sorting through the gifts she'd been sent for us, selecting enough items to make up an extra box, and I felt a wave of love toward her. Alyssa had bath bombs and luxury skincare minis like I did, although fewer of each, and some of the lipglosses and one of the water bottle kits the twins had received. And she'd been absolutely thrilled with it, too, the perfect amount of enthusiasm for Mum to film.

The four of us took our gifts up to our respective rooms—Oliver and Opal still clad in the matching Christmas pajamas they'd worn for the video, me and Alyssa in our own festive sets—and then gathered back in the living room to enjoy our usual Christmas Eve dinner.

It was a feast of what my dad liked to call "picky bits"—swirls of smoked salmon with a dill and mustard dip, crunchy breadsticks with different types of hummus, a baked camembert, caramelized mushroom tarts with buttery pastry, miniature sausage rolls with cranberry sauce, and chocolate brownies dusted with icing sugar snow for dessert.

Once we'd all finished and loaded the dishwasher, we gathered in the living room for the Shaw family's annual Christmas film tradition.

My favorite Christmas film was *The Holiday*, but every Christmas Eve we had a decidedly un-Christmassy *Shrek* marathon.

Mum dimmed the lights, Dad got a fire going in the fireplace, and we all curled up together side by side on the big corner sofa, Alyssa's leg pressed against mine. I liked having her here. I wished she'd come with me every time I came home.

On my other side, Opal rested her head on my shoulder. As the shenanigans started onscreen, I could feel her shaking with laughter beside me. And then I was laughing, too. Happy in the light of the fire and the Christmas tree, surrounded by my family and Alyssa, I wondered why I'd been so desperate to escape from the island in the first place.

Christmas Day was always a big production in the Shaw household.

Mum and Dad always put a lot of effort into cooking an incredible meal, something that I'd always felt lucky for—if not sometimes just a *little* bit put out that it seemed less for us and more for creating envy on the channel.

Our routine was to make a start on cooking Christmas dinner, get dressed, open our gifts, and then sit down together for our celebratory meal, full of gratitude for time with family. But first, something else had to happen. Something I always dreaded.

Oliver, Opal, Alyssa, and I sat on the floor around the Christmas tree, which was absolutely piled with immaculately wrapped presents. There were silver parcels with pale pink satin ribbon for me and Alyssa, brown paper with gold spots and a shiny gold ribbon for Oliver, and deep blue with a bottle-green ribbon for Opal. And, between my presents and Opal's, there was a gap.

Mum set up the tripod, as she did every year, so that it focused on us, the perfect family gathered in the living room. She secured her phone and hit record, before going to sit on the sofa.

Dad came in from the kitchen, still clad in his apron (it said *I'm Not Old, I'm Well-Seasoned* in big white letters, a recent birthday gift from the twins) and sat beside Mum. They held hands tightly.

"Twelve years ago," Mum began, her voice trembling only slightly. "We celebrated our last Christmas with your sister Lexie."

The sentence was the same as always, the only difference the number of years Lexie had been gone. And, as always, Mum's words brought back visions of that final Christmas. It snowed that year. Lexie and I had shared a friendship bracelet kit. She'd opened a soft toy rabbit that I'd envied—gray fur, with pink velvet on its paws and inside its long, floppy ears. It sat in my childhood bedroom now. Silly to think I'd ever wanted it. After she died, I would've given anything to hand it back to her.

"As you all know," Mum said, "it's important that, as a family, we never forget Lexie. That's why we always leave a space under our tree—a space where Lexie's presents would have gone."

Overcome with emotion, she pressed a hand to her face.

Dad continued for her. "So let's just take a moment to sit quietly, before we open our presents, to think about Lexie and appreciate how lucky we are to be here, all together."

Oliver's gaze was fixed on the carpet, his mouth downturned, picking at a hangnail. Beside me, I felt Opal reach for my hand. Her palm was clammy when I squeezed it. Alyssa looked down, her expression somber. I realized it was maybe odd to include Alyssa in this, Alyssa who'd never known Lexie and who only wanted to enjoy her Christmas with us.

I wanted to say something to her, but before I'd plucked up the courage to interrupt the solemn silence it was over.

Mum took a deep breath. "Okay," she said. She was smiling now. "We've had so many beautiful memories as a family, haven't we? It hurts sometimes to think that Lexie isn't included in the ones we're making now. But we are making memories, aren't we, the five of us? Six of us, including you, Alyssa! Happy memories. I love you all. Merry Christmas, my babies."

"Merry Christmas, Mum," we all replied in sync. "Merry Christmas, Dad. We love you."

"Merry Christmas," Alyssa echoed.

One by one, we opened our presents. I didn't expect a gift from the twins, but they usually got me one anyway—generally something homemade, or a trinket from the shop in the village. Once, it had been a pack of novelty bubblegum with a cartoon island sheep on it. That kind of thing.

This year, I'd received a hand-painted mug (*To the best sister ever at Christmas*) and some ginger snaps baked by Mrs. Dunstone down the lane, carefully wrapped in tissue paper. Oliver explained proudly how they'd saved up their pocket money to pay Mrs. Dunstone for them, since she usually sold them to the bakery or popped them into the little tourist honesty boxes dotted around the island.

My gifts from Mum and Dad weren't too dissimilar from the sponsored ones. I had some skincare products, including a moisturizer I'd been coveting; some fancy chocolates; and a new scarf and hat, the scarf a wonderful checked pattern with big squares in white, gray, and deep blue, with a blue hat to match.

The twins had bought a pack of biscuits for Alyssa, too, and Mum presented her with some chocolates and a tub of the same moisturizer I loved. I was surprised to see Alyssa flush, and then her eyes fill with tears even though she was smiling.

"Thank you," she whispered. "Thank you so much. You didn't have to get me anything."

"It's not Christmas without presents," Mum said simply, something that I knew she didn't necessarily believe but apparently thought would be comforting for Alyssa. Once again, I warmed toward her.

Once all our presents were opened and the wrapping paper had been put aside for recycling, we thanked each other again. Mum got to her feet to stop the recording, seemingly satisfied that our Christmas morning video was complete. Now that we were free, the twins and Alyssa and I disappeared to our separate rooms to get ready while Mum and Dad took turns keeping an eye on the food. Mum always insisted we dress in what she called our Sunday best for Christmas Day, and although part of me wanted to rebel and shove on a pair of jeans, another part of me was genuinely excited at the thought of dressing up a bit with my siblings.

I was the first ready, wearing a favorite black dress patterned with gold stars, so I headed back downstairs—only to freeze halfway down at the sound of my parents whispering harshly at each other. It was like they were having an argument, but one that they didn't want any of us to hear. If I'd been less cynical, I might've thought it was because it was Christmas Day and they didn't want to ruin the festivities. I crept closer.

Dad sounded both furious and exhausted. ". . . The credit cards are still maxed out; we're two months behind on the mortgage—"

"You think I don't *know* that, James?"

"I think you're burying your head in the sand, Marjorie. That's what. It's not working. The traffic on the vlog, the engagement on socials—it's still going down, not up. Maybe it's time to end all this."

I held my breath. Could he actually be suggesting ending *At Home with the Shaws*? Is that what they were talking about?

A hiss from Mum. "Don't you *dare*. After everything we've done? After everything *you've* done? It was your idea, remember. Besides, we've worked too bloody hard to—"

I didn't hear the rest of the sentence because Oliver—dressed in a crimson shirt and dark jeans—came pelting down the stairs and very nearly ran into me.

"Watch it!" I said.

He pulled a face. "Maybe don't lurk on the stairs like a weirdo and I wouldn't run into you."

I put a finger to my lips and, as annoying a little brother as he could be, he understood immediately that I'd been lurking for a reason. He nodded once, solemnly, then continued into the kitchen where Mum and Dad immediately started acting normally again.

I tiptoed back upstairs, keen to try to absorb what I'd heard before I put on a brave face and joined in the Christmas celebrations. My parents' credit cards were maxed out, and they were two months behind on the mortgage. Was that why Mum was being so controlling and fussy about my content—because *At Home with the Shaws* was failing?

Maybe it would collapse all on its own, and I wouldn't have to do anything.

On one hand, that could be a good thing. It would bring an end to the relentless pressure I'd been under my whole life, give the twins a life outside of social media. But then . . . what if my parents went bankrupt? They could lose the house, and what would Oliver and Opal do then? Where would they live?

For the first time, it occurred to me that what I wanted to do—to expose Mum's shady behavior—might have the same effect. A negative one, rather than the positive one that I wanted.

But if it brought peace in the long run, it was a good thing. Wasn't it?

Pushing those thoughts aside, I re-enacted my first walk down to the living room. Oliver winked at me, but Opal was none the wiser. She was wearing a lovely black velvet dress with sparkly tights and a hair ribbon, and the sight of the ribbon made my chest ache. Lexie used to love those.

Alyssa joined us a few minutes later wearing tight black jeans with a glittery silver top, and it took me a moment to realize that it was the same top I'd worn to the club the other night. Not the *exact* same one, obviously—that one was still in my laundry basket. But Alyssa must have tracked it down and bought her own one. I was impressed at her tenacity; she could've just asked me where it was from.

Mum stuck her head through from the kitchen to take a look at the four of us and nodded approvingly. Despite the apron she'd put on for cooking, she looked elegant in a tight red dress with dangly gold earrings—and a dash of scarlet on her lips. Dad wore a shirt that matched Oliver's. There was no trace of the animosity I'd overheard in the kitchen. Christmas Day was, once again, picture perfect. And, apparently, the world had to know it.

Before Christmas dinner was served, my parents removed their aprons and Mum returned her phone to the tripod in the living room. Together, we gathered in front of the tree, its lights glowing despite the bright day outside, and posed for the camera. After we'd taken a few timed family pictures, Alyssa standing close beside me, I went into the kitchen to help Dad serve the food while Mum added her pre-written caption and posted the festive picture on all the family accounts. The thought of my other new university friends—Jasper, Zoe, Rowan, and the others—seeing me posing in that way, like one of those dated, awkward family pictures that people like to parody, made me cringe, but I focused instead on the meal. It smelled fantastic; my mouth was practically watering at the combined aromas of roasted turkey, honey-glazed root vegetables, roast potatoes sprinkled with rosemary, herby stuffing, and the steam wafting from the huge jug of rich gravy.

The twins set the table with plates, side plates, cutlery, and napkins, and Dad and I carefully carried the steaming assorted stainless steel tureens and Le Creuset dishes through.

Once the rest of us were seated, Mum insisted on taking picture after picture of our feast from every angle. I could feel the twins getting impatient, Oliver's legs kicking under the table, but they forced smiles that gradually became grimaces.

Finally, Mum was done. "Okay," she said. "Let's dig in!"

Nothing could've stopped me. I didn't pile my plate high, but continued adding little tidbits here and there as I devoured the rest: an extra roast potato, another helping of turkey, some more honey-glazed carrots and parsnips. Alyssa, too, was demolishing her plateful.

We ate quietly for a while, the only sounds the scraping of our cutlery and faint Christmas music from the kitchen radio, until Mum spoke.

"Are you okay, Opal?" she asked, her forehead creased with concern.

I glanced across at my sister, who was looking unusually pale.

"I'm okay," she said. "I just feel a bit sick."

"Do you need to go and have a lie down?"

"That would be nice," she said. "If that's okay?"

"Of course it's okay," Mum said. "We'll pop your plate in the oven in case you want it later."

"Don't lie down too long," Oliver said. "I might eat it."

"No, you will *not*," Dad said, and Oliver grinned.

"Nah," he said. "There's plenty of leftovers."

Opal rolled her eyes, and got up. "I'll be back in a bit," she said. "Love you all."

The door closed behind her, and she was gone.

Chapter Twenty-Two

ALYSSA

I'd never had a Christmas that was so family-orientated, so peaceful.

As per the Shaw family's lifestyle, everything was warm, comfortable, pleasant—and, most important, aesthetically pleasing.

Even so, on Christmas night, Crystal convinced me to try to call my parents. She'd crept into my room when the twins were in bed and perched on the end of mine in her festive pajamas, looking like a little blond elf.

"Just to say hi," she wheedled. "To let them know you're safe."

"They know I'm safe," I'd said.

Crystal was beginning to understand me, though, because her next suggestion was: "Maybe you could rub their faces in it a bit. Tell them it's the best Christmas ever."

And *that* did appeal.

Once she'd left to give me privacy, closing the door gently behind her, I waited a moment and then slid from my bed. I knelt beside my suitcase and lifted the clothes I'd carefully folded, revealing the treasures hidden beneath. A red lipstick. A silver cufflink. A flower-shaped earring. A keyring. A translucent glass paperweight with a pink swirl inside. One item from each of the Shaws. With these little mementos, I could keep each of them close. I picked up the lipstick and removed the cap, then twisted the bottom until bright crimson peeked over the metal edge. Slowly, reverently, I applied the color to my dry lips and then put it away, tucking it back into its hiding place.

And then, in case Crystal happened to be listening, I picked up my phone and finally video-called Mum. I knew Dad wouldn't answer because a) it was me calling, and b) it was the end of Christmas Day, which meant he was probably asleep in his armchair after drinking too much wine.

The camera stayed black, the ringing sound repeating over and over—until something blurry appeared on my screen, and along with it the sound of Mum's voice.

"Alyssa?"

"Hi, Mum," I said. "Happy Christmas."

The camera moved into focus, and I saw my mum. She was sitting on the sofa from the look of things, the wallpaper behind her the flocked pattern of the living room. Her face was lit dimly by the Christmas tree lights, and I could see the flicker of the television in her glasses.

It took her a moment to speak, and when she did she sounded tired. "Happy Christmas."

"Have you had a nice day?" I asked.

Mum sniffed. "The meal was terrible."

My parents never cooked Christmas lunch; they always ate out, and every year the meal was subpar. According to my parents, anyway—I'd always enjoyed it. The food, that is, not the predictably tense atmosphere at our table.

"Oh," I said. "Why?"

Without any preamble, she launched into it. First her roast beef was "raw," and then it was "as tough as a strip of leather." The vegetables were overcooked and mushy, the mashed potato lumpy.

"And your father," she said, "drank two bottles of wine. He nearly got us thrown out; he was so disruptive. It was embarrassing."

I realized that she, too, must have had a drink, because she usually wasn't so open about my dad's failings—at least not to me. I'd heard her complaining about him on the phone to her friends many times. On cue, she took a long drink from a glass tumbler, filled with a clear liquid I assumed to be gin, her usual tipple.

"It's your fault, you know," she said unexpectedly, her expression sour as she looked at me on the screen.

"My fault?" I repeated. "But I'm not even there."

"What you did to that girl," Mum said. "It's haunted him."

"Oh, come on," I said. "It was hardly that bad. I set her bed on fire."

"When she was *in it.*"

"She was fine. She didn't even have any burns."

Mum didn't say anything for a while, and when I looked back at the screen she was shaking her head. She looked sadder than I'd ever seen her. "How did my life come to this?" she said, almost to herself. "A monster for a husband, and a monster for a daughter."

"If I'm a monster," I said, "it's only because you made me one."

"We've always done our best. But it was never good enough for you, was it?"

There was another painful silence.

"For the record," I said. "I've had a great Christmas."

Mum's lips twitched into an attempt at a smile. "Good," she said. "I'm going to go now. Goodnight, Alyssa. And by the way, I don't really care for the lipstick."

I didn't have time to respond before she'd disconnected the call.

The house was quiet around me now, the only sound the wind rattling the roof tiles.

I tucked myself under the covers and, on my phone, typed in the familiar handle. The Christmas post was already uploaded, of course. No doubt the videos would come later. I brought the screen closer to my face, zoomed in to make each picture bigger.

There they were, the perfect Shaws: Marjorie and James, proud as punch of their beautiful family. In front of them there were Oliver and Opal, both cute as buttons, and then myself and Crystal, side by side. It was like a glimpse of a different universe, one where Lexie hadn't passed away and there were two older Shaw siblings, two perfect daughters.

My eyes widened in realization. This was how I would join the family. I could never *be* Lexie, of course, but I could take on her role—another older daughter for the Shaws to dote on, the foil to Crystal. And I wouldn't complain about the attention, like Crystal did. I wouldn't complain about being filmed, having thousands of people adoring my every move. I would embrace it; I would love it.

I would love the Shaws.

And they would love me.

Chapter Twenty-Three

CRYSTAL

If I'd known what was going to happen only a short time later, I would have made sure to commit every moment in the days between Christmas and New Year's Eve to my memory. I would have treasured every second I spent with the twins. Instead, I let it flash by in a blur, focusing on Alyssa and trying to ignore the niggling voice in the back of my mind that insisted what I planned to do to my family was wrong.

Mum always recorded some post-Christmas island activity videos during this slower period, and this year was no different. Both videos did well, totting up thousands of views each within a few hours. The first focused on rockpooling at the beach, all of us wrapped in waterproof layers and investigating what lived in the tidal pools along the shore. The highlight was when Opal found an enormous hermit crab and it emerged partway from its shell, its eyes on their strange little stalks black and beady as it took us all in.

The second video was an hour or so of horse riding at the local pony-trekking center, a #sponsored post paid for by the center itself. That, I genuinely had enjoyed. The four of us did a dozen practice circuits around the manège before we were released out onto the moor, Mum and an instructor riding their own ponies following behind. Oliver and Opal regularly went there for lessons, but I hadn't ridden in years—probably since before we lost Lexie—and I'd forgotten how much I'd once loved it.

"I've never ridden a horse before," Alyssa had told me beforehand, tremulously, but by the time we were out on the moor she was laughing.

It was a foggy day, and the soft leather of the reins was slick between my chilled fingers. I leaned forward, enjoying the quiet blend of island sounds: the crash of distant waves, the creaking of the saddle, the sound of slow hoofbeats as our horses plodded over the short grass and through dry, spiked heather. In eight months or so, I knew, the entire moor would be blooming purple with it, loud with the buzzing of bees and the cries of skylarks and curlews. Maybe I would be back here, riding out again with Oliver and Opal, soaking up the sun, far away from the oppressive heat of the city streets.

It all depended on what I did when I returned to university, whether I continued with my plan. I'd been so solidly set on it when I'd left the island, even to the point of recruiting Alyssa—but now, I was beginning to doubt myself. Was it possible I'd somehow misinterpreted my parents' love and affection? That I'd twisted it in my mind so it was something painful instead of something wonderful? Did they really *mean* to treat me badly? This was their livelihood, after all—even if it was something I'd never asked to be part of. Kids grew up helping on the family farm, didn't they, or in the family store or takeaway. Was this really so different?

My creeping doubt continued until New Year's Eve. Mum, Opal, Alyssa, and I dressed to the nines in our sparkliest clothes, our hair smooth and glossy and our eye makeup glittery. Alyssa borrowed one of my dresses—a black sequinned one that brought out the silver in her eyes—and we shared my shiniest eyeshadow palette, taking it in turns to make each other up. Oliver hovered, watching us, until I put some shimmery eyeshadow on his lids, too: a deep navy blue that matched his button-up shirt perfectly. We recorded our obligatory family #NYE video in front of the Christmas tree, with a fake countdown to all of us shouting, "Happy New Year from the Shaws!"

And then the real New Year's Eve started: my parents' annual party, to which they invited most of the island, plus pretty much anyone from their former city life who could be bothered to get the ferry across for the occasion. The number of attendees from the city was generally quite low, but we'd see familiar faces—some of Dad's old business partners, or vlogging colleagues. FiveKidsAndCounting, aka Eliza, came every year—she'd known Mum and Dad since Lexie and I were little, and she now had a total of seven kids, a hit reality TV series, *and* a spin-off. I knew that that was what Mum wanted for us, and I also suspected that, secretly, Mum was undoubtedly doing her best to sabotage Eliza and her family's success. To their faces, though, she was the perfect host.

Eliza and her husband arrived early, as always, and greeted me with a tight hug.

"Here she is!" she said. "The university student! How are you liking city life, my lovely?"

"It's great," I said, careful not to be *too* enthusiastic since Mum was looking on. "I'm really enjoying it!"

"Good, good. I'm so glad! We'll have a catch-up later on, okay?" she said, and I nodded and smiled and let her move on.

"Wow," she said, gazing around the living room. "I swear, Marjorie, these parties get better every year!"

Mum's cheeks were flushed with pride. We'd spent hours that day cleaning the house from top to bottom while she decked out the living room and kitchen: shiny foil banners, streamers, confetti scattered on every flat surface shaped like the numbers of the upcoming year. Dad had ordered dozens of canapés for our guests to help themselves to, plus cases of wine, Prosecco, and crates of beer, and they were all set out on the kitchen island.

At seven o'clock sharp, we switched on a throwback hits playlist, turned the lights off, and threw open the doors to the rest of the guests. Freezing air slipped in with them, the flames in the fireplace flickering, and I shivered.

I was the star of the evening, of course. Everybody loved the Shaws. The clean-cut and doting father, James, beautiful and warm mummy, Marjorie, the cutesy twins dressed in their best festive sparkles. And Alyssa, too, the intelligent, witty city girl come to the island for Christmas, the new best friend. But everybody melted when it came to me, Crystal, the little girl they'd watched grow up, lose her sister, grieve . . . and then thrive. I was a comeback story, and who doesn't love a comeback?

I mingled, my smile so constant and fixed that my cheeks started to ache, laughing at jokes and blushing at compliments, complimenting others in turn ("I love your dress!" "Your eye makeup is amazing!" "Wow! Where did you find those shoes?") and lapping up their adoration. It wasn't so bad, was it, being loved? *Maybe*, I thought, *I could get used to this.* I could put more effort into my online presence, my platform—build my own brand as an off-shoot of the Shaws, do what my parents had wanted me to do all along.

At eleven o'clock, I found Opal sitting on the sofa, her legs tucked up. She looked pale and clammy, her eyes heavy.

"Hey," I said, "what's wrong?"

"I'm just feeling a bit weird again," she said mournfully.

"Why don't you go to bed?" I asked.

"It's still ages till midnight!"

"It's only an hour," I said. "It's basically the new year now."

She pouted. "I want to stay up!"

So, despite the music and the crowd and the general party atmosphere, I didn't dance or socialize with our guests. I stayed where I needed to be, sitting on the sofa with my little sister until the clock struck twelve.

When Opal heard the guests counting down to midnight, shouting and cheering, she realized she'd made it and leaped up. I laughed and jumped up, too, then spun her around, her hot hands clutched in mine and her hair flying out behind her.

I lowered her to the ground and she hugged me tight. I hugged her back.

"Happy New Year," I said to her.

And for the first time in what felt like a long time, I was actually happy.

The next day, the house was quiet. We didn't have any filming planned, so I took the opportunity to stay in my pajamas for as long as possible. I lounged in bed for most of the morning, and emerged from my room just before noon.

The rest of the family was downstairs. Dad and Oliver were playing *Mario Kart* on the games console, Mum was scrolling on her phone, and Alyssa was reading. It struck me how easily she fit in with us, like the last piece of a jigsaw puzzle. Maybe she fit in here better than I did.

I said good morning to everyone, then went into the kitchen to make myself a cup of coffee and a bowl of cereal. I took them back to the living room and squeezed onto the sofa beside Opal, who was watching TV. She nudged me with her knee in a complaining sort of way but eventually shifted over a bit to make room. "Are you feeling better after last night?" I asked her.

"Yeah," she said. "I think I was just tired. I don't think I've stayed up that late since that Marbella trip when we had the early flight."

I remembered it well: fighting to keep my eyes awake, the grittiness in them, the spiderweb of lights thousands of feet below.

"We're all just resting today," Mum said, with a reassuring hand on Opal's knee. "I'm sure you'll feel better once you've had something to eat and a nap this afternoon."

She nodded, and rested her head on Mum's shoulder.

"I might go back up and have a bath, actually," I said, as I munched the last of my cereal. "If that's okay, Mum?"

I only had one more day to enjoy the luxury of a bathtub with a sea view. Soon, I'd be heading back to Statue House.

"Go for it, lovely."

I took my bowl back through to the kitchen and rinsed it, then left it on the rack to dry.

"I was thinking about creating some content," I said, as I went back into the living room. "You know, with the bath bombs from the Christmas Eve box?"

"Oh!" Mum looked both surprised and genuinely thrilled. "That would be fantastic! For your channel, or for ours?"

"Both, I guess," I said. "I'll post it, and tag you as a collaborator? Then you can share it, too."

I caught Alyssa watching me with interest, probably wondering why I was suddenly so enthusiastic about social media, and I tried not to meet her gaze.

"Perfect!" Mum said. "Thanks so much, Crystal. And don't forget to tag the brand."

I rolled my eyes as I reached the living room door. "*Obviously*," I said, but I was grinning. "What am I, a beginner? I won't be too long."

As I stepped through the door, I heard Dad speak in a low voice. "I told you she'd get back on board," he said. "She's a good girl."

Usually, that sort of comment would rankle me, taste sour in my mouth, but it didn't. For the first time in a long time, I was flattered at being the good girl, the good daughter. It was a role that was easy for me to slip into, the mold long-formed.

Upstairs, I set the taps in the family bathroom running, then went to find the bath bomb set. I thought I'd put the box in my bedroom along with my other presents, but after opening and closing several drawers I still hadn't found them. Mum must've moved them. They were probably in my parents' bathroom or something.

I went through their bedroom to the ensuite, marveling as I always did at the floor-to-ceiling window, the upper half of the one in the living room. Outside, just a couple of fields away, I could see the gray sky and below it the sea: churning waves topped with foam, tossing themselves onto the shore. At the press of a button, the glass turned frosted for privacy, but whenever I'd bathed in my parents' bathroom as a kid I liked to turn all the lights off so nobody could see me and then defrost the window so I could stare out at the sea and the stars from the tub.

Now, as I gazed at the layers of gray upon gray—slate, charcoal, gunmetal, ash—for a moment I wondered how I could ever have felt trapped looking out at that water. The city, the university's campus, my whole life there felt a million miles away, as unreachable as if it were the dusty, cratered surface of the moon.

I opened the cupboards under the sink first, finding plenty of beauty products (moisturizers, serums, body scrubs), but no bath bomb sets. Next, I tried the woven baskets on the wooden step shelves beside the bathtub, which did have some bath bombs—but not *my* bath bombs. And, finally, I opened the mirrored cabinet above the sink.

Inside, there were the usual items—wrapped packets of soap, spare tubes of toothpaste, Mum's daily moisturizer, a box of tampons—as well as several bottles and packets of pills. I pulled some out, caught a glimpse of Lexie's name on a few of them, and sighed sadly. My parents must have kept them, all these years later. There were vitamins, too, and some painkillers for Dad's budding arthritis, but no bath bombs.

As I started putting the bottles back, defeated, a sticky note slipped out from underneath a box and fluttered to the floor. I picked it up, glanced at it, and then, unable to make sense of it, read it again.

It was a handwritten list of medications, words I couldn't even dream of pronouncing, and beside them in brackets were what looked to be side effects. *Causes nausea and vomiting*, read one. *Brings on fever*, said another.

It was probably something left over from when Lexie was around, I thought, something that Mum or Dad couldn't bear to throw away. She'd been on loads of medications, and some of them were really dangerous if you took too much or mixed them together. Before she'd died, my parents had had instructions all over the house, written on scraps of paper, warning them to give one tablet with milk, one spoonful of this medicine with a main meal, to not take these two at the same time—all sorts of things.

This note wasn't dissimilar. What seemed strange to me, though, was that whoever had penned the note—and it looked like my mum's handwriting—hadn't written down what the medicine was for, only what side effects it could have. Why would that be written down? There were some dosages, too—one beside what I recognized as an iron supplement that said *50mg per kg+, potentially deadly*.

I wasn't a medical professional, but I had been a bit anemic from heavy periods before and been prescribed some iron supplements, so I knew that wasn't a safe dose. It was nowhere *near* a safe dose. It even said, right beside it, *potentially deadly*. So why had Mum made a note of it? And more to the point, why had all this been hidden away? I wasn't sure but, for some reason, this note felt important. It also felt important that nobody knew I had it.

I glanced around furtively, listening to confirm that everybody—including Alyssa—was still downstairs, and then tucked the note into the waistband of my pajama bottoms. I neatened up the bottles and boxes of medication so they looked just as they had before, and went back to my bedroom. I slipped the sticky note between two pages of one of my novels, and then tucked it under some clothes in my sloppily half-unpacked suitcase, out of sight. It was there, in my suitcase, that I found the bath bombs I'd been looking for.

I chose a sparkly white one from the box that claimed to smell of freshly fallen snow, and took it back through to the bathroom where the tub was just under half full of hot water. I pushed the odd feeling and the note to the back of my mind, and picked up my phone, ready to film the bath bomb disintegrating into a million glittering, foaming pieces.

I didn't let myself think about the note again until I was back in the city.

The reverse journey of my homecoming was unexpectedly painful: the drive to the tiny airport, loading my bags onto the little propeller plane with Alyssa and the other passengers, hugging my family goodbye.

It was nothing like my first journey to the city, when I'd been so thrilled to leave the island for a new life. Instead, this leaving smarted, and I felt an ache that pushed tears from my eyes as Oliver and Opal wrapped their arms around me and Dad squeezed my shoulder. Both my parents hugged Alyssa, and told her that she was welcome back anytime.

"Thank you, Mrs. Shaw," Alyssa said shyly, and Mum laughed.

"Call me Marjorie, love," she said. "And look, girls—it'll be the end of term in no time," Mum said. "You'll be back here before you know it."

"I know," I said. "I already can't wait."

I meant it, too.

Alyssa took the window seat, and I gazed over her shoulder out of the window as the plane taxied along the runway and gathered speed, soaring up into the thick cloud cover. I stared down at the island, at the rocky coastal cliffs and whitewashed farmhouses, at the great swells of the mountains like giants sleeping under the island's surface, until it disappeared behind a bank of gray.

"Don't worry, petal," a woman with a dandelion clock of white hair said to me from across the narrow aisle, her accent local and full of warmth. "The island will be waiting for you when you get back."

I smiled at her. "Thanks. I'm glad."

She shifted in her seat, leaning to hear me over the sound of the propellers. "Where are you off to so soon after Christmas?"

"We're going back to university," I told her. "What about you?"

"The hospital," she said, matter-of-factly. "My husband's dying."

"Oh," I said, feeling my heart drop. "I'm so sorry to hear that."

The woman smiled, the creases around her eyes deepening. "Thank you, love. There's nothing to be sorry about, though. It gets us all eventually."

It was an interesting way of looking at it, I thought—acknowledging the very real fact that death, for all of us, was inevitable.

I wondered if that helped it to hurt any less.

Chapter Twenty-Four

ALYSSA

Being back in the city was like falling to earth with a thump.

Crystal and I shared a taxi, which let her out at Statue House first. We awkwardly hugged goodbye around seatbelts and backpacks, and promised we'd text each other later. The trip had bonded us more than I ever could have dreamed.

"We should talk about the project before lectures start again," she said before she closed the door, and I nodded and smiled.

Our project. Crystal's project. What a cute little way to refer to it, as if it weren't damning the very family we'd just spent a perfect Christmas with. She was right—we did need to talk about it. We had to talk about how to start it, so that I could get ahead of the game and put a firm end to it.

There was nobody else in the flat when the taxi dropped me off, so once I'd dumped my bags in my room I stole one of Niamh's coffee pods and made myself a latte. It would be another black mark against my name, but I couldn't bring myself to care.

I wondered what Crystal wanted to talk about. I was surprised she'd brought it up so quickly. Perhaps she'd enjoyed being home so much that she'd changed her mind. Or maybe she hadn't—maybe she'd seen how much I'd bonded with her family, how I'd fit into the gaping hole there like hot wax filling a mold, and decided she didn't need my help anymore. That was a worry, though, because what if she went to somebody else? Somebody who'd actually help her to carry out her plan?

I showered, changed into comfortable clothes, and treated myself to a nap with an archive episode of *At Home with the Shaws*—

Christmas 2011—playing on my laptop. When I woke, it was dark, and I could hear voices downstairs. Great. My flatmates were back.

I padded down the staircase, but when I entered the living room my flatmates were all waiting for me, grave expressions on their faces. I froze, trying to make sense of it.

"Has someone died?" I asked, only half-jokingly. The mood was that severe.

"Alyssa," Niamh said, leaning forward, her big brown eyes as gentle and earnest as a cow's. "We need to talk."

The four most anxiety-inducing words in the English language. "Right," I said, drawing out the middle sound in a questioning sort of way. *Riiiiight.* "What's going on?"

"We know you've been stealing from us," Toby said. "Food. Drinks. Niamh's coffee pods."

Niamh cast him a look, as if he'd stolen her moment.

I frowned. "*You* steal coffee pods from Niamh, too," I pointed out. "You take all the mocha ones."

"And you take all the vanilla," Niamh said, before Toby could respond. "It's not just that, Alyssa. You use up all the milk and you don't replace it. You take people's leftovers, birthday chocolates, things we were saving for later. And then there's the stuff from our rooms."

Alex, who generally tried to stay out of flat debates and had clearly been drafted in for manpower, said, "I don't want to blame you, but I keep losing things in my room, Alyssa. And I'm not a forgetful person."

Things. Insignificant, insubstantial *things*—but things that, for some reason, I just had to have. A creamy white cockleshell plucked from a jam jar filled with them. A single piece of blue confetti, shaped like the number 18. A pin badge that said, *Do No Harm, But Take No Shit.*

"I can't help it if you misplace things in your own room," I said.

"See, I think you can," Niamh said. "I think you go into our rooms when we're not here, and you take whatever you like." She folded her arms. "Does a pressed flower ring a bell?"

It did. It was a daffodil, slipped out from between the covers of a classic novel. I'd carefully hidden it inside a novel of my own. I hadn't thought Niamh would notice it was missing.

"Let me get this straight," I said. "You think I'm breaking into your locked rooms while you're away, and stealing from you? And not anything actually *worth* stealing, either—just random weird shit like a dried daffodil?"

There was a silence. "I never said it was a daffodil," Niamh said coldly.

Toby shook his head, and I hated the look on his face. It was no longer angry; it was pitying. And I hated pity. "You need to leave, Alyssa," he said. "We've all agreed. You have a month to find somewhere else to stay. We've settled it with the landlord."

I stared at him, disbelieving. "You've already settled it with the landlord without settling it with me?"

Toby shrugged. "He wants a quiet life. So do we. And it'll be a lot quieter for all of us with you gone."

My parents didn't want me. Now my flatmates didn't want me. This was becoming an unfortunate pattern.

"Fine," I said, trying to sound unbothered. "This place is a shithole anyway. I wouldn't stay here any longer than that if you paid me."

"Great," Niamh said brightly. "Then there's no hard feelings."

I turned to leave, tears smarting in my eyes. I had one month to find somewhere to live, one month to find a flat, view it, meet the roommates and pack up my sad excuse for a life and relocate it to somewhere new. All without falling behind on my university work right at the start of a new term. Fantastic.

"Oh, and before you go," she added from behind me, "we want our things back."

I slammed the door behind me so hard it rattled the hinges.

Chapter Twenty-Five

CRYSTAL

Compared to my parents' house, my apartment was bare and quiet. Every sound I made seemed to echo, and everything I did—unpacking my suitcase, putting the milk and cheese I'd bought at the shop down the road in the fridge—was as if I were just going through the motions, acting without a script for no reason at all.

When I'd first come here, it had felt like freedom. Now I just felt alone. On the island, you often felt small—but that was because of the enormity of the space, the wide skies, the mountains towering above you, the expanse of the sea. In the city, I felt small because I was anonymous. No one knew that I was here, nor did they care. I was just another person, and nobody minded if I stayed in the city or if I went. My phone buzzed and I picked it up too quickly, embarrassingly grateful, hoping it was Alyssa even though we'd only just said goodbye. But it was my mum.

Can I ring you?

Weird. But it wasn't like I was doing much.

Of course. xx

My phone rang barely ten seconds after I'd replied. I pictured Mum standing at the kitchen counter, waiting for my reply, and sympathy stabbed in my chest.

"Hi, Mum," I said as I picked up. "Everything okay?"

"I wanted to talk to you about something," she said.

Dread started to creep into my bones, chilling me. "Okay."

"It was hard to do at Christmas, with a house full and no alone time . . ." she trailed off.

"Okay," I said, again. "What's going on?"

"Well," Mum started. "You might've noticed that Opal was a little unwell when you were home."

Leaving the dinner table early. Looking pale and drawn. Not feeling herself on New Year's Eve. "I did a bit, yeah."

"When I fell pregnant with the twins," Mum continued, "they warned me that there was a chance that the twins, at a later date, could fall ill."

"Why would they say something like that?" I asked, a half second before understanding clicked into place. *Oh, no.* "Is it because of Lexie?"

"Yes," Mum said, and her voice was thick with tears now. "It's because of what happened to Lexie. They were concerned that her condition, since they couldn't identify it, may be genetic. We're taking Opal to the mainland next week for testing. But her symptoms are the same as Lexie's."

I closed my eyes, pressing the phone hard to my ear. *Not again. Please, not again.*

"It might not be that," I said. "It might be something else. A bug. She could've caught it at school."

"She might have," Mum agreed. "That's why we're going to the hospital. To find out."

I swallowed. It wasn't the end of the world. Not yet. "Does she know?" I asked.

"She knows she's going to the hospital for some more tests," Mum said. "She's been to the GP; she knows she's a bit unwell."

"But does she know what you think it could be?"

There was a long pause before Mum spoke. "No."

"*Mum!*" I was aghast. "You have to tell her!"

"She's eleven years old, Crystal," Mum said. "I'm not going to tell her until there's something to tell. There's no point in frightening her."

I pictured Opal—sweet, sensitive Opal—being faced with the news that she might have the same mysterious condition that killed the big sister she'd never known.

"No, you're right. When's the appointment?"

"Monday," Mum said. "I'll let you know how it goes, okay?"

"Okay," I said. "Thank you. And give her a big cuddle from me."

"I will," Mum said. "I'm sorry I had to tell you this way. I just didn't know how to do it with your friend here."

"That's okay."

"I love you."

I sighed. "I love you, too."

"Bye, my darling."

A click, and then silence.

What had happened to Lexie couldn't happen again. It just couldn't. It was so *unfair*. I knew that genetics were complicated, that some things could affect one person and none of their relatives, or a load of relatives could fall ill and one person would be okay. But it would just be cruel for us to lose Lexie, and then Opal, too.

I hoped I was right, that it was something with a simple explanation—something the doctors *could* explain and find a treatment for. Unlike poor Lexie, who tried what felt like a million medications with minimal improvement. No matter how a medicine started to work, it always failed in the end—a sort of torturous trial and error, each update recounted on the vlog with such high hopes and then crushing devastation that I still couldn't bear to watch those videos back.

I wondered if Mum would vlog about Opal now, whether her illness turned out to be something serious or not. Was it callous to wonder that? It had been a big release for her when Lexie was sick, when Mum's cathartic videos had changed our lives.

It was then that I realized something—the kind of something that feels like you've been punched in the sternum, all your breath forced out of your lungs.

Those conversations that I'd overheard, panicked whispers about the late payments, about the overdue bills. Mum and Dad's relief when I was enthusiastic about making content again, Mum asking if I would be contributing to both channels, not just to my own. What if this was all a lie, just a way to make money? What if my parents were only *pretending* Opal was ill so they could take advantage of it to draw in sympathetic subscribers?

What was I *thinking*? I wanted to hit myself. What kind of person thought these things about her own family?

Opal was ill. Of course she was ill—I'd seen her at Christmas, the sallow sheen of her skin, the tiredness in her smile. There was no doubting that she was really ill, just like Lexie had been.

So why did something feel so off?

And then something caught my eye: the yellow corner of the sticky note, the one I'd found in the bathroom cabinet and tucked into a book, out of sight. Now, the tiny triangle beckoned me, and I took the book from the shelf. I flicked it open to the sticky note, and read my mum's handwriting once again.

The only medication I'd recognized was the iron supplement, because it was the same one I'd been prescribed. The one with the warning: *potentially deadly.*

I typed the name of it into my phone, scanning the results to confirm what I already knew. It was a type of iron, a pill you could take if your body didn't have enough. I continued to skim read. And then I reached a paragraph that chilled me.

> *An iron overdose is a medical emergency. Symptoms include abdominal pain, diarrhea, nausea, vomiting, or vomiting blood. Symptoms may get better and then return.*
>
> *An extremely high dose of iron can result in convulsions, coma, organ damage or failure, or death.*

This last part, I knew from Mum's note—that a high dose could be dangerous, even deadly. But why had she written that down? And besides, what was an appropriate dosage for an eleven-year-old anyway?

I went back to the search engine to find out. The results varied, but one thing stayed the same: the numbers were completely different from what Mum had written down. There were lots of different tablets, but no matter the dosage the actual elemental iron content of each was a tiny percentage—far, far smaller than the number on the sticky note. And Opal was eleven; she wasn't even old enough to take these tablets yet.

Slowly, horribly, it dawned on me. My earlier suspicion had been right; this wasn't a treatment.

This was a way to deliberately make Opal ill.

I ran to the bathroom, throwing my phone down beside me as I leaned over the toilet bowl and heaved. Through streaming eyes, I could see it was still open on the page I'd been reading. The black-and-white text on the screen was undeniable, the list of symptoms and effects of the poisoning stark. And that was only *one* of the medicines. There were so many of them listed, each one with its side effects right there on the paper. Fever, nausea, vomiting . . . all things that would make someone appear to be unwell.

I slumped back against the bathroom door; my parents' earlier conversation about money ran through my head on repeat. They'd said engagement on their socials was down, and I could understand why—there were more creators now, more platforms, and with the twins' babyhood in the past and me away at university, it was becoming harder for them to keep hold of their audience. There were hundreds of other family vloggers, if not more, that focused on clean living and vegetable gardens. But if they had a sick daughter . . .

If Opal was ill, my mum could vlog every second of it. Every hospital appointment and medicine trial, every care package from sponsors and kind offers of free family holidays to spend some quality time together and recharge. The videos would show our every emotion, the tears, the bravery, the hope.

Views would go through the roof.

They always did, during family tragedies. Other channels would make somber videos sending thoughts and prayers; magazines would run glossy photos of lovely Opal looking pale and delicate by the shore; my family's devoted fans would track every update; and even casual viewers would get sucked into our story.

That's what had happened before, with Lexie.

And if my parents created a fake illness for Opal to mimic what had happened to Lexie, it was likely it would all happen again—the views, the sponsorships, the money. Although if they were poisoning Opal with different medications, I realized, it could hardly be called a fake illness. She'd really be sick, and getting sicker. Just like Lexie.

And suddenly, I had a thought so dark, so awful, that I shook my head to clear it. My stomach lurched, unwilling to even let the idea materialize. But I read the note again. There it was, in stark lettering: the word *deadly*.

I didn't want to consider it. I couldn't. But I had to.

Had my parents killed my sister?

Chapter Twenty-Six

ALYSSA

I was lying on my bed, lazily flicking through a horror novel I couldn't quite be bothered to read, when my phone buzzed.

URGENT. SOS. I know we've literally just got back, but please can we meet up?

Crystal. I frowned. She was right—we literally *had* just got back. Something was obviously wrong.

Rose & Crown, one hour?

Crystal's reply came instantly.

Perfect. Thank you so much.

I was ten minutes early, but Crystal was already there when I arrived, sitting at a corner booth with a steaming mug. I waved to her then went to the counter to order a caramel latte. Once I joined her, I realized how awful she looked. She was pale, and her fingers trembled when she picked up her mug.

"No offense," I said, "but you fully look like you've seen a ghost."

Unexpectedly, Crystal burst into tears.

"Oh, no," I said softly. "Crystal, are you okay?"

"I don't know," she said, swiping at her tears.

"We've only just got back," I said. "What could possibly have happened?"

There was a long pause before Crystal started speaking. "When Lexie fell ill," she began, "my parents, my mum mostly, focused on her journey on the vlog. It got them a lot of attention. And I mean, a *lot*. It's what launched the vlog, really, made it into what it is today." She hesitated. "Do you remember on Christmas Day and New Year's Eve, when Opal wasn't well?"

I remembered. Opal, pale and subdued.

"Well, Mum just rang me—like, before I texted you. Mum thinks Opal has whatever Lexie had, and they're going to do some tests to try and find out."

"Oh my god," I said. "I'm so sorry."

I put my hand out to rest on Crystal's, but she wasn't finished.

"The thing is, the doctors never really figured out what was wrong with Lexie. She always seemed to initially respond to treatment, but then she'd get ill the second we were home again. Her symptoms would change. The doctors were completely flummoxed. And over Christmas, I found this."

Crystal reached into her bag, and laid a butter-yellow sticky note on the table between us.

"What are we looking at?" I asked her slowly.

"It's a list of medications," Crystal explained. "And some of their side effects. I don't know all of them, but I do know this one," she said, pointing. My gaze roved over the text, spiky with consonants. "It's an iron supplement. It has a dosage, too. And right beside it, it says it's a potentially deadly one."

"Right," I said, trying to understand. "But why would your mum have written that down?"

"Exactly," Crystal said. I saw her take a deep breath. "I think they were giving these medications to Lexie. And I think a dose like that is how she died. I think my parents killed her."

There was an awful silence.

I couldn't believe what I was hearing. "You think . . . your parents . . ." I struggled to get the words out. "You think your parents *murdered* your sister?"

"I know how it sounds," Crystal said quietly. "I never would have said it if I didn't seriously think it might be true. I don't think they *meant* to kill Lexie. I think they'd been making her sick, and then they . . . accidentally upped the dose too far, or something. And now I think they're doing the same thing to Opal, using these same medications. I mean, I always thought the doctors were confused about Lexie because medicine's challenging, you know? They can't know everything. But maybe her symptoms didn't match what they were trained to look for."

"Why would they do something like that?" I asked, aghast.

"The vlog, I guess," Crystal said. "You have no idea what Lexie's illness did for it back then—the views shot up, the engagement, everything. The money was pouring in. It changed my parents' lives. And while we were at home . . . I heard them talking. I know they're worried about money."

"So you think they're doing the same thing again? For money?"

"I do," Crystal said, and I knew as soon as she said it that she believed it was true. She had a look in her eye, a pained resignation that was also grittily determined. It worried me. What was she going to do?

"It might not be what it looks like," I reasoned. "Maybe it's an alternative treatment or something? Parents get desperate when their kid's dying. And if they did it to Lexie, if they're doing it to Opal, why didn't they do it to you?"

She stared at me. "You don't believe me."

"It's not that," I backtracked. "I believe you. I'm just trying to think about this from all angles. That's all."

"I don't know why they didn't do it to me," Crystal said. "Maybe they thought it'd look suspicious if both of their kids had this mystery illness? And now I'm out of the picture, living in London, they've chosen Opal."

I gestured to the sticky note. "Will you go to the police about all of this?"

Crystal sighed, and slumped back in her seat. "My parents are basically celebrities," she said. "And they've got friends everywhere, high-up connections from their lives back in the city—from lawyers to PR specialists. I'm scared that no one would believe me. Or, worse, that they would and they'd keep it quiet anyway." Crystal's voice shook. "I barely have a shred of evidence unless they test Opal's blood, because Lexie was cremated. And surely they'd need to get permission from my parents to do a blood test in the first place, right? So my parents would know what I was accusing them of, and by the time it was tested Opal's blood would surely be clean anyway. It'd end up being my word against my parents'."

My mind was still racing, trying to put together the pieces; the James and Marjorie that I knew, and the picture of them that Crystal was painting. "What if you're wrong?" I asked.

"I'm not," she said. "I know I'm not."

"Okay," I said slowly. "What do we do?"

Crystal sat up straight, her shoulders back. "We go ahead with the plan," she said firmly. "But we tell the world about this, too. It's not just lies anymore. It's not just about trying to get rid of other influencer families. It's murder."

"And what then?"

"Then," she said. "It all comes crashing down."

I left Crystal at the coffee shop with a promise that I would do some research and make a list of publications we could pitch Crystal's story to. It was a promise I already planned to break, which had to be a record.

I didn't know what to think. I knew parents were capable of doing things like what Crystal suspected. I'd seen it on the news before, or in true crime documentaries—parents who were dangerously ill, who craved the attention that having a sick child brought them.

I could see where Crystal was coming from, sort of. It made a horrible kind of sense, that somebody who made money from having a sick kid would want their kid to stay sick, and then later, when they were in financial trouble, make *another* of their children sick in the hope it'd have the same effect.

I just couldn't imagine that James and Marjorie would ever do something like that. At Christmas, they'd invited me in as if I were one of their own. They'd cooked meals for me, involved me in family pictures—they'd even put together a Christmas Eve box for me, and Christmas presents, even though I'd brought nothing, not even a card, for them in return. They were kind, generous, loving parents who clearly adored their children. I was certain they wouldn't want to hurt them.

But I could hardly say that to Crystal. When I'd pressed her for more, questioned her theory and tried to get her to be realistic, she'd shut me down.

And it went without saying that if Crystal published this story—whether it was true or not—that would be the end of it all. The Shaw empire would crumble, their updates would disappear from their feeds, and my surrogate family would only be a series of old videos, getting older as the years passed. I'd be utterly alone.

I might still have Crystal, after the dust settled—if she didn't decide that my job was done and cast me out like everybody else. Like my parents. Like Bradley and Davina. My flatmates.

But even if we did stay friends, would that be enough? No. *Crystal* wasn't enough. I wanted her family. I wanted, more than anything, to be a part of it. I wanted to be another daughter for them to dote on, to love.

I wanted it more than Crystal did.

Until now, her entire plan had been based on no longer wanting to be an influencer, on her parents being cruel and obsessive and forcing her to churn out content. And now this?

Was Crystal telling the truth about her suspicions, or had she sensed my reluctance after such a perfect Christmas? Perhaps she just wanted to twist my arm into helping her. Did she even believe it herself?

And, if it was true, what did that mean for me and my happy ending?

By now, I was back at the flat—and as I walked up the narrow stairs, each one creaking underfoot, I remembered my predicament. Soon, if I didn't find anywhere to live, I'd be homeless. I was sure that, if it came to it, I could sleep on Crystal's sofa. Or Jasper's, maybe. I'd rather that than show up on my parents' doorstep after what happened at Christmas.

I tiptoed past the living room door, but paused when I heard my name.

"What about her?" Niamh was saying.

"We can't leave her homeless." Of course that was Alex, our resident Switzerland.

Then Toby: "She won't *be* homeless. She'll find somewhere."

"Look, Alex, you don't know her as well as you think. She doesn't steal because she's poor. Her parents are loaded. She steals because she's a freak."

Ouch, Niamh. Harsh. And how did she know about my parents' financial situation, anyway? Toby said something that I couldn't quite hear, and I leaned in closer.

". . . do you know?" he was saying.

"I knew some of the girls from her old school," Niamh replied. "Before she moved after the *incident*."

She said "incident" mysteriously, presumably to draw them in. For me, it had the opposite effect; the whorls in the door spun in front of my face. Niamh continued speaking.

"I didn't know it was her when she moved in here, *obviously*. Or I would have told the landlord, you know. But this girl, she's a risk. She's nuts."

"What was 'the incident'?" Toby asked. I could hear the quotation marks around the words, knew he was probably doing bunny ears with his fingers as he spoke.

And even though I knew the answer, I still stayed there, to listen—to find out just what Niamh thought she knew about me.

"She went to this fancy boarding school, right—the same one a couple of girls on the uni hockey team went to. That's how I found out. Anyway, apparently she was best friends with this girl, her roommate, and eventually they drifted apart or had a falling-out or something. Whatever. Alyssa supposedly couldn't handle it, and one morning the girl woke up and Alyssa was trying to set her on fire."

There was a shocked whistle from somebody, probably Toby. It seemed like the sort of thing he'd do.

"How did she try to set her on fire?" Alex asked.

"*I* don't know. I wasn't there, was I? But don't tell me you couldn't see that happening. She's such a weirdo. And she carries that lighter around with her all the time."

"Do you think that's the lighter she used?"

I'd had enough. I chose that moment to push the door open, slowly, casually, and lean against the doorframe. Niamh's expression was stricken.

"For the record," I said. "I didn't try to set *anyone* on fire. I set her bed on fire."

None of them said anything. With the sweetest smile I could muster, I turned and left, heading up the stairs to my room.

What did it matter if I told them the truth? My days here were numbered anyway.

It was hard to describe what fire meant to me. Or what it once meant, anyway. I didn't really do that anymore, find solace in the flames.

If you grew up in a house like the one I did (big and empty) with parents like mine (cold and usually absent), you'd have learned to seek out warmth wherever you could find it, too. Plus, you'd be spending a lot of time alone, bored and desperate for something to break the tedium.

It wasn't exactly surprising that I came across a pack of matches one day when I was seven or eight, and spent an hour or so striking each one. I'd let the tiny flame fizzle down so it just barely grazed my fingertips, a brush of heat, and then dropped them one by one into the kitchen sink.

Over time, I progressed from matches to lighters. First, I bought a cheap red plastic one in the corner shop—they didn't ID me for it, which made me wonder if I looked old for my age or if they simply didn't care. Then, later, I stole my dad's favorite silver lighter after he quit smoking.

And it was this lighter, engraved with my dad's initials, that I used to set fire to Rachel's textbooks, her bedsheets, and, best of all, the picture of her and her new best friend—my replacement—on their summer girls' trip to the coast.

I knew I was going to get caught. I didn't try to hide what I'd done. Besides, it was obvious—I was Rachel's roommate, her recently cast-out friend, and I had already had a bit of a reputation as someone who liked to snuff out the candles they set out for fancy dining hall events with my fingers. I suppose they just didn't expect me to move on to full-blown arson.

Unfortunately, that morning, Rachel hadn't got up early for hockey practice like she usually did. She'd appeared from beneath her sheets when she smelled the smoke, and by then it was too late. She ran from the room in her pajamas, screaming. All I could do was run after her.

In the end, it wasn't just our bedroom that went up in flames (my belongings carefully removed beforehand, of course, and hidden in my locker). Half the building burned down.

Nothing was hurt except for bricks and mortar, feelings, and the school's coffers. The repairs made a significant dent that my dad generously filled, plus extra in return for the school not pressing charges. But he'd never really forgiven me for that. Nor had my mum.

They didn't know what they'd done wrong, to have a daughter like me.

And that knowledge only made me lean closer to the fire, take solace in the destruction it could cause, my life turned to ash and reborn again.

I hadn't set another fire since then. Now, I wanted to. Desperately.

The following day, I put together a list of news contacts. It wasn't extensive, but hopefully it would be enough to placate Crystal—at least for now.

I had:

Bradley and Davina—*Local Times.*

Yeah, right. Like I'd give them anything after what they did to me.

Steve B—*City Gazette.*

One of Bradley's "pals." I knew that Steve was firmly committed to the "if it bleeds, it leads" style of journalism, but only if it brought in enough #ad clicks.

Amelia—*Daily Sun.*

More of a "knew of" than "knew personally." Amelia was their much-lauded Real Life reporter, the one who tracked down the mums who'd shed ten stone with a miracle diet and given their kitchens a DIY makeover that cost just £20 at the same time. But she also covered darker material: stalkers, abusive partners, teenage cults. She'd be a perfect fit for Crystal's story—*if* I ever pitched it to her, which I wouldn't. But my targets had to at least look realistic.

I slid the list, carefully copied down on notebook paper, across to Crystal in our first lecture of the year. She'd been running uncharacteristically late, and had jogged up the rows of tiered seating and slipped in beside me with literal seconds to spare.

Her eyes, which seemed less sparkly than usual, widened slightly as she read it. She met my gaze and, almost imperceptibly, nodded. Then she passed the list back to me with a small, grateful smile.

Maybe it was cruel to go through the motions with Crystal like this, but I didn't care. I wouldn't let her destroy her family's reputation, and my dreams with it, over pettiness and suspicion. I *would* be one of the Shaws. No matter what.

I looked back down at my list, at the names I'd written there. My gaze was drawn to the top one, the first name I'd thought of.

And suddenly, I knew how to quench my thirst for action.

Not long after I'd first started at *Local Times*, once Bradley had got over his kind, welcoming façade and become the bitter, miserable man he'd be for the rest of my time there, I'd done something. Something bad.

I'd hoped it would all play out while I was still there to see it, but unfortunately that hadn't been the case. Now, though, I had my finger on the metaphorical red button, ready to trigger a series of wonderful events.

I was not a drug user. I didn't have anything against party drugs necessarily, but they very much weren't my thing. However, Alex—the Switzerland of the flat—absolutely was. In one of my many casings of his room, I'd come across a biscuit tin under his bed stuffed with a veritable cocktail of narcotics. There were some bits and pieces, little plastic packets of this and that, but the main thing I noticed was a small supply of a white, powdery substance that looked significantly like a certain Class A. Gently, I'd pocketed it, and awaited a good time to use it.

I had expected a bit of backlash, but Alex hadn't said anything. I assumed this was because he was hoping I wouldn't tell the others. Famously straight-edged Niamh was all up in arms about the coffee pod theft—what would she say if she knew someone had drugs in the flat?

Anyway, one shift a couple of months earlier Bradley had been particularly ridiculing about something I'd written. So, when I went in the next week, I took the suspected Class A with me. I'd really thought it through—I'd sprayed it clean and bought some plastic gloves to handle it with, just in case.

Then, later that day when everyone went into a meeting that I apparently wasn't important enough to attend, I'd wandered over to his desk, ducked down, and slipped the bag behind a desk drawer.

For the first few days, I'd hoped they'd bring sniffer dogs in, have a random drug search, something like that. No luck.

My shifts passed, and by the time he'd dismissed me for the nail polish incident I'd pretty much forgotten about that little bag of something-or-other, hidden away in the dark. Until now.

I walked directly from my lecture to *Local Times*, anticipation bubbling beneath my skin as I traversed the city. There were two little cafés within sight of the once-familiar office building where the *Local Times* office was based: one directly underneath, next to the door, and another across the road in front of the bus stop I used to get off at. That one was quiet, just the barista behind the counter, so I chose it as I didn't want to be overheard. Inside, I ordered a coffee, selected a table with a good view of the building, and waited until the barista had gone into the back. Then, I dialed the police non-emergency number.

"Hi," I said in a low, trembling voice when the call handler answered. "I'm really sorry to bother you. I don't know if it's something you'd deal with, but, well . . . a couple of days ago, I heard my boss bragging about doing cocaine while he was at work. And I think he's actually keeping it there, too. I know people can get violent and aggressive when they do drugs, and he's my boss so I'm really scared. Can you help me?"

The call handler was kind and reassuring, and told me they'd send some officers out to have a look.

"Thank you so much," I said, my eyes actually welling up with my false gratitude. And when they asked for my details, I told them my name was Davina.

It took a few hours before anything happened. I'd brought my laptop with me so that I could work from the café, looking for all the world like a diligent student and not what I actually was: an ex-volunteer with a vendetta, waiting for Bradley's life to implode.

When the police car pulled up and two uniformed officers got out, I smiled. I watched as they went inside the building, and then I leaned back in my chair and waited.

It took longer than I expected. After all, I hadn't hidden the drugs *that* well. Bradley would never find them—why would he ever think to look?—but I knew the police would. They'd search everywhere, every potential nook or cranny a drug-using boss might secrete away his stash—like deep inside his desk, behind drawers filled with office stationery and old printed press releases.

Nearly forty-five minutes after the police had arrived, they escorted Bradley out of the building in handcuffs. His face was red with what I was sure had to be a combination of fury and embarrassment, and he stumbled over the pavement as he was frogmarched to the squad car and guided inside.

Behind the glass doors of the building, I could see a crowd gathering to watch as Bradley was taken away. And there, right at the front, just behind the glass, was Davina. Even from a distance, she looked rumpled and vaguely tear-stained. I imagined her wondering how she could possibly explain this to the news editor, that Bradley—their voice against crime—had been arrested for cocaine possession.

As the police car pulled away with Bradley inside, I leaned back in my seat and sipped a fresh, hot coffee. Finally, my *Local Times* saga had come to an appropriate end.

Chapter Twenty-Seven

CRYSTAL

I spent a whole week ignoring my parents' phone calls. Last year, this would have been totally unheard of; just the thought would've made me feel ill, guilt pouring through me whenever I saw the missed call notification.

Now, I didn't care. I couldn't bring myself to.

Once my phone stopped ringing, I'd wait a cursory five minutes and text back with a **Sorry, in a lecture! x** or **Out at the min, can I ring you later? x**

And they couldn't even call me out for lying, because I'd switched off the location tracker they'd installed on my phone. Mum did text me a few times, asking why the little blue dot that represented me wasn't showing up on the map, and I'd pleaded ignorance. Maybe it was just a glitch? Had she tried updating the app on her end? How strange.

At Christmas, I'd felt so close to my family. Now, I was more distant from them than I had ever been before. When it came to my parents, that was a good thing—sometimes I could barely resist ringing them up, screaming at them, demanding answers. Demanding to know what had *really* happened to Lexie.

For Oliver and Opal, though, it made my heart hurt. Neither of them had their own smartphones yet, and they had carefully monitored internet access—which was ironic, considering how much of their lives was plastered online. For that reason, neither of them were able to text me, or message me on social media, so we simply didn't have contact. And that, I felt guilty about.

Because of the way I'd been avoiding speaking to my parents, it was no surprise that when news came about Opal's health, I completely missed it. Mum rang me twice, and then resorted to leaving a voicemail, her voice thick with tears.

"Hi, darling," she said. "Sorry I seem to keep missing you. I know you're very busy this term. I just wanted to let you know about Opal's hospital appointment today. She had some tests done, and she was very brave. They're going to contact us with the results as soon as they can, but the doctor told me privately that she thinks Opal does have what Lexie had. I just hope that this time, they can find something to help."

Crocodile tears, I thought as she sniffled into the phone. *You're nothing but a liar.*

"Anyway, I just wanted to let you know. Ring me soon, okay? I miss you. Love you."

A click as the voicemail ended.

If the hospital wanted to start treatment, though, that meant that my parents' plan was working. I had to do something about it—and fast. I called Alyssa.

"Hello?" she said.

"Hi, Alyssa. It's me," I said, unnecessarily. "Crystal."

"Oh. Hi."

She sounded reserved. "Sorry," I said. "Is this a bad time?"

"No, no," she said. "I'm just in the library. Let me step out for a sec."

I heard the rustling as she stood up, her footsteps echoing in the stairwell, and then the smooth swish of the library's automatic doors as they opened out onto the quad, distant conversations and laughter.

"That's better," she said. "Sorry. I was on a quiet floor."

"No worries. Sorry for bothering you," I said. "What are you studying there? We technically don't even have any assignments yet, unless you've been looking ahead at the schedule?"

A light snort. "I have not," Alyssa said. "I'm doing research. For our project."

"That's actually why I'm ringing," I said. "I just spoke to my mum."

Okay, it was a voicemail, but Alyssa didn't need to know that.

"Oh," Alyssa said. "Is everything okay?"

"Not really," I said. I looked out my apartment window, at the tall buildings and people bustling around below. Did everyone have a secret like this, a private horror story all their own? If they did, how did any of us cope?

"She took Opal to the hospital on the mainland. They're still waiting for the test results, but they do think she has the same illness that Lexie had. Apparently."

"What does that mean for us?"

"It means that they're poisoning Opal, too," I said. "If Lexie wasn't really sick and Opal now has the same symptoms, then that's it. That's our confirmation."

"Unless," Alyssa said slowly, gently, "they weren't poisoning Lexie."

I leaned my head back against the wall. "Alyssa," I said, exasperated. "Do you want to help me or not?"

"Of course I want to."

"Then you need to believe me. We can't do this if you don't believe me! If you don't believe me, who else will?"

"I do believe you," she said. "I do, I do. I'm sorry. It's all just so . . . shocking. Unbelievable. And after we all spent Christmas together, too . . ."

"I can hardly believe it myself, sometimes," I admitted. "I can't believe this is my life." I shook my head, trying to snap myself out of it—self-pity would get us nowhere. "How's the project going, by the way? Have we had any responses to the pitch?"

"Nothing concrete," Alyssa said. "But I reckon Amelia from the *Daily Sun* will be all over this like a rash once she's read it."

That made me laugh unexpectedly. "There's an image that'll stick in my mind."

Alyssa laughed, too. "Sorry," she said. "What I mean is . . . it's very much her kind of thing. I'd be really surprised if she doesn't get back to us."

"Who are you, in the pitch?" I asked. "It's coming from you, right? Not me?"

"Right," Alyssa said. "I'm an enterprising journalism student, working with a well-known former child influencer to expose some seriously sordid behind-the-scenes behavior."

"Wow," I said. "I hope whoever does take this story on gives you credit. Actually, I'll insist on it. I really couldn't do any of this without you."

I could practically hear Alyssa's smile through the phone.

"If no one replies by the end of the week, maybe send them all a follow-up email?" I suggested. "Or could we find some back-up publications, just in case?"

"Why?" Alyssa asked.

"I'm worried about Opal. What if they start trying to treat her? The sooner this all comes out, the better it is for her—the fewer horrible treatments she'll have to go through for no reason."

I remembered Lexie, her skin so pale she was practically translucent, swallowing what seemed like endless pills and spoonfuls of medicine in a tired, resigned motion. I couldn't let that happen to Opal. I wouldn't let it get that far. Not this time. This time, I could do something about it. With Alyssa's help, of course.

"Yeah, okay," Alyssa said. "I'll see what I can do, okay? I'll find some more contacts."

"Thank you, Alyssa," I said. "Seriously. You're the best."

I hung up, then slid down the wall. I curled my knees to my chest, suddenly exhausted. I couldn't help but worry about Oliver and Opal, though. Would I be able to become their legal guardian? If I did, what would that mean for me—for my life, my goals, my dreams? But if I didn't, what would happen to them?

That is, if it ever went to trial. If my parents were ever found guilty for what they'd done. Maybe, by the end of all this, nothing would happen. Maybe they'd wriggle out of any charges, their throats raw with emotion and unshed tears. Nobody had suspected the heartbroken Shaws in the first place—why would what I'd said change anything?

I hoped, beyond anything else, that the article, the piece—whatever Alyssa's journalistic magic wove—would be enough to destroy their public image. Even if the police didn't believe me, even if the courts sided with them, I needed to know that their lives would never go back to the way they were.

I wanted them to lose their reputations, their brand deals, their sponsorships. I wanted them to lose everything they'd built from our stolen childhoods, from Lexie's stolen life. And they would; I would make sure of it.

All I had to do was bide my time.

Chapter Twenty-Eight

ALYSSA

I wasn't sure how much longer I'd be able to bluff for. Every day, Crystal would ask me—over text or in person if we had a lecture, seminar, or radio session that day—if any of the publications had got back to me yet.

And my excuses were no longer good enough. *Nothing yet!* changed to *I'll start pitching to more publications*, which became *I'll keep chasing them, okay?*

I'd underestimated Crystal's determination—the privileged influencer energy that ran through her veins. She'd grown up with a family who "got things done" and now here she was, snapping at my heels, pushing me to "get things done," too.

But destroying Crystal's family wasn't currently my main priority. It was finding somewhere to live.

My landlord had contacted me, as promised, and I'd officially been asked to leave. And, despite my rage at Niamh, Toby, and Alex, I didn't actually mind. They'd barely been able to look at me since my outburst, and whenever I entered a shared space—like the living room, or the kitchen—they'd each find an excuse to retreat. They'd disappear into their respective rooms, or else I'd see them go out to the back steps, Toby lighting a cigarette to feign smoking even though I knew—from the leaflets and nicotine patches I'd seen in his room—he'd been trying to quit. Apparently, I was so unbearable to live with I'd driven him back into the arms of his addiction.

I had a long day of viewings ahead of me. I'd originally had five scheduled, with two different agents, but one of the spaces in the house and/or flatshares I was planning to look at had already been snapped up. I wasn't feeling particularly positive.

The flat was silent as I left, even though I knew only Niamh was at work. Toby and Alex were hiding. I imagined that the second the door clicked closed behind me they'd emerge, like sneaky vermin—rats, mice, or particularly putrid cockroaches—to discuss how much they hated me.

The first viewing was a twenty-minute train ride away, and I settled in my seat and tried to enjoy the sights from the window: houses and trees flashing by, parents pushing buggies and holding hands with toddlers, smiling spaniels and Labradors chasing balls on grassy fields still dull and muddy from the long winter.

I disembarked at a station I'd never heard of before. It was very quiet—cars crawled by, and pigeons cooed on rooftops. The suburb was close to the river, and I could smell the brine of it on the breeze, an undercurrent of diesel smoke from the boats that traversed its brown waters.

The agent was impeccably dressed and well-groomed, as they all seemed to be, and he smelled of aftershave as he shook my hand.

Advertised as a house share for "young professionals or sensible students," I don't know what I'd expected. A higher standard, maybe? Instead, the terraced house the agent showed me to was scruffy—the windowsills were in need of a paint, dandelions and thistles forced their way through cracks in the path in the front garden, and there was what looked very much like a muddy boot print from a well-angled kick on the front door.

Inside it was dark and musty, and somebody's bicycle leaned against the wall in the hallway, wallpaper peeling behind it to reveal a big patch of damp. The kitchen sink was piled high with dirty dishes, the living room smelled of old cigarette smoke, and upstairs wasn't much better. The bedroom that I'd be renting—for four figures a month, no less—was a box room on the first floor, and it had barely enough room to fit the double bed that had somehow been squeezed into it. And the highlight of this property: seven other people lived there. I would be the eighth and final tenant.

The agent didn't look surprised at all when I told him then and there that I wouldn't be putting in an application.

The second property was only a couple of streets away, so we walked there together, making conversation about the weather which was unseasonably mild—enough to trick you into thinking spring was on its way, before battering you with rain for another two months.

When we arrived, I noticed that this terraced house was smaller—as was the number of tenants, just three of us in total. The two other girls were home when we went in, sitting together at opposite ends of a sofa. They paused whatever it was they were watching on Netflix, and they both glared at me as if I were already intruding.

The bedroom in this place was better; it had enough room to fit a bed and a desk, and had a view along the street with the city skyline in the distance. Even so, the last thing I wanted was to live with more people who hated me, so I decided not to offer on that property either.

The rest of the day followed suit. Every property I viewed was either essentially uninhabitable, had tenants who clearly did not want me there, or was overpriced to the point of hilarity. If I'd known that the rental property market was quite so dismal, maybe I wouldn't have refused my parents' offer to help me out with rent when I'd found my first flatshare. And now it was too late; I'd rather die than go back and beg them for money.

I got the Tube back to my current (but not for long) flatshare, deflated, defeated, and with sore feet. I didn't think my day could get any worse.

Until I received yet another text from Crystal.

Hey!! Can we meet up? xx

How many more times did I have to tell her to be patient? Obviously, I hadn't *actually* pitched her story to anybody—but even if I had, she needed to understand that these things weren't instantaneous. She wasn't going to have a tell-all article appearing in a newspaper or a magazine less than two weeks after I'd sent the first pitch. I tried not to make my frustration with her obvious in my response.

There's not much to talk about right now. Still working on it though! x

That's okay! I just think that there might be another option if this doesn't work out? Can we meet up to talk about it? xx

I groaned in frustration. I'd had a horrible day, I was exhausted, and I didn't want to leave the flat again. But I had to indulge her, and carefully consider my next steps—because clearly, she was getting impatient.

Sure. Usual spot? x

Yes, please! In 20? xx

Twenty minutes? I checked the time on my phone. I could just about make it.

Sounds good. x

It did *not* sound good.

Crystal was already there when I arrived at the pub turned coffee shop, with a half-drunk iced latte in front of her and a somber expression.

"Alyssa," she said slowly as I sat down, "I don't think this is going to work."

At her disappointed tone, my mind flashed back to a million and one parents' evenings, *Local Times* meetings with Bradley, and every other negative experience I'd had with an authority figure—which was plenty.

"You don't think what is going to work?" I asked her.

"*This*," she said, and waved a hand around vaguely. "Our project. Nothing's happening. Nobody's biting."

"It's only been a couple of weeks," I said. "You have to be patient."

Both Crystal's hands were raised now, a gesture of exasperation. "I know," she said. "I know two or three weeks is a normal turn-around time. Maybe even a quick one. But it's not quick enough! This is important—it's literally life or death. We can't wait around anymore."

"So what do you want to do?" I asked. "Should we stop?"

Crystal looked at me as if I'd suddenly started speaking another language. "Why would we *stop*?"

"You said—"

"I know what I said. We're not stopping. We *have* to do this. We just need to try a different tactic, and I have an idea."

I leaned forward. "I'm all ears."

"If nobody's interested in covering my story," she said. "We'll *make* them interested. We'll use what power we already have. Me." Crystal grinned at me triumphantly. "We'll use my socials, my new channel. I've changed all my passwords so my parents can't access the accounts. We'll script a video, film it together, and we'll share it everywhere. We'll go viral. And then no one will be able to ignore us."

"Isn't that risky?" I asked. "What if nowhere picks it up? If that happens, your parents will know what you've done—and you won't be any further forward."

"They'll pick it up," Crystal said firmly. "I know they will. And I'll say in the video we contacted loads of press, and no one ever replied.

No one cared. The public outcry will be huge! Can you imagine? They'll *have* to cover it."

I'd never seen Crystal like this: so steely, so determined. And so eager to use social media for good—or evil, depending on your perspective.

Besides, Crystal was right. The public outcry over something like that would be unavoidable—and, undoubtedly, it would eventually come out that not a single publication had received a pitch from us. I was a bystander here, an assistant. Crystal was the one with the social media following, the skills, the clout. And I knew that if she did post a video detailing her allegations, the media—local, national, maybe even international—would jump at the opportunity to cover her story. They already would have, if I'd actually pitched it to any of them.

I smiled at her. "I think that's a great idea," I said. "If you like, I can go back to my pitch and edit it so it reads more like a script? Then you could use it for the video."

"Perfect," Crystal said. Her eyes were glittering with excitement, an emotion that I honestly felt was a bit inappropriate given the situation. "I'll write around it a bit, too—some anecdotes, stuff like that."

"I could go through the channel, too," I suggested. "Maybe harvest some clips?"

Crystal shook her head. "Those will only show us being happy. My parents would've never let anything else onto the channel."

"Well, yeah," I said. "But there are still all those videos of Lexie, right? The beach trip, the picnic, the one where you're both gardening . . ."

The words were out of my mouth before I realized just how badly I'd slipped up. I hoped Crystal wouldn't notice, but of course she did. She stared at me.

"I thought you hadn't watched any of the videos?"

"I've watched a few," I lied. "Only since we started working together on this, though. I needed some more context, you know? To understand more about what you've experienced."

"Right," she said slowly.

"I never knew Lexie," I pushed on. "I wanted to find out more about her, watch your family's dynamic while she was still . . . here. Try to look for signs or something."

Crystal seemed to relax minutely, her posture slumping in her seat. "You wouldn't have seen any signs," she said. "No one did."

"No one else *knew*," I argued. "Maybe if someone had suspected something at the time, things might have ended differently."

Crystal's answering smile was sad. "Maybe."

She sipped the last of her drink, the melting ice cubes in the glass clinking as she lifted it. Her lipstick, a rosy pink, had left a ring around the striped paper straw. Then she stood up, hitching her tote bag up onto her shoulder. "I'd better get going," she said. "Thank you for this. As always."

I got up, too. "You don't have to thank me."

I followed her outside where she moved as if to walk away—and then, at the last second, turned and wrapped her arms around me.

My face was pressed into her woolen-clad neck, and I could smell the fresh apple fragrance of her shampoo, the jammy sweetness of her rose perfume overtaking the gritty scents of the city around us. I closed my eyes and inhaled.

"Thank you so much," she said again. "I couldn't do this without you."

"You could," I told her. And then, because it's what a best friend would say, "You could do anything. You're so strong. And I'm proud to be your friend."

When she stepped back, her eyes were wet. "You're the best, Alyssa. Text you later, okay? And don't forget to send me the pitch."

"I won't," I said. "Text you later."

She gave me a little wave, as always, as she left. I stood on the pavement and watched her until she was nearly out of sight, her soft hair bouncing on her shoulders.

Crystal's new plan was a good one, and she knew it. There would be no convincing her otherwise. And if it went ahead, all my hopes for the future—a new, loving family, the beautiful island home that I deserved—would crumble into dust.

I had to stop it.

I had to stop her.

And I knew exactly how I'd do it.

Chapter Twenty-Nine

CRYSTAL

The morning after my conversation with Alyssa, I woke up feeling elated. I opened my eyes to falling snow, unexpected after the warm spell, and a sense of both peace and determination. I knew what I had to do; all that there was left was to do it.

When I checked my phone, I saw there were two texts from Mum, which I left unread, and zero new emails. That was weird; I'd assumed Alyssa would send the edited pitch across as soon as she could.

We didn't have any lectures or seminars scheduled, and my mind was racing. I desperately needed a distraction. The library? Too quiet. Shopping? I didn't need anything, and I didn't want to give my parents the satisfaction of checking my bank statement and seeing I'd been treating myself. And then I thought of something: the radio studio.

I'd been so distracted by everything going on, plus my January coursework and the upcoming spring term, that I hadn't been to the radio studio in a while. If nothing else, it would be good for me to practice reading a script off-air. And if somebody else was already in there, it would be nice to be an assistant to them and forget about everything outside the studio for a short while.

I had a shower, dressed in a comfortable sweatshirt and jeans, swiped on my favorite tinted lip balm, then popped my headphones in and selected a cheerful morning playlist for my walk to campus.

By the time I arrived, I had almost forgotten who I was and what I was trying to do. The media building was quiet when I swiped my student ID, and at first I thought I might have the studio all to myself. But the light was on when I reached it, the red lettering declaring OFF AIR. I knocked once, and waited for a shout before I opened the door.

Rowan was sitting behind the desk wearing the obligatory enormous radio headphones, and a navy-blue sweater with an embroidered gray cat on it. Beside them, leaning over to show them something on the screen, was Jasper.

"Hi," I said. "Love the jumper, Rowan."

"Thanks!" Rowan said. "And hey, long time no see!"

"I know," I said. "It's been forever. Hey, Jasper."

Jasper looked a bit sheepish. "Hi, Crystal."

"Do you mind if I hang out?" I asked.

Rowan shook their head. "I'm not live or anything," they said. "Just practicing. I want to do a radio program for our next assignment, I think, so Jasper's been giving me a refresher."

"I'm just about to leave," he said.

I shrugged. "You don't have to."

Rowan looked between us with interest.

"I need to," Jasper said. Then, a little softer, "I've got to get back to the flat. It's Greek night tonight, and I promised I'd cook. I need to prep." He rolled his eyes.

"Let me walk you out."

"Sure," he said. "See you later, Rowan. Text me if you need anything."

"Will do," they said, and when Jasper turned away, they raised an intrigued eyebrow at me.

I shook my head, silently asking them not to say anything, and then followed Jasper out the door.

Once it had shut behind us, we stood in silence for a moment. And then we both spoke at the same time.

"I'm sorry," I said. "I overreacted—"

"I was being totally insensitive," Jasper said. "And I'm sorry—"

"No, seriously, I was being—"

"Your feelings are valid, Crystal—"

"Anyway," I interrupted, louder to shut him up. "Can we please be friends again?"

Jasper smiled, and it was so soft and open that I found myself instinctively leaning in toward him a little. "Of course we can be friends," he said. And he stuck his hand out for me to shake.

I laughed, but took it. His palm was warm and dry, and something about actually *touching* him, the most innocent brush of skin, made my cheeks flush. I shook his hand, once, and then let go. "Friends," I said.

"Friends," Jasper confirmed. His smile had widened, showing crooked front teeth. "I'll see you around, yeah?"

"Yeah," I said. "See you around."

He sloped off along the hallway, but just before he got to the end, I saw him glance back. My stomach filled with butterflies.

I took a deep breath, and went back inside the studio.

Rowan looked up as I entered. "Are you going to tell me what *that* was all about?" they asked with a grin.

"We had a falling-out," I explained briefly. "We made up. We're friends again."

"*Just* friends?" I waited just a second too long to confirm or deny, and Rowan squealed. "I called it!" they said. "I knew it."

I laughed. "There's nothing to know! Look, enough about me, anyway. What have *you* been up to?"

I could tell Rowan wanted to keep fishing—but apparently, the temptation of sharing good news was too much for them.

"I've been working!" they said. "As a photographer for *Local Times*. It's not permanent or anything, but I've been freelancing with them for a while and they needed someone to cover some proper shifts for one of their usual photographers."

"No way!" I said. "That's amazing, Rowan! Congratulations."

"Thank you," they said, eyes sparkling. "It's meant missing a couple of lectures, but it's regular paid work—and hopefully they'll keep me in mind for future jobs, too."

"It's awesome," I said, honestly. "I didn't know you worked for *Local Times*! Did you ever get to hang out with Alyssa?"

I imagined it'd be pretty fun, being in a newspaper office with Alyssa. Matching photographs to articles, grabbing coffees for each other, that kind of thing.

But Rowan shook their head. "Nah, Alyssa was always in editorial. I saw her sometimes, but . . ." Their tone took on a shade of guilt. "I sort of avoided her in the office."

"Oh," I said. It seemed a bit uncharacteristic of Rowan, who always seemed kind and generous with their time. "Why?"

They sighed. "Well, you know she got fired, right?"

"Yeah," I said. "She said it was for no reason. That her boss—Bradley, I think?—had something against her."

Rowan puffed out their cheeks. "Wow. That's what she told you?" When I nodded, they shifted in their seat. "That's not *entirely* the truth. Bradley did fire her, but it was because she was being super weird. She'd been copying people in the office for weeks, their looks—clothes, hair, makeup."

This wasn't news to me; Alyssa had already told me something about being fired for wearing the same color nail polish as a colleague. I said as much to Rowan, instinctively prepared to defend Alyssa.

"It wasn't just that," Rowan said. "It got *intense*. She copied this senior reporter called Davina right down to the exact brand of clothing she wore. She came in wearing the same lipstick as her, the same nail polish, the same bag. Everything. And it was a pattern—by that point, she'd done it to practically everyone in the office, and people were getting seriously weirded out by it."

I *had* privately wondered how wearing a similar shade of nail polish to someone else was a fireable offense. What Rowan was telling me made far more sense—and yet, why had Alyssa left out such important details? Did she think I'd think it was strange? Because . . . well, really, it was. It was very strange, actually.

I liked Alyssa. I liked her a lot. But sometimes, I had to admit, the way she acted was a little bit odd. Maybe that was why she didn't get on with her sister, because of something like this.

"Why would she do something like that?" I asked, thinking aloud. "*Local Times* was so important to her."

"Honestly? I think she just wants to be anybody but herself."

Rowan's evaluation struck me as terribly profound—and terribly accurate.

In the relatively short time I'd known her, Alyssa had never seemed happy and confident in her own skin. She'd always been striving for something more, to become somebody else. It was sad, in a way, but also concerning.

Rowan was looking at me somewhat searchingly, and when I met their gaze, they quickly glanced away.

"What?" I asked.

They hesitated.

"Go on," I said. "It's okay. What were you going to say?"

"I was going to say . . ." Rowan shifted uneasily. "Well . . . haven't you noticed who she's trying to become now?"

"What do you mean?"

"Crystal," Rowan said, their brow furrowed with concern. "Don't you see? Alyssa's trying to become *you*."

Chapter Thirty

ALYSSA

Once I'd decided what I was going to do, it was simple, really. Marjorie wasn't exactly difficult to find on social media—and when I messaged her the following morning, she accepted my request almost instantly.

Hi, Mrs. Shaw, I'd written. Can we talk? I'm really worried about Crystal. Alyssa x

In response, Marjorie sent her number, along with a note that said Please call me. x

I rang her less than five minutes after she'd sent the message, and she picked up straight away.

"Hello, Alyssa," she said, her voice kind with an undercurrent of worry. "Is everything okay? Why are you worried about Crystal? Has something happened?"

"Hi, Mrs. Shaw—"

"Marjorie, please."

"Marjorie," I corrected. "Crystal's okay, she isn't hurt or in trouble. But . . . well, it's really hard to say . . ."

A sigh of relief on the other end of the line. "As long as she isn't hurt," Marjorie said. Then, gentler, "Please, Alyssa, tell me what's going on. I'm sure we can help to fix it, whatever it is."

"Crystal thinks you hurt Lexie," I blurted out. "That you are somehow responsible for her death. She thinks you're going to hurt Opal. And she's going to post a video all about it."

"She thinks—she—*what?*" Marjorie sounded understandably blown away by the accusations, stuttering into the phone.

"She says she found a dosage written down that you could've used to poison Lexie. She thinks you made her sick on purpose. And that you're doing the same thing to Opal now."

"I can't believe this," Marjorie said faintly. "After everything we've done for that girl, the success we've given her, that she'd throw this, of all things, back in our faces."

"I'm so sorry," I said. "I know it's awful, but I had to tell you."

"No, no," Marjorie said. "Of course you had to tell us. I'm glad that you did. I'll book a flight, okay? I'll come over, and we'll talk all of this through."

I thought back to when Crystal and I had returned from the island together. "That'll take hours," I said. "What should I do?"

"Distract her," Marjorie said. "Make sure she doesn't have time to film anything. Keep her somewhere busy, out of her apartment, for as long as you can. And I promise, we'll clear everything up, together, once I'm there."

"Okay," I said, thinking hard. "I will."

"Thank you again for this, Alyssa," Marjorie said. "I can't thank you enough for telling me. Just don't let her post it—do whatever you have to do."

"I just didn't want her to ruin everything," I said. "You're like my family."

"Well, you're like our family, too," Marjorie said. "I'll keep in touch, okay? Speak soon."

She hung up. I was left staring at my phone with something like wonder, my heart pounding. Joyful fireworks burst inside me, colors sparkling in front of my eyes.

I'd done it: I'd told Marjorie what Crystal was going to do. Marjorie was coming here to stop her—*and* she'd said I was family. That was all I'd ever wanted.

But I couldn't bask in happiness for long, because it wasn't over yet. There was still work to be done. Marjorie had said to distract Crystal, and so I would. I opened the group chat I had with the members of the Journalism Society, one Polly had set up for arranging library dates and discussing assignments and other boring things. I'd long since muted the notifications. Now, though, it would come in handy.

I typed a quick message, and sent it.

Anyone up for a night out? xx

One by one, everybody read the message. Thankfully, Sadie was as predictable as she was blond.

YES!!! When??

What about ten-ish? Same place as last time? x

My phone buzzed with a message from Ravi.

I'm out, seeing my sisters tonight. We're going bowling. RIP me.

Jasper gave Ravi's response a thumbs-down, then replied to me.

Sounds good to me!!

If Crystal said no, I would have to think of something else, a different way to distract her.

But, at the same time, something else occurred to me. Yes, Marjorie was coming here, but what if that didn't make a difference? What if Crystal still wanted to go ahead with her plan?

If I wanted to prevent my dreams being crushed once and for all—especially now that Marjorie had confirmed I was practically part of the family—I had to stop Crystal from revealing her suspicions to the world. But how?

I'd fought for this for too long, trying on different skins, trying to figure out where I fit in the world. Finally, I'd found it—I'd found who I wanted to become. And Crystal's plan would ruin everything.

Maybe I could insist she isolate herself from her family for her own good, convince her to ignore every call and message and never go back home. Even as I considered it, I knew Crystal would never agree; she loved her siblings too much to abandon them.

What if I suggested she went no-contact with her parents and continued speaking to Oliver and Opal? No—her parents would never allow that.

Slowly, a dark thought dawned on me. I had to get Crystal out of the picture. Permanently.

She'd left me no choice. I had to kill her.

Murder was a drastic measure, one line I'd never crossed, but I knew what I had to do. And I knew exactly how I would do it.

Ten minutes later, everyone had responded aside from Crystal. I itched with anticipation. And then, finally, she replied.

Okay, let's do it. x

I raised my fists in the air, victorious. And while I waited, while I showered and styled my hair in lovely loose curls and applied my pink shimmery eyeshadow, the clock ticking ever closer to nine thirty when I would have to leave, I considered the finer points of my plan.

By the time the taxi came, parked outside the flat with its hazard lights on, I was ready to put it in place.

Arriving at the club, I was giddy. Within just a few hours, my new, exciting plan would be complete. Crystal would be gone. And there I'd be, waiting for Marjorie, ready to pick up the pieces of their once-again shattered family.

Imagining it, the way she'd hug me so tightly like she had at

Christmas, filled me with longing. I wanted it so, so much, and I wasn't going to let anybody—not even her daughter—stand in my way.

A queue was beginning to build outside the club, but none of the other journalism students, including Crystal, were here yet. Or had they gone in without me? I checked my phone, but the group chat was silent. I hovered outside for a while, wishing that I smoked so that I had something to do other than hunch over my phone, and was filled with relief when I spotted Zoe.

"We the first ones here?" she asked as she got closer. She was wearing a startlingly sparkly champagne dress, with glossy black heels. She caught me admiring it, and grinned. "Do you think it's a bit much for somewhere grungy like this?"

"Not at all," I said honestly. "I love it."

She did a little twirl. "I never get to wear it," she said. "So, I thought, why not tonight?"

"Why not tonight indeed," said Polly as she joined us, Rowan beside her. "You look hot."

"Thanks, babe," Zoe said, blowing her a kiss. "You two look great."

They did. Polly was wearing a royal blue minidress, and Rowan was in a particularly sharp suit.

"Who else are we waiting for?" Rowan asked.

"Just Jasper and Crystal, I think," Polly said.

"Should we go in, then?"

"Might as well join the queue," Zoe said with a shrug. "We can save them a space."

We headed to the end of the queue, which wasn't so much long as it was bulky; seemingly everybody had come as part of a crowd, and the queue slid forward quickly as different groups made their way in.

We were nearly at the front, Polly mid-flow in a story about a friend's disastrous set of hair extensions ("They literally pulled out chunks of her scalp. Her *scalp*!") when Jasper and Crystal arrived.

Zoe made a loud *oooh*-ing sound. "Look at you, arriving together!"

"I came with Polly," Rowan said. "It doesn't mean anything."

Zoe stuck out her tongue. "Spoilsport."

But her teasing had worked. Jasper was visibly pink in the face.

"We just bumped into each other getting out of our taxis," he explained.

He and Crystal merged into the queue with us, causing a bit of muttering from the people behind.

"You can't hold spaces for your friends," one girl, who was chewing what I thought was probably gum with exaggerated jaw movements, said. "It's not fair."

"Oh, who cares? We're all going to get in anyway," Polly said. The girl huffed and tutted, but didn't pursue her point. Satisfied, Polly smirked.

We were coming to the front of the queue now. We all flashed our IDs to the doorman, who nodded us in one by one.

"Entry's a fiver," said the bored guy behind the counter, and we dutifully handed over the notes.

"Anything for the cloakroom?" Jasper asked.

"I'll shove my suit jacket in there, two secs," Rowan said. They disappeared around a dark corner, and reappeared a minute or so later without it, revealing a partially unbuttoned white shirt. It looked very cool.

"All good, yeah?" Zoe checked, glancing around at us all. "Cool. Can we get in there now? I'm *dying* for a drink."

As we stepped through the doors into the main room of the club, stage two of my plan launched into action.

I wasn't obvious about it. I was just generous, making regular trips to the bar from the dance floor, taking everybody's drink orders before I went. And we were drinking a lot; the club was hot and sweaty inside, a sharp contrast to the cold, late winter night.

Whatever drink Crystal asked for, I would get for her, but I'd always make it a double. A double vodka and Coke, a double gin and lemonade. If it was a big order, I'd usually recruit somebody to help me carry the drinks, but I always kept hold of the strongest one until I could make sure it had gone to Crystal.

The first drink I bought her, she winced. "It's a bit strong," she said.

I glanced at the others, but none of them had heard her over the pounding bass. It wouldn't matter if they did, anyway, I supposed, since Crystal didn't drink. What did she know?

"It's the cheap booze," I told her with an air of authority.

"It's rancid," she said, but she stirred it with her straw a bit then took another sip.

I laughed. "It just takes a bit of getting used to."

As the night wore on, I kept my eye on Crystal. She finished her first drink, so I bought her another. And then another. The fourth drink, I allowed Jasper to get—a single, like Crystal had asked for. I needed her to get drunk, but not *too* drunk too quickly.

And Crystal was perfect—all bubbly and smiling, holding hands and dancing with Polly, Zoe, and Rowan, laughing at Jasper and his self-conscious, stiff dancing. I observed them all from the bar, finishing the dregs of a Red Bull. The caffeine joined the adrenaline running through my veins, keeping me alert.

I returned to the group with another tray of drinks, gently pressing a double measure into Crystal's grateful hand.

"Thank you so much for this," she said, her words falling over one another as they came out of her mouth. "You have no idea how much I needed this. It's like a last hurrah, before . . . before . . ." She lifted her drink aloft in emphasis and wobbled on her feet just a little, spilling some. "Whoops." She laughed.

This drink would be the one to do it, I reckoned.

I took hold of her empty hand, and gave it a tug. "Come on," I said. "Hurry up and finish that so we can go and dance!"

Crystal grinned sloppily, and swallowed down the rest of the drink in one gulp. "Let's dance!"

I let her drag me back toward the dance floor, where Polly, Zoe, and Rowan were dancing as a trio. Jasper appeared to be talking to a girl.

I nudged Crystal, and when she caught sight of them she sighed. "He's still so into Hayley, isn't he? I wish he was into me."

And then I remembered: Hayley, Crystal's neighbor. Perfect. Hopefully, she'd stay here awhile longer with Jasper as I carried out my plan. No witnesses was always best.

Abruptly, Crystal stopped dancing. She was looking faint.

Rowan approached us, with the others—sans Jasper—following behind.

"Hey, Crystal," they said, leaning close to her. "Are you okay?"

"I feel a bit sick," Crystal replied, in a thick voice that I knew meant vomiting was imminent. "I think I need to—"

"Come on," I said, taking her by the arm. "Let's get you outside." I turned to the trio. "I'll get her some fresh air, and we'll be back in five. Okay?"

"Sure," Zoe said, but Rowan frowned.

"What?" I asked them, half challenging.

"Nothing," they said, but I could feel their eyes on us as I led a stumbling Crystal away.

The doormen didn't look twice at us as we left, a sober girl leading her far more drunk friend out of the club. No one looked at us as I sat Crystal on the curb near the taxi rank and instructed her to take some deep breaths while I tried to flag down a taxi.

And no one looked as I promised a frowning taxi driver that Crystal would absolutely *not* be sick—and handed him a wad of cash to cover any cleaning fees just in case she was. Once Crystal was safely belted in, I gave the driver her address and slipped Crystal's phone from her bag. There was a text from Rowan.

You okay??

I tapped a message back, doing my best impression of a drunk Crystal.

Was siclk otside. Alyss help get me a taxi. On wy home.

Rowan's reply came through seconds later.

Be careful. Let me know when you're home? :)

That text, I chose to ignore. Later, when somebody undoubtedly put together a timeline of the night, a drunken Crystal would be passed out by now—and she was, just about, slumped against the seat, her face pressed against the cold window.

And in no time at all, we arrived at Statue House.

I thanked the taxi driver, gave him a tip, and put my arm around Crystal as she got out of the car on unsteady legs. She was like Bambi on ice, and she held on to me tightly as we wobbled our way up to the main entrance.

On CCTV, this would look good. I was just a kind girl, helping her horrifically drunk friend back to her apartment. I made sure I kept a sympathetic expression, just in case the cameras could see, even though Crystal's clumsiness was beginning to annoy me. She tripped on the entrance mat and I gripped her tightly by the arm so she didn't fall to the ground.

"Careful!" I said.

Crystal just glared at me. "I *am* being careful."

Finally, I got her to the lift, then along the hallway, her feet shuffling along the soft carpet. I reached into her bag for her key, unlocked the door, and allowed her to lurch across to the bathroom. I heard her vomiting.

As the horrid noises continued, I looked in her kitchenette cupboards and retrieved a glass, which I filled with water from the tap. And then, from my pocket, I added a little pill—courtesy of Alex. I let it dissolve for a few seconds before I carried it across to the bathroom and lightly tapped on the open door.

"I've got you some water," I said.

I expected Crystal to take the glass from my hands and down the whole thing in one with the urgent thirst of the drunk. But she didn't. Instead, she carried it across to her bed in the corner and sat down. Her gaze was worryingly clear, and she frowned at me suspiciously.

"What?" I asked.

She narrowed her eyes. "What have you done?"

"I haven't done anything." The water in the glass was clear. Surely, she couldn't tell there was something in it?

But that wasn't what she was talking about. "You don't want to be part of my plan anymore," Crystal said. "You've been weird about it lately, but now you're being all . . . kind. I think you've done something, and I think you feel guilty about it."

I was surprised that Crystal, several drinks down, was that perceptive. Unless . . . I glanced toward the bathroom. Of course—she'd vomited up the alcohol. She was beginning to sober up.

I supposed I could still tell her the truth. Soon, once she'd drunk her sedative-laced water, it wouldn't matter.

"Fine," I said. "Yeah. You got me. I did something." I grinned, allowing myself a moment of triumph. "I called your mum, Crystal. I told her everything."

Crystal's look of heartbroken dismay was the icing on the cake. "Why? Why would you do that?"

"Because I think you're ridiculous," I told her. "You have no idea how lucky you are to have grown up in your family! Your parents have given you everything, Crystal—love, money, fame—and you don't even appreciate it. You don't appreciate them. All you want to do is destroy them."

The volume of Crystal's response surprised me. "I want to destroy them because they killed my sister!" she shouted. "Or have you conveniently forgotten that part? They're not good people, Alyssa! They didn't give me a good upbringing—they used me to make money. They deserve everything they get!"

"Lexie's just an excuse," I spat. "You found some stupid circumstantial evidence, and now you're planning on using it against them because you want to ruin their lives."

Crystal shook her head slowly. "I can't believe this," she said quietly. "All this time, I thought you were on my side."

"I *am* on your side," I said. "I'm on your family's side. I won't let you ruin your life—or theirs. Or mine. You're not going to take this away from me, Crystal. Not when I've waited for so long."

Something in Crystal's expression seemed to click into place. "Take this away from you? You've always known who I was, haven't you?" she asked. "That's why you wanted to be friends with me—you wanted to use me to get to my family. And—for what? To rub shoulders with them, bask in their so-called glory?"

"All I wanted," I said, "was to be one of you. I wanted to be your friend, your *sister*. I wanted to be part of your family, it's why I joined this university, and then you threatened to tear it all to pieces."

"You'll never be part of my family."

"Your parents love me," I said. "Oliver and Opal love me."

"You're insane!" Crystal said. "You stayed with us for Christmas. You were there, what, a week? Do you really think that makes you one of us?"

I gritted my teeth. "Yes, because you don't *want* them. And I do. I want loving parents, a brother and a sister."

"You already *have* a sister," Crystal said. Then her face fell. "That was a lie, wasn't it?" she whispered, "You said you don't talk to your sister—but I bet she doesn't even exist. Does she?"

I shook my head.

"I should've known. That is sick, Alyssa. You're sick." Crystal laughed bitterly. "So what do you think happens now? My parents are *so* grateful to you for being my friend that they take you in as one of their own? In what world would that happen? You're eighteen years old, Alyssa. It's time for you to grow up."

And then she drank the water. All in one.

My satisfaction soothed the sharp sting of her words.

Once she was finished, she slammed the glass on the bedside table and leaned back against the wall, staring at me venomously, cheeks pink with fury. But seconds later, her eyes started to droop, a confused frown appearing on her face.

I moved closer to the bed, sat down beside her, and spoke directly into her ear. "What happens now, Crystal, is that I *replace* you. Believe me, it's for the best. I'll be a better daughter to them than you've ever been. I'll be a better sister to the twins. I promise."

Her eyes widened momentarily as she fought to keep them open, but the drug won. Gradually, she slumped over. I helped her lie down, her head on her pink-patterned bedspread. Alex's drugs had worked—she was out.

Still breathing heavily from my outburst, I tried to calm down, to think with a level head. I had to finish what I'd started.

I left Crystal on the bed and went across to her kitchenette. First, I washed out the glass so no evidence of any drugs remained, then I switched on the biggest ring on her electric hob. I added half an inch of water to a pan, opened a packet of instant noodles, and dumped the lot in. I discarded the crumpled plastic on the floor as evidence of drunken sloppiness, and slid the pan onto the ring.

As a final safeguard—or, rather, the opposite—I grabbed the tea towel Crystal had neatly folded beside the sink, and laid the edge of it on the hob, too.

I hoped it would happen quickly; if the flames took too long to catch, the drugs might wear off and Crystal might wake up. Alternatively, the pan and tea towel might just smoke a bit and do nothing else. If I tried to accelerate it, it might look as though it was deliberate—as if somebody like me, an arson aficionado, had started it. All I could do was wait.

I perched on Crystal's bed beside her prone body, and watched.

After a few minutes, the pan—the water now boiled away—started to smoke. I stayed there as the smoke grew thicker, as tiny orange flames started to appear over the silver rim of the pan. As the tea towel finally caught alight.

In a space this size, it wouldn't take long for the fire to spread.

The smoke was growing heavier, the flames larger, and when I glanced toward Crystal she hadn't moved a muscle. She was unconscious. Good.

I clamped my sleeve over my nose and mouth to block out the worst of the smoke and, smiling beneath it, got up. I stopped to look down at Crystal for a final time.

"It's okay, Crystal," I said gently. "Go and be with Lexie."

Then I left.

Chapter Thirty-One

CRYSTAL

The moment the door closed behind Alyssa, I was on my hands and knees with my fingers clawing at the back of my throat, forcing myself to vomit all over my apartment floor.

I hadn't been as drunk as she'd thought, and through the open bathroom door I'd seen her slip something into the glass of water after she poured it. I was feeling woozy already, like my eyelids were being pulled down by lead weights, but I was nowhere near falling unconscious. Drugs didn't kick in that quickly; clearly, my act had fooled her.

I sat back on my heels. And it was only then, with my lurching stomach empty, that I realized I had a far bigger problem than Alyssa's attempted drugging.

My apartment was on fire.

I squinted, smoke stinging my eyes. I could see a burned and blackened pan on the hob, and flames had already started to lick along the counter. I leaped up and ran toward the door, but skidded to a stop at the sound of a sharp crack, followed by a loud bang. I instinctively threw my hands up to protect my face, and when I put them down again it was obvious what I'd heard.

I kept a glass bottle of olive oil beside the hob, and it had exploded. Shards of glass littered the countertop and the floor, and the oil had sprayed everywhere. As I watched, horrified, the flames absorbed it hungrily, spreading faster than I could think—to the cupboards, the floor, and then across to the door. My only exit.

The realization hit me all at once. Alyssa had tried to drug me, and she'd set my apartment on fire.

She'd tried to burn me alive.

And now, I was trapped in here.

Desperate, I ran back across to the window and looked out. I was three stories high. Could I survive falling three floors? I didn't know.

But the alternative was staying here, and the flames were slowly growing.

I hit the window with my fist once, then again. And again. It was no good; I wasn't strong enough to break the glass.

I spun around to find something that I could use, but my apartment was sparse—I still hadn't decorated it properly, had no heavy furniture or knickknacks tucked away on a shelf that I could use. In the kitchenette, though, right at the end of the counter nearest to me, there was the microwave. That would be heavy enough, surely? But it was very nearly on fire.

Then again, so was I.

I grabbed a bath towel that I'd left to dry on the radiator beside the window and used it as a clumsy shield as I clamped my hands around the metal. Even through the thick, fluffy material, it was burning hot. I dragged the microwave from the counter, its plug dangling behind, and heaved it toward the glass as best as I could. It bounced off, and landed on the floor with a crack.

"Come on!" I screamed, hearing the fear in my own voice along with the frustration.

Somewhere outside I could hear sirens, but I couldn't wait to be rescued. The smoke was growing more dense every second, and it was starting to get harder to breathe.

I heaved the microwave at the window again with all my strength. And it smashed. I dropped the towel and pulled myself up onto the windowsill, shards of broken glass sticking into my knees and the palms of my hands as I gripped tightly onto the frame and breathed in the fresh air. I looked down at the street, so far below, packed with fire engines and people. By the time the firefighters reached me, it could be too late.

I prepared to let myself fall.

And then I heard a shout from somewhere behind me.

"Crystal!"

I turned around. Through the crackling flames, I could see the silhouette of an advancing figure. They were brandishing something. And all at once, it exploded into a burst of foam and the flames began to recede. A fire extinguisher. It was a fire extinguisher.

I scrambled down from the windowsill as the flames slowly died, the kitchenette and doorway blackened and covered in foam. And there, holding a red canister in both hands, sweaty hair stuck to his forehead and eyes bright with fear, was Jasper.

"Rowan said you'd been sick and Alyssa brought you home," he said shakily. "I wanted to see if you were okay, but I didn't think . . ."

I didn't let him finish. I ran to him and buried my face in his chest. He squeezed me tightly, but our reunion couldn't last long—we were still in danger, the smoke around us still choking.

"Come on," he said. "Let's get you out of here."

With an arm around my shoulders, he guided me through the burned shell of the doorway and out into the corridor.

The firefighters met us on the stairs and escorted us out to where an ambulance was waiting. Reluctantly, I was separated from Jasper and given some oxygen while the paramedics checked us both over. The adrenaline was fading, and I was suddenly aware of searing pain in my hands, my knees. My surroundings—the flashing blue lights, the gathered onlookers, the firefighters in their uniforms, and, up above, the soot-stained window I'd nearly been forced to jump from—began to blur. Overwhelmed, I passed out.

Chapter Thirty-Two

ALYSSA

I made it back to the flat in record time. The lights were all off. I was the only one home.

I locked myself in the bathroom and quickly undressed, then washed every inch of myself and shampooed my hair twice to get rid of the smell of any lingering smoke. My clothes went straight into the washing machine, with a large scoop of powder.

Afterward, I'd left Crystal's building completely normally. I'd made a show of flicking through some apps on my phone, strolling along the pavement at a casual pace until I was out of sight of the building's CCTV. I kept up my air of nonchalance as I walked, aware a hundred cameras could be watching, careful not to rush but also not to dawdle. I was a girl alone at night. I still had to be alert, didn't I? Even if I was the person that everybody on these dark city streets should fear.

I was electric. Every single one of my veins was alight with the signature buzz, the kick I only ever got from setting fire to something. Plus, my plan had actually *worked.*

Soon, Crystal would suffocate in that flame-filled apartment. Tomorrow, or later this week, investigators would piece the story—*my* story—together.

Crystal had been drunk. She'd maybe even taken drugs. A friend had taken her home from the nightclub, put her to bed, and then left. With the logic of the drunk, Crystal had tried to cook herself a meal, passed out on her bed, and the resulting burned food had caused a kitchen fire that, tragically, she was too unconscious to be aware of.

What a sad cautionary tale. Crystal's parents would get some mileage out of this on their channel, that I was certain of. And then I would nudge my way in with sympathy, become the active, involved, appreciative daughter that the Shaws had always longed for.

Perhaps, at the same time, I could even become an online fire-safety campaigner, extolling the importance of sobriety when cooking to university students just like poor, unfortunate Crystal. The potential side hustles were endless, once I'd secured my perfect family. I wanted to rub my hands together with glee, like a cartoon villain.

Back in my bedroom, I ran some oil through my hair and climbed into bed. My laptop was still set up beside my pillow, already on the *At Home with the Shaws* channel. Serendipity.

I clicked on to the first video that appeared ("Visit Embervale Zoo with us!!!") and let myself drift off, smiling, to the sound of my new mum's soothing voice.

It wasn't her voice that woke me, though, hours later. It was my own.

"All I wanted was to be one of you," I was saying. "I wanted to be your friend, your *sister*."

I sat up, blearily, and reached for my laptop. Still dazed from sleep, I couldn't understand what was happening, why I was listening to echoes from earlier that night. I pulled the laptop closer to me so that I could see the screen properly. And what I saw filled me with abject horror.

Crystal's apartment, on its side. It was her phone, beside her on the bed. There I was, fists clenched at my sides as we argued. I couldn't see much of Crystal on the screen, just a slice of her arm, but I could hear her clearly enough.

"You're eighteen years old, Alyssa," she said. "It's time to grow up."

There were still five or so minutes left on the livestream, which had now ended. I didn't have to watch it, though. I knew what happened next. I knew what the camera had seen. I knew what it had heard.

Me, setting the fire.

Me, whispering to Crystal, *Go and be with Lexie.*

It was over. Everything was over. My dream was officially dead.

I buried my face into my pillow and screamed.

Chapter Thirty-Three

CRYSTAL

My body felt as though I'd clawed my way to the surface after being buried underground. There was a crushing pain in my chest, and my head throbbed with every beat of my heart.

Gradually, my other senses started to awaken. I was in bed, my covers draped over me. But why did I feel so ill? Was I hungover? If I was, it was the worst hangover I'd ever had. Had I really drunk *that* much in the club?

My ears registered a rhythmic beeping off to one side, and a smell—a strange smell, like chemicals, disinfectant, old food—all mingling.

I started to sweat, my body recognizing the mixture of scents before my brain had caught up. I fought to open my heavy eyelids, and, once I did, the light was blinding. I waited until my eyes adjusted, and a slow glance around—my neck was incredibly stiff—confirmed my suspicion. I was in a hospital. What was I doing here?

I took in my surroundings. I was in a private room, not a ward. I had various things stuck in my nostrils and in my arm.

There was a window to my right, and outside the sky was glowing the deep, bronze-orange of sunset. I felt like I'd been asleep for a long time, my thoughts syrup-slow. I couldn't remember how I'd got here.

I started to register more pain, a strange, hot tightness to the skin on parts of my arms and hands, the backs of my legs. There was a stinging sensation, too—especially in my knees—like somebody was poking me with something sharp. Like a knife. Or a shard of broken glass.

And then I remembered. I remembered everything.

The club. Alyssa. The fire.

I wanted to cry with sheer relief. I'd survived. I was alive.

But where was Alyssa?

At that moment, a shadow filled the open doorway.

Mum.

I knew it was her, because her face was covered by her phone. She was holding it up in front of her at arm's length, talking—presumably to her camera—and it took her a moment to register that I was, in fact, awake.

"Crystal!" she said. She didn't run to me, overcome with emotion, and envelop me in her arms. She didn't cry, didn't laugh with sheer relief, didn't so much as kiss me on the forehead. She continued to film, talking to her followers rather than to me.

"As you all just heard, our darling daughter is finally awake. I'm sure we'll discuss everything that's happened together, and make some sense of this terrible misunderstanding. We owe you, our lovely followers, the truth." Mum held the phone in my direction. "Wave hello, Crystal! We're live!"

I didn't move a muscle. I could feel every emotion I'd been holding back—the frustration, the anger, the sense of injustice—beginning to build up inside my chest. I'd just been through a horrific, terrifying, painful ordeal, and her first priority was this? Not to comfort me, not to love me—but to try to protect herself and her lies and mine my life, once again, for content?

"No."

Mum looked at me, eyebrows raised in surprise, the phone lowering slightly in her hand. "What did you say?" she asked in her nicest voice, still performing for her followers. She hadn't heard me, but she was about to.

"I said no," I repeated. "I won't wave hello. I won't do anything—not for you, not for your stupid channel. Not anymore. I'm done. And I'm clearly *not* okay! How could you even ask that? How could you do this?"

Mum's hand fell to her side, her live broadcast forgotten in her shock. Her mouth opened and closed, but no words came out.

Mine did, though—I'd finally unstoppered my feelings, and they poured out of me like water. "I'm lying here in a hospital bed, after being betrayed by my closest friend, hurt in a fire she set, and the *second* I'm awake you come in here and start filming me? Have you been filming me while I've been unconscious? What the fuck is wrong with you?"

Mum stared at me, stunned.

"You ruined my childhood. You've ruined my life. I was never your child—I was just an actor, a content creator you employed without paying. And it stops now. Do you hear me? I won't let you ruin Oliver and Opal's life like you did mine—and like you did Lexie's." I looked Mum in the eye as I said her name.

"I'm aware you think I've ruined your life," Mum said tightly. "I saw the video you posted, Crystal. I saw the lies you've told the world about us—about our family. How could you?"

"How could *I*?" I burst out. "How could *you*? You killed her, Mum! You poisoned her. And now you're doing the same thing to Opal, feeding her all sorts of medications she doesn't need to make her sick. I found the list."

"The list?" Mum repeated, sounding dazed. She glanced down at the phone in her hand, and I knew then that she hadn't stopped broadcasting. Perhaps she'd been trying to save face, to protect her reputation by challenging me on the accusations in the best way she knew—only to be blindsided. For the first time in my life, I was standing up to her, and she hadn't expected it. And, by streaming this live, she was damning herself.

I doubled down. "The list of medications, with all the side effects?

You know what I'm taking about, don't you? You had it hidden in the bathroom, but I found it. You gave all these medicines to Lexie, and you killed her. And now you're trying to kill Opal, too."

Now that my video had posted and the allegations were out there, everything would undoubtedly change. My parents' follower count would rapidly decrease, sponsors would put an end to their partnerships with *At Home with the Shaws*, and true-crime obsessives would start scripting their deep-dives into the channel's content—what remained of it, anyway, after it was taken down.

Coming here, Mum had been making a last-ditch attempt to curry favor with her followers, to slow the collapse, but it was inevitable. Everything had already been set in motion. It had been set in motion when she posted that first video so long ago, triggering an addiction to attention that would prove fatal.

It was a long moment before Mum spoke. When she did, she was gentle, persuasive. "I know losing Lexie has been hard for you, darling. But making up stories won't solve anything. I need you to take the video down. *We* need you to, as a family."

I stayed stony, determined.

"We're going to lose everything," Mum said. "Everything we built, for you and Oliver and Opal. Don't you care about us? Don't you care about your brother and sister?"

Still, I said nothing.

"Please, Crystal. You have to understand. I didn't mean to kill her."

Her words hit me like a battering ram, the air punched out of my lungs. And only then did Mum realize what she'd said, what she'd admitted to. Her façade dropped, the mask slipping away. I saw her hit the end broadcast button, her fingers fumbling frantically, but it was too late. Her face crumpled, and she began to sob.

"I didn't mean for it to happen, Crystal. I didn't mean for Lexie to die. I loved her. I loved her so much."

I was right—I'd been right all along. But I felt no sense of victory in it, only a dark, devastating sadness.

My mum had killed my sister.

Mum looked at me, her eyes reddening, tears streaming down her cheeks. "Lexie was sick," she croaked. "She really was sick. And when she was ill, the views, the money . . . it all went up. The vlog was so popular suddenly—I thought it would change our lives. We barely had any money; it was like a lifeline. But when she started to recover, everything just . . . stopped. So I pretended she wasn't improving, got her more and more treatments. I got carried away, Crystal—I took it too far. And one day I . . . I gave her too much of something. I don't even know what." Mum slumped over, her head in her hands. "But I killed her. I killed my baby girl."

"If it was an accident," I asked, my mind reeling, "why would you do the same thing to Opal?"

"It wasn't my idea," Mum said. "It was your father's. We were desperate—we were going to go bankrupt. And he remembered what Lexie's illness did for us back then, how it saved us from rock bottom." She swallowed. "He didn't know about Lexie. I'd never told him. How could I? But I think . . . I think he always suspected something. So I agreed to do it, but I knew I had to be more careful this time—that's why I wrote all the side effects down. I couldn't let it happen again."

The realization that Dad suspected what Mum had done to Lexie all those years ago and had chosen to stay by her side, had even suggested doing it again to Opal, broke my heart. And then Mum's next words stamped all over the shattered pieces. "We did it for all of you," she said. "You have to understand, Crystal. We did it for our family."

I thought about Opal on Christmas Day and on New Year's Eve, how pale and drained she'd looked. I pictured Lexie's white coffin, piled with flowers, and Opal lying in one just the same.

"You didn't do it for our family," I said. "You did it for yourselves. And now everybody knows the truth. It's over. And I will never, ever forgive you."

When I pressed the call button, Mum didn't try to stop me, didn't try to convince me not to. She stayed where she was, her head in her hands.

Less than a minute later a doctor entered the room, closely followed by a nurse.

"Hello, Crystal," the doctor began. "How are you . . ." But she trailed off when she saw Mum.

"I need you to take her into another room, and make sure she doesn't leave," I said. "And then I need you to go and get the police. I know they're here." I took a deep breath. "I'm ready to make a statement."

The police had been waiting for me to wake up.

I told them everything—a lot more than they expected, frankly, considering they were only there to investigate the fire.

I told them about what had happened to Lexie, about the list of medications I'd found. I told them about Mum's confession, how she'd admitted to accidentally killing my older sister all those years ago, and how she'd implicated Dad. I told them how her confession was now online—inadvertently broadcast on her own social media account. I told them about Alyssa, how she'd helped me home from the club and then tried to drug me, how she'd set the fire because she wanted to become me. I told them to check my social media account for the livestream of it all, so they could hear Alyssa's final words to me, the ones that had clearly communicated her intent to kill me.

Once the police had left and Mum had been escorted away with them, still crying, the doctor returned. Her shiny black hair was pulled into a bun, not unlike the ones Mum liked to wear, but her expression was infinitely softer, more caring.

She sat in the plastic chair beside my bed, and introduced herself as Dr. Lewis.

"How are you feeling, Crystal?" she asked in a smooth, deep voice. "You've had quite a challenging couple of days."

I snorted. "You can say that again."

She smiled gently and nodded, encouraging me to continue.

"I'm okay," I said. "I mean, I'm sore."

"You might be sore for a little while yet," Dr. Lewis said. "Burns take time to heal. You'll have scars, but otherwise there's no permanent damage. You're very lucky that your friend got there in time."

Jasper. I pictured his face, his initial horror and then relief once he'd quenched the flames, how gently he'd led me away from the shell of my apartment toward safety. He'd saved my life.

"What about emotionally?" the doctor asked. "How are you feeling?"

"Shaken," I said. "And . . . I guess I'm grateful, too."

"Grateful?"

"That the police believed me. I didn't think they would. My parents are so perfect, you know? They have friends in high places; they always told us that when we were kids, and I was scared that the police would think I was making everything up. I didn't want Oliver and Opal—my brother and sister—to get hurt somehow because of me."

"Have you considered," Dr. Lewis asked gently, "that your parents implied they had powerful friends for that exact reason—so you'd be scared of going to the police?"

I sank back against my pillows. I *hadn't* considered that, but it made sense.

Dr. Lewis smiled sympathetically. "I think what you did was very brave, Crystal."

I smiled, but couldn't bring myself to thank her. If I did, I thought I might cry. And if I started, I wasn't sure I'd be able to stop.

Dr. Lewis nodded, and stood up. "I'll let you get some rest. Oh, before I forget." She reached into her pocket, and handed me something smooth, rectangular: my phone. "I thought you might like it back," she said. "Someone put it on charge at the nurses' station for you."

"Oh," I said, "thank you."

"You're welcome."

Dr. Lewis left the door open behind her, and I sank back into my pillows, listening to the voices and electronic beeping. It still filled me with tension, brought painful memories to the surface, but that was all they were now—memories.

From now on, everything would be okay. I was sure of it.

I took a deep, calming breath, and then unlocked my phone. I had hundreds of notifications, and I scrolled through them carefully.

Some were texts—I had several from Jasper, Rowan, Zoe, and the others, asking if I was okay and promising to come and visit soon. I replied to Jasper's first, telling him that I was awake and I wanted to see him. I desperately needed to thank him in person, although mere words would never be enough.

The overwhelming majority of notifications, though, were because of the video. My video.

I'd recorded my exposé, which I'd clumsily titled "The TRUTH about the Shaws" before I'd left for the club the night of the fire. I'd poured out my thoughts, my suspicions, my doubts—and I'd scheduled it to post at midnight.

I hadn't known what chaos would ensue later that evening—what lengths Alyssa would go to—but I had suspected time might be running out. Alyssa's growing reluctance to discuss the pitches she'd sent and Rowan's revelation had made me wonder if her resolve was crumbling, so I'd taken action. And that action had saved me.

The video had been out there for less than twenty-four hours, and it had nearly half a million views. There were thousands of likes, too, and just as many comments. And as I watched, they continued to pour in.

You're so brave!!! xx

This is shocking! This is why kid influencers
should be ILLEGAL.

I KNEW there was something off about this family. WTF!

So will the parents be done for the murder of their other daughter or??

We love you, Crystal, we will always support you. No matter what <3

I read all of them. Every single one.

After a while, I couldn't keep up. I just lay on my side, my phone propped up on my pillow, to watch as the supportive, gushing words filled my screen.

I'd done it.

Later, after I'd eaten my evening meal, I checked my other apps. The follower count on all my socials had increased by thousands. I had emails from publications and news channels from all over the world, begging for an exclusive interview, offering me money.

It was addictive, this kind of engagement—this intense, unquestioning adoration. I could almost understand why my parents had become so obsessed with it, allowed their desire for approval, love, and money to twist their hearts into cruel things, capable of poisoning and killing a child.

Only *almost*, though.

I would never do something like that.

But it wouldn't do me any harm to indulge in it, to enjoy it for a while.

Would it?

Chapter Thirty-Four

ALYSSA

One Year Later

Life in prison was nothing like on TV. There was no drama, no excitement, little conflict—just mundanity and routine, unhappy women, and the combined smells of body odor and cafeteria food permeating the gray walls.

My dad refused to visit, naturally, but Mum came occasionally, sitting stiffly with her hands clasped as we talked, every conversation strained. During one of these uncomfortable occasions, she told me that Marjorie Shaw had confessed to killing her oldest daughter. I couldn't believe that, after everything, Crystal was actually *right*.

I tried not to get my hopes up in case they were dashed, but then the rumors started. It appeared that the Shaw family's loss was to be my gain. Marjorie's confession had led to a prison sentence—which, in turn, would lead her to me.

The first day I saw her, sitting at a table in the dining hall with a tray of food, I made a beeline for her. I slowed as I approached—she wasn't the Marjorie I remembered, glamorous and glowing. She was tired, drained; I supposed it was the stress. Her hair was stringy, and our prison clothes were unflattering on her, shapeless.

She's still Marjorie, I told myself. And so I treated her as such.

"Hi, Marjorie," I said. "I heard you'd be joining me in here. Isn't this great? I mean, obviously it sucks you're in prison. But at least we're both here together, right?"

Marjorie just looked back at me, her expression unreadable. She hadn't eaten any of her food, her cutlery untouched.

I tried a different tack. "I know it's been hard for you," I said gently. "Lexie's dead, Crystal betrayed you, you can't see the twins anymore, and your husband's probably going to end up in prison, too. You must feel horrendous. But look—this is a silver lining. We can plan, work together, come up with ideas for when we get out. Maybe we could even set up a channel together—'cause, you know, by then we'd be family. I could be a Shaw!"

Finally, Marjorie spoke. "Are you joking?" she asked. "After everything that social media has cost me, you think I want to go back to that?"

That was the opposite of what I'd wanted to hear. "Well . . . I . . ."

"I don't know who you think you are, Alyssa, but you are not a Shaw," Marjorie said icily. "And you never will be. I know what you did to my daughter. Crystal is worth a thousand of you, betrayal or not. Now go away."

She looked down at her tray. I had been brutally dismissed.

Cheeks flaming with humiliation and fury that I would never get what I deserved, that I'd been thwarted yet again, I left my tray on the table and stormed out of the dining hall.

I still had some free time left before I had to go back to my cell, so I went to the library. It was nothing like the university's library, no tiled floor or old wooden shelves or dusty leather-bound tomes to bury myself between. It was institutional and boring, gray-carpeted, dimly lit, but it was a safe haven for me in the prison. I liked to go there and flick through the stacks of magazines and newspapers. They were usually new every week or so, but not always—sometimes they'd already been thumbed through by fingers grubbier than mine, the crosswords and word searches filled out by some bored prison officer or another. I was never really bothered about that, though—there was only one thing I was looking for, which was any mention of Crystal.

I'd seen a few snippets: Crystal's release from hospital, her reunion with the twins and the grandparents they'd all gone to live with, my own sentencing. The courtroom illustrator's drawing had made me look like a crazy person, wild-eyed with unruly hair. Of course I'd received the maximum sentence.

Those glimpses into Crystal's life on the outside were never enough, though—I was always hungry for more. Especially now that Marjorie had outright rejected me, I knew it was over; I would never be Crystal. I would never be a Shaw.

But I could still live vicariously through her like this.

I flicked through a new edition of *In the Know* magazine, barely breathing, desperately craving news, and when I saw it my heart stopped. Jackpot! It was a feature, an entire double-page spread featuring Crystal—and it was written by none other than Davina Lawrence.

I thought fondly of Davina, with her black fingernails and her piercings. I was glad she'd moved on, finally escaped from under Bradley's dark shadow. Where was Bradley now? Still in custody, I hoped.

I leaned forward, poring over the glossy images of Crystal. She looked happier and healthier than I'd ever seen her, posing and pouting, decked out with designer fashion and shiny pink lipstick.

The wide-legged pink trousers and long-sleeved sparkly dresses and denim pinafores layered with tights she was wearing in the various photographs were cute, but carefully chosen, too—they covered the scars left from the burns.

It was soothing to know that they were there. I'd left my mark on Crystal and her family, even if her mother claimed I would never be one of them. That was okay. I was sure I'd change her mind, anyway—after all, I had all the time in the world to do it.

I gently ran my fingertip across Crystal's printed face, smiling to myself. I would never forget Crystal Shaw. And she would never be able to forget me.

EPILOGUE

IN THE KNOW

The UK's #1 lifestyle & entertainment magazine

15 May 2022

"I JUST DON'T WANT THIS TO HAPPEN TO ANYONE ELSE": CRYSTAL SHAW SPEAKS OUT

Thirteen years after her sister Lexie's death, Crystal Shaw uploaded a video to her channel that shocked the world.

In the video, Crystal—teary-eyed and visibly drained—explained in horrifying detail how she believed her parents were responsible for killing her older sister—and how she suspected that they were trying to kill her younger sister, too.

That very same evening, Crystal was rushed to hospital after being injured in an apartment fire. And the following day, in Crystal's hospital room, her mother, Marjorie Shaw, finally confessed to the long-term poisoning and accidental killing of her oldest daughter.

In the year since her world imploded, life has transformed dramatically for Crystal. Our reporter Davina Lawrence sat down with the influencer turned activist to find out just how much has changed.

DL: Hi, Crystal. How are you doing today?

CS: I'm doing great. Thanks.

DL: And how are Oliver and Opal?

CS: (smiles) They're amazing, thank you for asking! It's been a big adjustment for them, but they're loving living in the city with our grandparents.

DL: That's so good to hear. For our readers who might not know all of the ins and outs, can you remind us of your story?

CS: Yes, of course. In brief, I guess, my parents, Marjorie and James Shaw, used to run a vlogging account focusing on family life. It was called *At Home with the Shaws*. When I was six years old, my mum killed my seven-year-old sister, Lexie, after deliberately making her ill for a long period of time. She'd hoped that Lexie's illness and her "treatment journey" would help to grow the vlog and make it profitable, which it did. Dad claimed he didn't know about what had happened to Lexie at the time, but years later when my parents ran into financial trouble he suggested doing the same thing to my sister, Opal, and Mum went along with it. They both made very bad decisions, and because of that they're now both in prison.

DL: I'm so sorry that this happened to you.

CS: (sniffles) Thank you.

DL: How did you find out about what your mum had done?

CS: I found a note in my parents' bathroom with a list of medications and their side effects. I recognized one of them, and the dose was all wrong—it was way too high. Later, Mum told me that Opal was ill and that she had the same symptoms as Lexie, and something just . . . clicked. That's when I first became suspicious, but it was only really confirmed for me when Mum actually admitted to it.

DL: And that's not the only trauma you've faced in the past couple of years, is it?

CS: (shakes her head) No, it isn't. When I started at university, I became friends with a girl called Alyssa Hayes. I didn't know it at the time, obviously, but it's since emerged [at court] that Alyssa had a history of arson. She was also deeply obsessed with my parents' channel, and chose to attend the same university as me in the hope that she could befriend me—and then use me to integrate herself into the family. When she found out about my plan to expose my parents' crimes, she tried to kill me by drugging me and then staging an accidental fire in my apartment. I managed to vomit up the drugs before I became incapacitated, and was rescued by my friend Jasper. I was very lucky to survive.

DL: You were injured, weren't you?

CS: Yes, I was. I had some burns that luckily weren't too serious, and lacerations on my hands and knees from trying to climb out of a broken window. I'm all healed up now, though, and I'm so grateful for everything my incredible healthcare team has done for me.

DL: We're so glad to hear that you've healed physically, but what about emotionally?

CS: I won't lie, it's been very difficult. It's been hard to trust anyone. I went to court for Alyssa's trial and sentencing, and I'm pleased to say that a livestream I managed to record that night was instrumental in the case. Alyssa won't be released for a long time. So that's brought some closure.

DL: That must be a relief.

CS: Yeah, it is. I was put in touch with a wonderful therapist, too, which has really helped, and I've been focusing on activism. As well as my original socials, I've set up a brand new vlog, which is called *Crystal Clear*.

DL: Oh, yes! Huge congratulations—how's it going?

CS: It's been amazing. I wanted to show everyone how we're rebuilding our lives, our journey toward growth and healing, and the reception has just been incredible. Oliver and Opal are absolutely loving being back on camera, too!

DL: So are Team #ITK!

CS: Thank you so much! It just means so much to me—I guess

I want to raise awareness of the dangers of family vlogging, and just how toxic and abusive it can become. Obviously, not everyone who runs a family vlog is like my mum—but I really want people who love vloggers to pay attention to what they're watching, and look out for any red flags, no matter how insignificant they seem. I just don't want this to happen to anybody else.

DL: Speaking of your activism, what's up next for you? I've heard there's a potential book contract on the horizon?

CS: (smiles) I can't share much about that yet—but honestly? I have a feeling my future's going to be bright.

DL: And finally, if any of our lovely readers want to check out your new vlog and your socials, can you share your handles with us?

CS: Of course! It's @CrystalClear, on everything. And as always, don't forget to like, share, and tell your friends!

ACKNOWLEDGMENTS

I can't believe I'm already writing the acknowledgements for my second book!

This last year, up to and following the publication of *The Goldens*, has been an absolute whirlwind.

First of all, I'd like to say a huge thank-you to every reader who bought, borrowed, gifted, or recommended my debut novel—as well as for showing your excitement about this one! I genuinely couldn't do this amazing job without all of you, and I really hope you enjoy *Tell Your Friends*.

Thank you to all the fantastic booksellers worldwide who've shouted about my books. I'd like to add a special thank-you to the teams at the Bound in Whitley Bay and to the Newcastle and Morpeth branches of Waterstones.

Thank you once again to everyone at HarperCollins Children's Books and the Harper Fire team, especially Megan Reid, Charlotte Winstone, and Laura Hutchison.

Thank you to the team at Flatiron Books and the Pine & Cedar imprint, especially Christine Kopprasch and Kate Lucas.

Thank you also to my fantastic international publishers and editors—it's been incredible to see my words translated, and I'll never take that thrill for granted.

Thank you all for quite literally making my dreams come true.

Thank you to my superstar agent Chloe Seager and the Madeleine Milburn Literary Agency team for changing my life.

Thank you to the journalists and newsreaders at Global and Bauer Media Group in the North East for taking me on as a freelancer when I was at university and showing me the rope—and for being very much the opposite of Bradley in every way.

Thank you to my wonderfully talented writing group, the North East Novelists, and to New Writing North for bringing us all together.

Thank you to Laura, Lucy, and Ellie for the love, the advice, the early feedback, and the endless cheerleading. You're all amazing.

Thank you also to Han, Oliviah, Marie, and all my online writing community pals. You know who you are.

Thank you to Grace for being the coolest cousin ever. I hope you enjoy!

Thank you to Nanna and Grandad for always indulging my love of storytelling—even if it meant buying me a new ninety-nine-pence notebook every week.

Thank you to Mam and Dad for your endless love and support, for reading everything I've ever written, and for letting me turn your loft into a library while I was growing up (I will move my books one day, I promise!).

Thank you to my incredible fiancé, Jack, always and for everything. I love you.

Thank you, lastly, to our spaniels Albie and Tilly. Beach walks wouldn't be the same without you.

ABOUT THE AUTHOR

Lauren Wilson is the author of *The Goldens* and *Tell Your Friends*. She has a degree in journalism and an MA in creative writing, both from Northumbria University. She previously worked as a freelance radio reporter and for *Mslexia*, a magazine committed to championing women's writing.